Barbara Seranella was born in Santa Monica and grew up in Pacific Palisades. After running away from home at fourteen, joining a hippie commune and riding with outlaw motorcycle clubs, she eventually became a mechanic.

UNWILLING ACCOMPLICE

Munch Mancini and her daughter Asia are doing just fine. Munch rejoices in being a car mechanic, but it's tough when people from her old life surface. Lisa Slokum, Asia's aunt, has bolted from a Witness Protection Programme with her two daughters and needs Munch's help. But when fifteen-year-old Charlotte disappears, Munch must call upon her ex-boyfriend, cop Rico Chacón. Why did her niece run away, and where is she now? Munch must unravel the mystery of Charlotte's life before it's too late to save her.

BARBARA SERANELLA

UNWILLING ACCOMPLICE

Complete and Unabridged

ULVERSCROFT
Leicester

First published in Great Britain in 2005 by
Robert Hale Limited, London

First Large Print Edition
published 2006
by arrangement with
Robert Hale Limited, London

The moral right of the author has been asserted

British Library CIP Data

Seranella, Barbara
    Unwilling accomplice.—Large print ed.—
    Ulverscroft large print series: mystery
    1. Mancini, Munch (Fictitious character)—Fiction
    2. Women detectives—California—Fiction
    3. Automobile mechanics—Fiction 4. Detective and
    mystery stories 5. Large type books
    I. Title
    813.5'4 [F]

    ISBN 1–84617–446–5

Published by
F. A. Thorpe (Publishing)
Anstey, Leicestershire

Set by Words & Graphics Ltd.
Anstey, Leicestershire
Printed and bound in Great Britain by
T. J. International Ltd., Padstow, Cornwall

This book is printed on acid-free paper

For all the kids who have broken the chain, and for all the counselors, teachers, and mentors who helped them.

Prologue

The man was everywhere. Asia Mancini first met him by the rabbit hutches. He gave her two carrots to feed the bunnies, which was nice of him. Then he squatted down next to her as she pushed the orange sticks through the wire mesh. She could feel his breath on her neck when he said, 'C'mere, bunny.'

It made her feel funny when he did that, gave her goose bumps all up and down her arms. She crossed her legs and brought her elbows down to her sides. She didn't know why she did that.

'How old are you?' he asked. 'Ten?'

'Eight and three-quarters,' she said, pleased that he thought she was older.

'Almost nine,' he said. 'My little girl is nine.'

'What's her name?'

'Taffy, like the candy. I bet you like candy.'

'But not taffy,' she said. 'No offense.'

He laughed and patted her arm. His fingers had hair on the backs of them and looked large on her forearm. She sank deeper into the cannonball position, her chin on her knees, arms holding them tight against her chest.

'You just have fun,' he said.

Asia was glad when he left and she could go back to studying the bunny's cute little whiskers, trying to get him to wiggle his nose at her. Next to the bunny pen, there were ducks. Asia liked the ducks in the Venice Beach canals near her godparents' house better. Their feathers weren't all tufted up and she didn't remember them smelling bad, like they'd been stuffed in a closet or something with a bunch of dirty laundry.

At the goat pen, the man was there again wearing the same blue windbreaker, his longish dark hair combed straight back, a friendly smile on his tanned face. This time he gave Asia an ice cream cone full of birdseed.

'No, thank you,' she said, being polite like her mom had taught her.

'G'wan,' he said, 'take it.'

She looked around, wondering where all the other kids and adults were. She felt like she was in trouble, like she might not get to go on another school field trip, but didn't know what she'd done wrong.

'I have to go,' she said. 'My mother is looking for me.' This was a small fib, but sounded better than saying one of her teachers.

She went to the gift shop and scanned the

souvenir racks for pencils with her name already stamped on them. There were plenty of Anns, Andreas, Audreys, Alices, even an Abigail, but none, as usual, with *Asia* engraved in the wood.

Audrey? she thought, trying to picture a kid her age named that. She shook her head. Abigail would be cool, though.

She saw her teacher, Miss Hopp, talking to Sister Margaret over by the bus. Sister Margaret was eating an ice cream cone. Today's outing was going to use up the whole school day so all the kids would get a chance to see the animals get fed and groomed.

Asia thought she'd seen the last of the man with the hairy fingers, but then, after lunch, when all the kids were sitting at the benches talking and acting stupid, she went for a walk along the tree line. She thought she might find something interesting. A rock or a piece of wood that she could take home to her collection, maybe some flowers for her mommy. She would like that.

Asia didn't even hear him come through the bushes. Then suddenly he was there on horseback.

'You want to go for a ride?' he asked.

Of course she did. More than anything. But that vague feeling stopped her. The sense that she was in trouble or would get in trouble. He was a stranger, even though he seemed to want to be friendly. His clothes weren't all dirty or torn and he didn't smell. And he had a kid, so he was like a dad, too. Still, she felt dry in the mouth and wished she hadn't wandered off alone. Again. The sisters and her teachers were always telling her about that.

He patted the saddle in front of him. 'C'mon, I'll take you for a ride.'

'Both of us at the same time?' she asked. What would it be like, sitting on the saddle in front of him? His breath would be all over her again. Her bottom would be touching him. The saddle would make that happen. She knew she wouldn't like that, being so close to his boy parts. She also knew he shouldn't be asking her. He must be a bad man. She remembered then something else her mom said once, something that she didn't really get, and her mom said she'd tell her more about it when she was older. Something about how being a parent didn't make someone good. Asia turned and ran back to the picnic tables. Forget good manners.

She spent the rest of the day alone on the bus, waiting for the others. Sister Margaret asked her if she was all right. Asia told her she was tired and didn't feel like seeing any more animals. Unsure what had happened or almost happened or might have happened, she said no more. She wasn't stupid. Why take a chance of getting punished for breaking some rule she'd probably forgotten?

'Look before you leap' was her new motto. Starting now.

1

Munch Mancini could hardly believe it. Richard Dean Anderson wanted to make love to her. MacGyver. All six feet and blond and holding her in his muscular arms.

She wasn't sure if she had become part of his television show or she had met him somewhere else. The only thing that mattered was his closeness now.

They shared a kiss that put every gland in Munch's body on high alert, then he whispered into her lips, 'Can we make a baby together?'

Munch wanted him bad then, already so turned on that she knew the sex was going to be good. But before they went any further she ought to address his question. She blathered on about the scarring on her fallopian tubes, completely ruining the moment. She woke up alone in her bed remembering the kiss, then nothing else.

Man she thought, not knowing whether to laugh or cry, *I screwed up my own wet dream.* Her policy of 'searching and fearless' honesty had once more proved that she could carry even a good thing too far. Had to be the addict in her. Sober or not, she still had that tweak in her psyche that never knew when to quit.

'Asia?' she yelled into the next room. 'You up?'

Asia bounded into her bedroom. Munch braced herself for her daughter's body block as the eight-year-old flung herself on the bed with a whumpf to Munch's solar plexus that knocked the air out of her lungs and damn near brought tears to her eyes.

Asia's enthusiasm was impossible to resist.

At least somebody was going to get her heart's desire today.

'I've been up for *hours*,' Asia said, her face rosy with anticipation.

'C'mon, it's Saturday.' Munch yawned and rubbed her eyes. 'I thought we'd just relax today. We don't have anything we *have* to do, do we?'

'Mooom, you promised!' Asia stood straddling Munch and tugged on her arm with both hands, remarkably strong for such a skinny little girl. 'Let's go. Up and at 'em.'

'Oh, right.' Munch stretched with feigned languor. 'We were going to look at dogs today.'

'We're going to *get* a dog today.'

Munch felt a smile pull at her cheeks. The kid was right. The day had come. They owned, not rented, their little house in Santa Monica. The homes on their street were mostly fifties-vintage wood cottages thrown up after World War II with a few triplexes mixed in. The property had already doubled in value so she was feeling pretty flush. It was October 1985. The economy was booming with no end in sight.

Her little house wasn't a fancy starter mansion north of Montana Avenue, but it had a yard, two bedrooms, and a garage. She and Asia, not some landlord, decided what color to paint it, what flowers and vegetables to plant, and who would share the space with them. Munch had never had a dog when she was growing up, had never had the continuity of living arrangements or the certainty that she could take care of one, so this was a long-awaited first for both of them.

Sometimes her life felt as if it were nothing but firsts. Other times she recognized how everything had a way of coming around twice.

She pulled Asia's squirming body into her arms and twisted her up in the covers, crying, 'Steamroll!'

Asia yelled for help.

Munch held her trapped for a moment longer, breathing in the scent of her daughter's hair. A wave of love bubbled through her.

'Get off of me!' Asia screamed, her words muffled by the bedspread, bucking again with that surprising strength of hers.

'Oh, all right.' Munch knew she had tortured the poor kid enough. 'Somewhere in this city is a dog with our name on it. Let's go find him.'

'Speaking of names,' Asia said. 'How come I have such a weird one?'

'Your name is pretty.'

'But no one else has it.'

'Someday you might like that.' Munch took a moment to consider Asia's ensemble of yellow pants, red high-tops, and a flowered pink blouse. Definitely a kid who marched to her own brass band.

'Is that what you were thinking?' Asia pressed.

'It's what I think.' Munch paused to study Asia's reaction and said carefully, 'You already had the name when I got you.'

'Oh, you mean my *other* mother gave it to me?'

'She and your dad both, probably.'

Asia wrinkled her perfect little nose in concentration. 'Who would name their kid Audrey?'

Munch exhaled, glad that Asia was dropping the subject of her parentage. 'I don't know. It sounds old-fashioned.' The hot

9

names of Asia's era, kids born in the late seventies and early eighties, were Shannon, Carrie, Jamie, and lots of Sarahs. Half the boys Asia knew were named either Justin or Jason.

Munch stared at her daughter, half-bemused, half-perplexed. She often wondered if she was doing a good enough job as a parent. Talk about operating without a manual. Or net, for that matter. She wished she could pry the little girl's brain open and see what she really thought. How much time did Asia spend during her busy day contemplating the origin of her brown skin and curly hair, the birth parents she'd never known, or the life she might have lived had either Sleaze John or Karen survived?

'Hey,' Munch said, pushing back those sweet brown curls from her daughter's eyes, 'you never told me. How was the petting zoo yesterday?'

'Boring.'

'Wasn't it fun, seeing all the animals?'

Asia looked down at her hands. 'They kinda smelled.'

★　★　★

Asia waited impatiently by the front door while her mother dressed. This Saturday had

10

taken forever to arrive. She'd wanted a dog since she was a little kid in first grade. It was all she'd ever really wanted, though she wouldn't turn down a pony, or a twin sister. Still, she felt her best bet was to focus on one big wish at a time.

So, every night she pretended her puppy was in her arms as she waited to drift off to sleep. Every wish she made on every star and birthday candle was to that end, and the wishes were finally going to come true.

She loved all animals. As far as the horse went, she understood that you needed a place to keep it. The horse she could wait on until she was ten. A dog was doable now. A dog didn't need a whole big ranch, just a spot on her pillow. They would be a team, a dynamic duo, each ready to aid the other when adventure called.

Thinking about a horse made her remember the man with the hairy fingers, and she had to rub her stomach hard to get rid of the icky feeling there. Maybe she'd been wrong about him, but she was glad she wouldn't have to see him again.

★   ★   ★

When Munch and Asia got back from the pound with Jasper, a gold-red cocker spaniel,

11

a message was waiting on the answering machine. For an insane instant, Munch thought it might be Rico, which surprised her. Not the expectation so much, but that she was hoping it was true.

We're mad at him, she told the committee in her head, *remember? He's an asshole. He chose someone else.*

Asia, too young for ghosts, marched straight to the machine and pushed PLAY.

'I hate talking to machines,' a woman's voice said.

Very original, Munch thought, brushing her bangs out of her eyes. 'This is the eighties,' she said out loud to the spinning reels, 'get over it.'

'Munch?' the voice queried, then waited a second for a reply.

'C'mon,' Munch said, 'you're wasting tape.'

Jasper barked, a deep boy bark that made him sound like a much bigger dog, and Munch and Asia jumped in surprise. It was the first sound they'd heard him make.

'It's Lisa. I'm back in town. Call me. My number is, uh, wait a minute . . . hold on . . . '

Asia rolled her eyes and looked at her mother as if to say, *What an idiot.*

Munch felt a guilty pride, knowing exactly where Asia had learned that look.

Lisa recited a number and ended the message with 'Call me, bitch.'

'Very nice,' Munch said as she scrawled the number on the pad by the phone.

'Who was that?' Asia asked, her arms locked around Jasper's neck in a choking embrace that the dog, rather than resisting, leaned into.

'Your aunt. Your dad's sister.'

'I have an aunt?'

'And two cousins by last count.'

'So you're an aunt, too?' Asia asked.

'Technically,' Munch said, but a warm flush was already spreading through her. *Auntie Munch.* She liked that. Then she considered Asia's end of the deal. Lisa. Munch wanted to add, *Don't get too excited until you meet her. With any luck, they're just passing through.* But her next thought was already defying that logic. Why would Lisa have a phone if she were just passing through?

'Why didn't you tell me?' Asia asked.

Munch sighed. 'Because when you were a baby, they all went somewhere and they weren't supposed to ever come back, and I didn't see any point in telling you about relatives you'd never meet.'

Asia lifted the receiver. 'Let's call her back.'

Munch took the phone from her and

replaced it in the cradle. 'We will, but let's get Jasper familiar with the house first. Show him the dog door, take him into the yard, and let him sniff around.' She went to the kitchen and filled the new dog bowl with water, dropping in a few cubes of ice. Her friend LAPD homicide cop Mace St John did that for his dogs. Asia had picked out the ceramic dish at the pet store, drawn to the images of the Disney character Pluto in his space suit painted on the sides of the bowl. Jasper's leash and collar were red with white bones. They'd come with him, along with the name. That's what sold Asia on the dog. He'd been someone else's first, and for whatever reason those people couldn't take care of him anymore.

'There's nothing wrong with him,' the lady at the animal shelter had said.

'Of course not,' Asia had replied, appointing herself the animal's champion, 'why would there be?'

Jasper had responded by rolling on his back and fixing them all with a bloodshot gaze.

'He's been neutered,' Munch said.

Asia wanted to know how her mother knew that and what *neutered* meant exactly but then the shelter lady mercifully changed the subject. 'He's not a big eater.'

'His eyes and nose look dry,' Munch noted.

'He's not a big drinker either,' the lady said.

'Perfect for us, huh, Mom?' Asia was already on her knees, scratching Jasper's ears and offering her face to be licked.

Twenty-eight dollars later, they had themselves a dog.

Now, as Asia trotted past Munch on the way to the back door, Jasper trailed at her heels. He glanced nervously back at Munch as if unhappy that the two of them were to be separated and his loyalty tested so early in their acquaintance.

Asia dropped to all fours and climbed through the dog door; Jasper squeezed through with her, bringing an exasperated 'Just wait' from Asia.

Munch chuckled with a parent's perverse pleasure at seeing her kid on the receiving end of a dependent's impatience. The dog was earning his keep already.

She stared at the paper with Lisa's phone number on it and sighed. She hadn't seen or heard from Sleaze John's sister since October 1977. Eight years to the month. The same month Munch's old lover Sleaze John had caught up with her at the gas station where she was wrenching and announced he was in a jam and had a baby daughter named Asia. The first fact hadn't surprised her. The second piece of news, however, had sent her reeling. Maybe she'd sensed that her life was about to be changed in ways she had never dreamed possible. Big, wonderful, beautiful, curly-brown-haired ways.

Hours later, Sleaze was dead. Days later, Munch took on Asia to raise as her own, and Lisa — lazy, ornery, selfish bitch Lisa — disappeared into the witness protection program with her worthless old man, James, and two young daughters. Charlotte would be fifteen by now, and little Jill eleven. James, well, who knew if ol' James baby was still in the picture. Eight years was a long time.

Munch had made a halfhearted attempt to find Lisa when she was going through Asia's adoption process and had been relieved to find no trace of her. The court and the child services people had understood the special circumstances and let the adoption proceed without the next-of-kin sign-off.

Maybe Lisa had changed, but somehow Munch doubted that.

'Call me, bitch' sure sounded like the same old sweathog.

2

Munch called the number Lisa had left on the machine. The prefix she recognized as a West Side exchange, possibly in one of the neighboring towns of Palms or Mar Vista. She listened to the first ring, promising herself to wait only four more rings before she hung up. Someone picked up at two.

'Who's this?' Munch asked.

'Who wants to know?'

'Lisa?'

'No.'

'Charlotte? You sound like your mom a little. This is your aunt Munch.'

'Really?'

Munch thought that an odd question. A voice in the background asked, 'Who is it?'

'Auntie Munch,' Charlotte yelled back, without apparently thinking to cover the mouthpiece of the phone or direct her voice away from it.

Still, hearing the phrase *Auntie Munch* gave Munch a small, unexpected thrill.

'Let me talk to her,' Lisa said in the background.

'My mom is being a bitch on wheels,'

Charlotte confided.

Teenagers, Munch thought. Some things never change.

Asia and Jasper came running back in the house. Munch pointed to the water bowl. Asia got on her hands and knees over the dog's dish and mimed lapping at the water. At least Munch hoped she was miming. Jasper dunked his face in the bowl and came up with an ice cube. He trotted off with it as though he'd found a piece of steak.

Lisa came on the line. 'Hey, how the hell are you?'

'You're not back in town, are you?' Munch asked.

'Yeah, missed you, too.'

'What about that thing?' Munch asked, referring to the dope-smuggling bikers Lisa had snitched out. That judicious piece of confidential informing had earned Lisa and family a one-way ticket out of Dodge, courtesy of the Feds.

'That blew over a long time ago. Those guys are all dead or in the joint. We're cool. I hear you're doing good. All Miss Straight and Narrow.'

Was this a prelude to getting hit up for money? 'We get by,' Munch said cautiously, wincing at using we instead of I. 'How're the girls? Jill and Charlotte?'

'Real good, getting straight A's. Growing up fast, think they know everything about everything.'

Munch laughed. It sounded familiar.

'They want to see their cousin,' Lisa said. 'They got a right.'

Munch looked at Asia, who was petting the dog, but obviously listening to Munch's half of the conversation. 'How you figure?' she asked, responding to Lisa's defensiveness with some of her own.

'We're blood.'

'Lisa, let me make this real clear. I'm eight, damn near nine, years sober. Asia is well adjusted and happy. I work hard to give us a good life. I'm not letting anyone into it who's going to mess up any part of that.'

'Hey, hey — '

'I don't give a damn what you think ties us together. I am not getting dragged down any slippery slopes because you suddenly show up and — '

'Fucking A, hold on a minute, will you? I just want the kids to meet. I don't even have to be there. It wasn't my idea anyway. Ain't no call for you to go freaking out on me.'

Munch looked down to see Asia and Jasper staring at her. Jasper was shivering and looking unhappy. Was this an omen or did angry voices upset him? Maybe his last family

19

had broken up because they couldn't get along and that was why he'd been abandoned. Asia's big brown eyes, her daddy's eyes, were wide and solemn.

'You want to meet your cousins?' Munch asked.

Asia nodded carefully as if not sure whether a yes would offend her mother. Munch hugged her, then ruffled Jasper's ears to reassure him.

'Okay, Lisa. Let's meet at the park on Seventh and Wilshire. Can you be there in an hour?' Might as well get it over with.

'Yeah, we're on the West Side.'

'I figured,' Munch said.

'See you.'

'Happy day,' Munch said after hanging up.

Picking a public place was no accident. Munch wasn't about to invite trouble to her home. She could always step up the relationship if this first reunion went well. It would be much harder to step back if she offered too much. Starting next year, she vowed, their phone number would be unlisted.

★ ★ ★

On the weekends Munch usually left her hair loose to give her scalp a break from the tight

20

braid she wore when working on cars. It also felt more feminine to let her light brown hair fall unencumbered across her shoulders and down her back. Feeling feminine, however, was the last thing on her mind as she got ready to meet Lisa. If anything, she had gone into warrior mode: jeans and boots, a ponytail that could easily be tucked in the collar of her sweatshirt if the need arose, and an attitude of deep suspicion.

Munch, Asia, and Jasper got to the park first. It was early enough in the afternoon that the bums were either still begging at the 7-Eleven or sifting through the alley Dumpsters. They hadn't yet migrated with their shopping carts full of bedding and keepsakes to surround the concrete restrooms and stake their claims for the night.

Homeless, she corrected herself, that's what they're calling themselves now, especially in the People's Republic of Santa Monica. There hadn't been such a polite name for it when she was living the life of a street person. She'd just been a junkie and maybe worse than that if she'd ever paused long enough in her self-destruction to worry about labels.

Lisa arrived twenty minutes late in a creaking Dodge Dart. Charlotte and Jill piled out first. If Munch hadn't been expecting

21

Lisa, she wouldn't have recognized her. The years had been downright brutal.

At five-five or five-six, Lisa had a few inches on Munch height-wise, but she had yards on her everywhere else. Never svelte, Lisa had bloated to twice her previous girth since Munch had last seen her. Most of her newfound weight appeared unhealthy; her flesh was pale and without tone. Her facial features looked as if they'd been transposed on to a lump of Silly Putty. The excess of her bilious cheeks distorted her eyes, nose, and mouth — until they seemed compressed upon themselves. Multiple chins gave way to a sagging throat. The hair that had once been brown and as long as Munch's was now gray and cut close to the scalp.

Asia's little face scrunched in disbelief. 'Is that her?'

'Afraid so.'

The short walk from the parking lot to the wooden bench where Asia and Munch waited left Lisa short of breath and sweating.

Jill skipped ahead of her mother, lithe and unconcerned, incongruously sunny, dressed in pink stretch capris and a flowered blouse. Charlotte, the second, older daughter, shuffled behind. If Jill was the sunshine, then Charlotte was permanent midnight. Dressed all in black, her hair was long and straight and dyed

Morticia Addams black with the exception of the last two inches, which were pumpkin orange. Face pale. Eyes dead. As the teenage kid of a loser like Lisa, Charlotte appeared to be appropriately morose.

'When you turn fourteen,' Munch said sotto voce to her daughter, 'I'm locking you up.'

'I know, I know, until I hit twenty.'

'Maybe longer. Depends.'

'Don't worry, Mom, I'll be a perfect angel always.'

'Uh-huh. We'll see.'

Lisa plopped down on the bench beside them with a force that bounced Asia an inch in the air. She covered her mouth with her hand and, to her credit, successfully fought off a giggle.

'Made it,' Lisa announced, fanning herself with pudgy, unjeweled fingers. They looked like raw sausages. Her nails were gnawed to nothing, the cuticles red and angry from constant assault.

'What happened to James?' Munch asked.

'James is history.'

'Is that right?'

'He split after the first year. We had to spend all this time around each other and got to fighting nonstop. Finally he just took off.'

'Yeah,' Asia said, sneaking looks at her

cousins, 'we haven't had much luck holding on to a man either.'

Munch laughed, amused even though it was true, maybe *because* it was true. They'd both thought Rico was going to be a keeper.

Encouraged, Asia nodded knowingly. 'All the good ones are taken.'

What Munch actually thought was that when guys got to be thirty-five, forty, and were still single, there was usually a good reason for that. Her best bet at this point was to catch a guy right after a divorce or breakup, but not too soon. And there would be a reason for his newly single status, too.

Jill performed a perfect cartwheel on the grass in front of them. Asia looked impressed, but made a big point out of petting Jasper's head and saying loudly, 'Stay. Good boy.' Jasper didn't look as if he had any intention of going anywhere. It was a safe command.

Charlotte remained standing, her mouth half-open.

'Sit down,' Lisa told her. The teenager sat with all the emotion of an amoeba. Munch remembered exactly what it felt like to be fifteen. Too bad the elevator had to stop on that floor. It was an ugly age.

Lisa then turned her attention to Asia. 'How about a kiss for your auntie?'

'I'm shy,' Asia said, looking her aunt

directly in the face.

Munch swallowed a smile. 'Why don't you and Jill take Jasper for a run?' She watched the two girls skip off to the monkey bars, then turned back to Lisa. 'So what's the plan?'

'What d'ya mean?'

'Are you staying? Are the kids in school? Do you have a job?'

'When did you get so fucking nosy?'

'Which question don't you want to answer?'

'Hey, you know, I don't need this shit. Here I am, trying to make nice, and you're treating me like some secondclass citizen. Maybe this was a mistake.' Lisa attempted a pout, but even that came across as duplicitous.

Munch glanced over to where Jill and Asia were teaching Jasper how to shake hands, then turned back to Charlotte and Lisa. Charlotte had not yet spoken word one. On closer inspection Munch realized that her eyebrows were drawn on, two nihilist black chevrons punctuating her white death mask.

'Charlotte? Do you remember me?'

'Yeah.'

'Last time I saw you, you were Asia's age and Asia was a little baby.'

'They grow up fast,' Lisa said. 'Enjoy 'em while you can. Show your aunt Munch what you did.'

Charlotte cracked a sheepish smile, showing off braces. The orthodontia surprised Munch. Maybe Lisa wasn't doing a totally terrible job. Charlotte lifted her long hair to reveal a scalp shaved clean from the ears down.

'Nice, huh?' Lisa said.

Munch wondered where Lisa found the room to judge, but said nothing. She looked at her watch.

'I'm cleaning houses,' Lisa said. 'Char's in high school and picks up spare change babysitting, not that I ever see any of that. Jill is in fifth grade at Palm Elementary. Happy?'

'Ecstatic.' *Ecstatic* had been one of the words on this month's 'Word Power,' the *Reader's Digest* vocabulary quiz. *Limpid, bucolic,* and *didactic* had also been on the test, but Munch had yet to come across a suitable context to put them to use.

'What about you?' Lisa asked, pointing vaguely north. 'We drove by your old gas station. It wasn't even there anymore.'

'They bulldozed that place six years ago. I'm in Brentwood now, at a Texaco station.' Munch didn't mention her limousine business. Lisa would only think she had deep pockets to plumb. And she couldn't be more wrong about that. Munch's refurbished stretch limo barely paid for itself. Munch had

26

started A&M Limousine thinking she would cash in on the '84 Olympics when they came to Los Angeles last year. Who knew that in anticipation of the crowds so many other wannabe entrepreneurs in the city would have the same idea? Or that so many residents of the city would exit en masse and that traffic would be the lightest in recent history? Now she was stuck with the car, the insurance, a Yellow Page ad, and a too short client list. Not to mention the competition of gypsy services who didn't bother with the legalities and subsequent overhead of the proper insurance.

'You're at a Texaco station?' Lisa asked. 'Which one?' As if there were hundreds of Texaco stations in Brentwood.

They spent the next fifteen minutes listening to Lisa bring up stories of what she thought of as the glory years. Munch remembered the names and none of the stories as Lisa remembered them. Charlotte kept looking at Munch with an unmistakable hunger. Occasionally her mouth would open as if she wanted to speak, then her thin shoulders would fold forward and she'd let that unnaturally black hair fall over her face.

If Munch had had an aunt to go to, anyone, in her teen years, it might have made all the difference. Hadn't Lisa said this meeting wasn't her idea?

Jasper broke free from the girls and came bounding over to sit at Munch's feet. Lisa reached out to pat his head, but he pulled away.

'Your dog shy, too?' she asked.

Munch saw the hurt in her face before the sarcasm took hold. She reached a hand out and laid it on Lisa's fleshy shoulder. Lisa flinched as if unused to human contact. Munch found a smile for her. 'We just got him. This is all new for him. Don't take it personal.'

'We should be going anyway,' Lisa said, using both hands to hoist herself. 'I got stuff in the Laundromat. I don't want nobody ripping us off.'

'We'll have to do this again sometime,' Munch said, sounding as vague as possible. This visit definitely counted as one of the three good deeds she tried to perform each day, maybe all three, although the good deed should really be anonymous.

Charlotte hung back and petted Jasper, her Halloween hair falling down over her face. 'We had a pact.'

Munch wasn't sure if she heard Charlotte right. 'What?'

'I guess you forgot.'

Munch was suddenly flooded with memories. Lisa's cruddy little clapboard house in Inglewood, 1977, eight long years ago. Jets taking off overhead, drowning out the television that was always running. Lisa smoking and drinking beers, in over her head with bad guys on both sides of the law. Sleaze John newly dead. Munch sitting on the floor of the kids' bedroom, trying to bring some order to the mess they lived in. Charlotte was only seven then, and Jill was three. Munch had the two little girls hold out their right hands and pledge to meet again on that very spot, ten years from the day. It was all she could think to do for them. She promised herself that on that future date she would explain to them the facts of their lives. That their parents were assholes and to let it go because it wasn't going to do them any good to feel sorry for themselves. They only had themselves to count on and account to. Maybe they'd figured that out already. You didn't get straight A's without a good work ethic and study habits.

Munch fished a Bel Air Texaco business card out of her wallet and gave it to Charlotte. 'No, I didn't forget. We said ten years, right? We're early.'

The card disappeared with sleight-of-hand speed, then Charlotte turned and followed her mother and sister.

Munch started to call for Asia, but the girl was already beside her instead of pushing her boundaries as usual. Asia slipped a hand into her mother's, and Munch wondered if she was going through one of her clingy stages again.

'Oh, no,' Asia said as they got in their GTO for the drive home.

'What?'

'Jasper's tags are gone.'

Munch cast one last backward glance at the park. *Strange*, she thought. 'Don't worry, Asia. We'll get him some more.'

3

Charlotte knew it was her fault. Not that she had pulled the trigger, but if she had left things alone, hadn't gotten involved, Steve might still be alive. Not *might. Would* be alive. Who was she kidding?

He was just a kid. Now he'd always be a tenth-grader. His framed yearbook picture atop his closed coffin would be her last memory of him. They'd closed the coffin because the body had been burned. Standing there for the service, touching the bronze box that would carry him into the earth, she thought she smelled the cooked flesh. Her mother said she was crazy. Her mother said that a lot.

Charlotte knew what she knew, though. She knew right from wrong.

Steve's life would not be in vain. His death would not be forgotten. That was her pledge to him.

He had wanted out, not dead. She had gone about it all wrong. She might as well have painted a big target on both their backs. It was all her fault. Everything was so screwed up. She banged her fist against her head. She

31

wanted to use the wall, but that would make too much noise, and her mother was in the living room. No doubt cooking up one of her schemes.

Charlotte didn't care about herself, but Steve had wanted to live. He cared. He cared. Look where it got him.

She twirled her hair around her finger, around and around, tighter and tighter. She needed something to focus on besides her unbearable guilt. She should have stopped him, should have asked him what he was going to do. She should have known what would happen.

As she thought, she paced. Eight steps, turn, eight steps.

Worrywart, her mother said, you worry about things that are none of your business.

But it was her business. Her mother never asked enough questions. She was happy in her ignorance. Charlotte wished she didn't know what she knew. Jill needed looking after every second, always had. So many things around to cause pain, to make her sick. Poisons, broken glass, a door left open, unattended pools where she could drown. Brakes failed, fires started, there were diseases with no cures. It was all real and it was all around them.

Pace and pull. Her scalp itched. Crazy as it

sounded, she wished she could reach up inside her skin and attack the follicles from within. Instead, she wrapped just a few strands from the back around her finger and yanked them loose. The tingling relief was short-lived before the shame at her weakness set in.

She needed to get out, but she couldn't leave her room until she had everything in order. What else hadn't she thought of? How much worse could one person feel? If only she could trade places with Steve, but then who would look after her mom and sister?

She realized she had lost count of her steps. That was just the kind of inattention to detail that let people get hurt. What kind of a monster was she? The more she tried to be a good, decent person, the worse things went. There were times she'd love to give up, but she didn't have that luxury and she certainly didn't deserve an easy way out.

★ ★ ★

Monday morning, two days after meeting Lisa and the girls at the park, Munch was paged over the gas station's loud-speaker. A call on line two. She punched the appropriate button. 'Munch speaking.'

'Has Charlotte called you?'

It took Munch a second to recognize Lisa's voice. Munch's boss, Lou, stuck his head out of his office and asked her if she'd heard yet from the alternator shop. She shook her head no, then covered her free ear to block out the sounds of revving engines and compressed air escaping the tire machine. 'No, why?'

'She's gone.'

'What are you talking about?'

'Her bed was empty this morning. She never made it to school.'

Munch looked at the clock. It was only ten. 'Maybe you're overreacting.'

'That's what the cops said.'

'You called the cops already?'

'They won't do anything until she's missing at least a day. The worthless fucks, but what are you going to do? So much for my tax dollars.'

Munch didn't get a big picture of Lisa filing a 1040. She was probably referring to sales tax. 'Lisa, it's not like she's a toddler. Teenagers do play hooky sometimes. I know you did.'

'Char's not like that, and she didn't run away. Nothing is missing from her room. You don't know this kid. She never misses a beat, everything's gotta be just so. She's kinda fanatical like that. Besides, if she was going to split, she'd take her Doc Martens and her music.'

Munch thought about her own police connections. Mace St John was in homicide and Rico . . . Rico was out of the question. 'Lisa, it's too soon to freak out. Wait until school's out. She'll probably come home pretending she was there all day.'

'Why won't anyone listen to me? Something's wrong. A mother knows.'

'I knew something was wrong the minute I saw her.' Munch looked at the Peg-Board full of work orders and briefly debated the value of expressing her honest reactions to Lisa and then decided to go for it. 'I understand that you're upset, but where do you get off acting surprised?'

'Are you going to help me or not?'

Munch sighed. This was how it always started. She pinched the bridge of her nose between two grease-stained fingers. 'If she doesn't come home by tonight, give me a call.'

Lisa hung up without telling Munch to have a nice day.

Munch stared at the phone for a moment then dialed Mace St John's number. She had met Mace St John in a biker bar in Venice. It was February 12, 1977. She remembered the date because it was her last day drinking and using. He was a homicide cop, there to arrest her for the murder of her father, Flower

George. Now he was her friend. He'd married her former probation officer Caroline Rhinehart, and the two of them were Asia's godparents. So much had changed. The only thing that hadn't changed was that Flower George was still dead. Thank God. George Mancini was the kind of guy you wanted to dig up so you could shoot him again.

Munch was surprised when St John personally answered the phone. 'West L.A. Detectives.'

'Slow day?'

'I'm not complaining,' he said. 'What's up?'

'Asia's aunt and two cousins have moved back to town.'

'She's got an aunt? You never said.'

'Yeah, well, I never expected to hear from her again. She went into the witness protection program. I always thought that was a lifetime commitment.'

'Not necessarily. What's her name?'

'Lisa Slokum. She might have gone back to her maiden name, Garillo.' Munch looked up as Lou emerged from his office. Lou mimed lifting a coffee cup to his lips and pointed to her. She pantomimed back, *Make it a tall one.* 'She's got two kids, girls. The older one is fifteen and Lisa thinks she's gone missing.'

'Thinks?'

'Apparently the kid didn't make it to

school this morning.'

'Fifteen you said?'

'Yeah.'

'Any signs of foul play?'

'Not that she said. She's claiming maternal instinct, but June Cleaver she's not.'

'What do you want me to do?' he asked.

'Nothing *to* do, right? Not till the kid's been gone for a while?'

'Well, yes and no. Just to be prepared, you might want to tell the mother to locate the most recent photo of . . . what's the missing girl's name?'

'Charlotte. I'll tell her. Thanks.'

'What's his face hasn't called, has he?'

St John was of course referring to Rico the Dumper, aka He Who Must Do the Right Thing When an Old Girlfriend Shows Up Pregnant. 'No, I didn't even get the wedding invitation. Where did the happy couple register? Condoms-R-Us? No, too late for that.' They'd probably had the kid by now.

'So you haven't heard?'

'What?'

'I don't know the whole story,' he said. 'I stopped in at the Pacific Division Station last week and ran into Art Becker.'

Art Becker had been Rico Chacón's partner when Rico had first moved to Los Angeles. He was also Rico's partner when

37

Rico and she fell in love and was still his partner when Rico broke her heart. 'And how was Art baby?'

'Good. Maybe I shouldn't say any more.'

'Oh, no, you don't. What do you know?'

'Turns out Kathy was never pregnant and the wedding never happened.'

Munch felt a funny buzzing in her ears and shooting sensations of heat radiated up her back. The feelings weren't entirely unpleasant, but then neither is that first second when scalding coolant contacts your flesh. In that first instant of getting burned, you can't even tell if the water is hot or cold. The blisters that form later are always a big clue.

'Munch?'

'I'm still here.'

'The guy's an asshole any way you look at it.'

'I know. I was there, remember?'

'Yeah, but I know how women are. They get stupid over this kind of thing.'

'I'm not most women.'

'You don't have to tell me.'

Munch smiled at the left-handed compliment. St John couldn't know that one of her secret beliefs was that other women, normal women, had very different instincts from her when it came to life issues, especially those concerning men. Some women were looking for a man to take care of them. She was more interested in the kind of guy who wouldn't get in the way of her doing her own thing.

'Thanks for the heads-up,' she said, and instantly regretted using the phrase. You give the guys at work a line like that and you were opening yourself up for a comeback like 'That's what she said.' To which her only response could be to walk away. Fortunately, St John wasn't that kind of guy, at least not to her.

She hung up and considered calling her AA sponsor, Ruby, but she had already spent too much time on personal business. It was time to get to work.

* * *

Come midday, she was on the gas island imprinting a credit card when some man spoke to her over the tops of the cars getting their tanks filled.

'You should be ashamed,' he said.

She didn't know who he was, but he was looking right at her when he spoke.

'You're taking advantage, holding me hostage,' he said.

A lady in a Buick stopped putting on her lipstick to listen.

The guy gestured to a Chevy Impala that

had been towed in an hour earlier. Munch put it together now. The guy needed a new starter.

'You're ripping me off,' he said, louder than was necessary to reach her ears, but he was playing to an audience. 'Eighty dollars for a new starter, forty dollars to put it in. You people are crooks.'

She could have explained to him that he was in Brentwood. That in an upscale neighborhood everything costs more, from gasoline to rent. That on whatever planet he came from the cost of a starter and solenoid might be cheaper. She could have suggested he go to the Chevy dealer if he thought her station's prices were unreasonable. No dealership would offer him a rebuilt unit, and they got a hundred and thirty for the part new. Never mind the labor.

But this guy was obviously just interested in being a jackass, was pissed off at having to spend unplanned money, and was venting his frustration by embarrassing her. She finished imprinting the credit card, put the slip on a small clipboard, and faced the guy.

'You're going to have to pay in cash,' she said. Since he was already being a big poop butt, she wasn't going to give him an opportunity to stop payment on a check or refuse the charge on his credit card bill.

He didn't like that either and walked away in a huff. Munch resisted the temptation to move the guy's job to the front of the line so as to be rid of him faster. She didn't believe the nicer, patient customers should be penalized for not being obnoxious.

As it turned out, he was out of there an hour later, much to everyone's relief.

At four-thirty the school bus dropped off Asia at the corner in front of the gas station. At five Munch called Lisa.

'Still no word,' Lisa said. 'I'm going nuts.'

'I need to go home and check on the dog. If you want, we'll come over and help you look.'

'It'll be dark by then.'

'I'm sure she's been out after dark before.' Judging from the girl's punk-goth look, she probably preferred it.

★   ★   ★

Jasper was waiting at the front window when Munch and Asia arrived home. His whimpers of delight sounded as if he were in pain with pleasure. Munch remembered making similar noises with Rico.

She and Asia sank to the floor with Jasper and indulged him with ear scratching and words of reassurance that he was the best dog

41

ever and they had missed him, too. The fur on his muzzle below each eye was darkened with streaks of moisture.

'He's been crying,' Asia said, using her white Catholic-school-uniform shirt to wipe the dog's face dry.

Munch went into the kitchen to check the answering machine.

'Mom,' Asia called from the living room, 'come here quick. You've got to see this.'

A stack of their shoes was piled next to where Jasper had stood vigil at the front window. They hadn't been chewed, but judging by the strands of red-gold hair and indentations on the tops, he had lain on the shoes for hours.

'Aww,' Asia said. 'He wanted to smell us.' She pulled him into a hug. 'Don't worry, boy, we're never leaving you. Ever.'

Jasper gave Munch a bloodshot, woeful look.

'You're going to be high-maintenance, aren't you?' she said.

He squirmed free from Asia and rolled on his back, hind legs flopping apart. She hoped he wasn't the kind of dog who did that in public every chance he got.

Munch pushed PLAY on the answering machine. Lisa's fatalistic-sounding voice reported that Charlotte had still not surfaced.

Munch called her back, got directions to her house, and promised to be over as soon as she had changed from her work clothes.

Munch and Asia brought Jasper with them. He'd already proven himself to be a good car dog. When he wasn't looking out the window, he curled up quietly in Asia's lap. And when they arrived at Lisa's ground-floor apartment in Palms, Jasper never strayed farther than two feet from his new family. Munch liked that he didn't need a leash. Mace St John's dogs, which she sometimes watched, couldn't be trusted not to gallop off to points unknown. Especially Brownie the hunter, who would chase a rabbit into the briars, thorns be damned.

Lisa was waiting for them on the concrete stoop. She wore black leggings, an oversize man's shirt, and tennis shoes with no socks. There were tears in her beady little eyes.

'Did you eat?' Munch asked.

'Not yet.'

Munch handed her a McDonald's bag filled with an order identical to the ones she and Asia had just consumed. Big Mac and fries for Lisa, a Chicken McNuggets Happy Meal for Jill.

Once inside, Jill immediately took Asia in hand. The two of them plopped down on the lone piece of furniture in the front

43

room, a beanbag chair. Jasper chewed burrs loose from his front paws as the girls watched MTV on a stack of televisions. The top set provided the picture, the bottom unit the sound. Janet Jackson strutted in black leather and pumped her fists while demanding to know, 'What have you done for me lately?'

Munch scanned the room. Lisa's home-making abilities hadn't improved any over the years. A stack of blankets and two pillows were in the corner under a floor lamp with three metal, cone-shaped shades — two of which dangled loose from their pivot plates. Neo-Dumpster motif. Someone was reading a Danielle Steele novel — Munch preferred Ken Follet or James Michener, or whatever abridged versions Reader's Digest Con-densed Books sent for the month. The carpet needed vacuuming. Lisa was probably waiting for someone to throw away a Hoover that still sort of worked.

'May I?' Munch asked, pointing toward the hallway leading to the other rooms.

Lisa shrugged. 'I don't know what you think you're going to find.'

'I don't either.' Munch glanced back at Asia and decided she was safe enough for the moment.

The first bedroom was obviously Jill's,

decorated with a jumble of color and bright plastic. Hello Kitty and Disney characters adorned the walls. Clothes almost covered the floor. The second bedroom was smaller and darker and suited the missing girl. There was no third bedroom.

Instead of taking one of the rooms for herself and making the kids share, Lisa chose to sleep on the floor.

Charlotte's walls were covered with punk-rock posters of bands that had taken a darkened and perverted twist on the sixties and seventies celebration of dope and free love. The bands' names said it all: Suicidal Tendencies; Black Flag; Circle Jerks. Sid Vicious and Johnny Rotten of the Sex Pistols glared with violent malevolence from the glossy depths of their two-by-four rectangles of immortality. Rock 'n' roll was going downhill.

Charlotte's bed was a mattress on the floor. The blankets were askew. A hair dryer was plugged into the top socket of the outlet next to her bed. A boom-box cord utilized the bottom socket. Her clothes were folded neatly in two plastic milk crates. In fact, on closer inspection every item in the room, with exception of the bedcovers, showed a keen attention to symmetry. The posters were arranged in neat rows, the cassettes in even stacks. Four glass thermometers in their plastic cases lay parallel on top of one of the clothing crates.

'What's this about?' Munch asked, pointing to the thermometers.

Lisa shrugged. 'Kids.'

Munch felt bad about invading the girl's space. It seemed to be about all she had. A narrow track of the carpet between the door and closet was worn to the wood beneath. The expression *someone's walking on my grave* came unbidden to her mind. They used to say that all the time back in her day, but she hadn't said or thought it for years. Must be Lisa's influence, pulling out the old memories. She shook it off.

'You got any recent pictures of Charlotte?'

'No,' Lisa said, around bites from her burger, 'we couldn't find that box.'

Munch considered again the sparsely furnished apartment. Apparently many boxes had gone 'astray.'

'Maybe the school would?' Munch stepped into the room and saw no desk. *What would St John be looking for?* she wondered.

Lisa brushed shredded lettuce from her shirt. 'Yeah, she said something about working on the yearbook.'

'How long have you been back?'

46

'You mean in L.A.?'

Munch made note of the stall and waited for Lisa's answer.

'About a year, but we've moved a few times.'

Munch picked up a cassette by the Dead Kennedys with their current hit, 'Too Drunk to Fuck.' That made her smile. Been there. Now the opposite was true. Too *sober* to fuck. Hell, she could barely dance sober.

She put down the tape and stood in front of a Boy George poster as he poutingly asked, 'Do you really want to hurt me?'

Yes, she thought, and felt herself take a firm step toward the next generation, the older one who 'just didn't get kids these days.'

Munch opened the closet and found it no wider than the door. Three pairs of identical black jeans hung from white plastic hangers. The shelf above the clothes dowel held two pairs of high-top tennis shoes, the favored black Doc Martens boots, a blender, two blackened bananas, and a jar of protein powder.

'Look at this shit,' Lisa said. 'She's gonna bring ants.'

Munch didn't answer. Ants were the least of their worries. True to form, a marinade of denial and nonresponsibility, Lisa had to keep

47

pretending that she was a normal mother faced with middle-class problems.

Munch pulled down a boot, surprised at its weight. She reached inside, closing her fingers around the neck of a glass bottle.

'What's that?' Lisa asked.

'Vodka.'

'Oh, God,' Lisa said, a fat, bloated hand moving theatrically to her throat. 'She shouldn't have that.'

Munch reached into the other boot and pulled out a month's worth of birth control pills. The ring dispenser was still full.

'I got her those,' Lisa said proudly.

'She hasn't taken any.'

'She doesn't like how they blow her up. Says she'd rather just not have sex. I said, 'Whatever.' I just want her to break the chain, you know?'

The chain of unwed mothers, teenage pregnancy, crime, and poverty? Or poor housekeeping and hygiene? Munch wondered.

She was starting to question if bringing Charlotte home was the right thing after all.

'Here's how I know something's wrong,' Lisa said.

Munch followed her into the kitchen. Lisa opened the refrigerator and produced a brown cardboard box. She opened it and showed Munch the rows of glass bottles with rubber tops. 'Her insulin. She can't go more than twenty-four hours without it. Now do you think I'm overreacting?'

'She's diabetic?'

'Yeah, it's been a real bitch, too.'

'What did the cops say when you told them that?'

'Uh, they, uh . . . '

'You did tell them, right?'

'I'm not sure.'

'That should have been the first thing you said. What's the matter with you?'

'Fuck them anyway,' Lisa said. 'We don't need their help.'

Munch pulled three vials from the cardboard box.

'What are you doing?' Lisa asked.

'I'm taking these with me.'

'It has to be kept refrigerated and you'll need these.' Lisa rummaged through a drawer under the counter and produced a handful of individually wrapped syringes. Munch froze. She was allergic to needles and drugs; they were liable to make her break out in addiction. *This is different*, she told herself. *This is medicine*. 'How will I know how much to give her?'

Lisa handed Munch an insulin test kit of a lancet and strips. 'She knows what she needs.'

'Write me a letter authorizing me to act as your agent,' Munch said.

'My what?'

'I'm going to go to the school and try to get a picture of Charlotte. They're not gonna want to help me without your say-so. You should be here in case she comes back or calls. Where does she go to hang out?'

'Don't you think I would have looked?' Lisa said. 'Believe me, no one's seen her because she didn't leave on her own.'

'Write me that note,' Munch said, remembering Charlotte's expression — how there had seemed to be something she wanted to tell Munch. She should have made some excuse to get the girl alone and hear what was going on.

Lisa had to go to Jill for a piece of clean writing paper. Ten minutes later, Munch, Asia, and Jasper were headed for Charlotte's school.

'Who do we know who has a truck?' Asia asked after strapping her seat belt on.

'Lou has a truck. Why?'

'Jill said most of their stuff was at a storage place and all they needed was a truck and then they could get it back.'

'A truck and the back rent, I'll wager.'

'Jill said it was the kind of place where you

can take it out in trade.' Asia scratched Jasper's ears and then, in a tone that implied that whatever she didn't understand would be a mystery to anybody else, rolled her eyes and said, 'Whatever that means.'

4

Munch drove to Venice High School on the chance that someone in charge might be working late. She knew the location well from the outside. Many of her old friends had gone there. She would have, too, if Flower George (her so-called father) hadn't insisted she start earning. She'd only been fourteen, but George said she was mature for her age. She had him to thank for that.

Venice High was only a few long city blocks from Lisa's apartment. Charlotte might have walked it if she gave herself enough time.

Munch was in luck. The front door was unlocked and lights still glowed in several of the ground-floor offices. Jasper had to wait in the car, which he didn't seem happy about.

Munch followed signs in the hallway to the administration wing, and after several turns with Asia in tow, she arrived at the registrar's office. An older woman with a sour expression greeted her warily.

'Can I help you?' The woman's tone and shaking head implied that she'd rather not.

Munch took a step closer to the high counter. It was her first time inside a high school office, never mind a classroom; she felt nervous and out of place. 'My niece didn't make it to school this morning and we still haven't heard from her. We're worried. The police asked us for a recent photograph and I was hoping you'd have one here.'

'Her name?' The woman had yet to smile or make any small gesture to put Munch at ease.

'Charlotte Slokum.'

Mrs Sourpuss rose to her feet grudgingly and disappeared into another room. She reappeared a long minute later with a well-coiffed lady in a skirt suit.

'I'm Tanya Lubell,' the woman said, extending a manicured hand. 'I'm the principal. Charlotte is your niece?'

'You know her then?'

'Very well. She's in the honors program and coeditor of this year's yearbook.'

'She is?' Munch realized her surprise wasn't serving her well. For a moment she felt guilty. Here she was playing the role of concerned aunt and she didn't know the first thing about the kid.

'We haven't seen them in years,' Asia said. 'Since I was a little kid.'

Munch put a hand on her daughter's thin shoulder and gave it a squeeze.

'Do you know who her friends are? Were

any of them also absent today?' Munch asked.

'It's been a hectic day,' Ms Lubell said. 'We had the memorial for one of our students, Steven Koon, yesterday, and we've been running counseling sessions nonstop since the news of his murder. I'm very concerned to hear that Charlotte is missing.'

Munch looked up at the black wreath on the office bulletin board and made the connection. Steven Koon. She'd read about the teenager's 'apparent' murder in the *Los Angeles Times*. His body was found in the trunk of a half-burned car in the alley behind the lumberyard on Lincoln Boulevard. The fire had burned itself out before completely destroying the corpse. The boy, according to the newspaper story, had recently been questioned by police in connection with a series of home burglaries. The police were calling the death a homicide. Ms Lubell seemed to agree with that assessment.

Munch remembered thinking as she read about the dead boy that the body had been found in Rico's jurisdiction. She had wondered if he caught the case and how it must have affected him since his own daughter was fifteen, maybe sixteen by now.

'Were Charlotte and Steven friends?' she asked.

'Part of a small group that ate lunch together sometimes. Her mother didn't tell you?'

'No, but she's, uh . . . ' Munch paused, unsure how she wanted to complete the sentence.

Tanya Lubell nodded sagely. 'I've met her mother.'

'How has Charlotte's attendance been in general? Has she missed many days?'

'Today would be her first. Sometimes we have trouble getting her to go home.' Ms Lubell paused to give Munch a meaningful look. 'I was told that you wanted a current picture. Do you mind if I look at your identification?'

Munch produced her driver's license and Lisa's note. Ms Lubell studied both and then said, 'Wait a moment, please.' She left Munch standing at the counter while she went back to her office to verify the information, Munch assumed.

Ten minutes passed before she appeared again. 'Which police officer asked you for her picture?'

'His name is Detective Mace St John. He works out of West Los Angeles. He's a family friend. I don't know if you know this or not, but Charlotte is diabetic and doesn't have any insulin with her.'

The principal studied Munch with a focus

that would have done credit to any law enforcement officer. If Munch had anything to confess, she was sure she'd be tempted under the scrutiny of this woman's steady gray eyes.

'I wasn't aware of the diabetes,' Lubell said finally, 'but I suspected there was something.'

'Her life hasn't been easy,' Munch said, wanting to tell this woman more, sensing an ally. Half her students probably had it rough at home. How much could she allow herself to care?

'Come with me,' Lubell said. They walked across the campus until they came to a building near the football field. The only sounds were the woman's high heels clacking on the concrete and the jingle of keys on her large metal ring. Munch and Asia practically had to trot to keep up. Asia put her head down and pumped her arms. She wasn't the kind of kid to complain or ask for special consideration. Munch wanted to scoop her in her arms and carry her, but Asia would hate being babied.

Ms Lubell unlocked a classroom full of drafting boards, paper cutters, and bulletin boards studded with photographs. The pictures were arranged in exact rows, as if rulers and levels had been put to the task.

'Charlotte's work?' Munch asked.

'Yes, your niece is rather ... exacting. Almost to a fault.' Lubell opened a filing cabinet and pulled out a folder. 'I called the Pacific Division Police Station.'

Munch felt her heart drop a beat. Rico's station.

Lubell handed Munch a sheet of proofs. 'They had no knowledge of this situation with Charlotte but seemed to know who you were.'

'Who'd you talk to?' Munch asked, scanning the tiny pictures for Charlotte.

'Sergeant Flutie, the watch commander. He said he'd have a detective get in touch with Lisa Slokum. Find the number and I'll give you the negative. You can have a print made from that.'

'Twelve.' Munch pointed as she spoke. Charlotte's hair was lighter and streaked in the picture, but the facial features were the same. 'Did he say which detective?'

'No. We can call back if it's important.'

Munch looked down and saw Asia watching her closely. 'That's all right,' she said, taking the negative, 'we've gotten what we came for.' Then another thought occurred to her. 'Is there a picture here of Steven Koon?'

Ms Lubell studied the sheet briefly and then said, 'Yes, here he is.' Her voice clotted with emotion.

57

'Maybe I should have that one, too,' Munch said gently.

Ms Lubell gave her the film after a moment's hesitation.

'You said you've been running counseling sessions,' Munch said. 'Is there any chance I can speak to Charlotte's counselor?'

'I don't think Charlotte's met with the grief counselor yet. Her school guidance counselor would be Mr Lombardi. He's gone for the day, but I'll leave a note in his box.'

'This is my work number,' Munch said, giving Ms Lubell a Bel Air Texaco card. Munch then opened her checkbook and tore off a deposit slip from the back, ripping out the square that her name, address, and telephone number were written on. 'And this is home.' The trading of deposit slips, sans the account numbers, was a time-honored AA practice. Most recovering alkies and addicts didn't have formal calling cards.

'Please keep us informed,' Ms Lubell said. 'Charlotte has made such strides since she's been here.' Her throat hiccuped with emotion. When she resumed speaking, her voice was too high and the words came out in a rush. 'We've already had one tragedy too many.'

Munch carefully folded the negatives into a sheet of loose notebook paper from one of the desks before slipping the film into her pocket. 'I'll get these back to you.'

Tanya Lubell could only nod. Asia looked as if she was about to cry as well. Munch gave her hand a reassuring squeeze and led her outside.

★　★　★

Munch took the negatives to a one-hour photo developer and then called St John at home from a 7-Eleven, where she also bought a small disposable ice chest for Charlotte's insulin.

'You want to meet our new dog?' she asked St John after determining he and Caroline had already had their dinner.

'Sure,' he said. 'I'm glad you called. I have some things to tell you about your friend Lisa Garillo Slokum.'

'Yeah,' she said. 'I need a few more friends like her.'

Ten minutes later she knocked on the door of his little house on the Venice canals. Brownie (their newest foundling) barked, but didn't run out when St John opened the door. Mace St John was wearing sweats and looked tired. She knew it was close to his bedtime. He worked the early shift and rose each morning at four-thirty. She was a morning

59

person, too, but it was usually at least light out when she got to work.

St John knelt down and greeted Jasper, more interested for the moment in the dog than in his goddaughter or Munch. Jasper was much more interested in sniffing after Brownie, who sat on her haunches to thwart him. Munch laughed. Samantha, St John's Lab/husky mix, approached slowly. She had aged drastically after losing Nicky, her soul and kennel mate. Munch petted her gently.

'He's a nice dog,' St John proclaimed, straightening to his feet. He ruffled Asia's curls. 'How's it going, squirt?'

Asia pushed his hand away, feigning annoyance, but clearly beamed under his attention. It struck Munch how hungry the girl was for male energy.

I'm working on it, she thought.

'Caroline's in the living room watching television.' St John directed his words to Asia while indicating to Munch with a tilt of his head that she should hang back. Asia trotted off to join the detective's wife, her god-mother. Munch followed St John into the kitchen.

'Want anything?' he asked.

'No,' she said, thinking of the many answers to that question, 'I'm good.'

He pulled a bottle of orange juice from the

fridge and took a drink. 'I talked to a friend of mine in the FBI.'

'About Lisa?'

He nodded. 'She tell you why she's out of the witness protection program?'

'Something about the guys she snitched out weren't a threat anymore.'

'Uh-huh. That's part of it.' He took another sip and wiped his mouth. 'She was kicked out.'

'They do that?'

'If you get caught running a scam on your handlers.'

'What kind of a scam?'

'She claimed to be in fear for her life, that she saw one of the bikers she turned state's evidence against. She needed to relocate, she said. Investigators learned that the man she had given a detailed description of — including his name and the threats he made — had died in a robbery two months earlier. The investigator grew suspicious when her testimony began vague, then sharpened in detail as she told it. In our experience, witnesses, truthful witnesses, begin with specific details and remember vague impressions later.'

'She's never going to win any awards for brilliance,' Munch said.

'What time did she call you this morning?'

'Around ten.'

'And what did she say exactly?'

'That Charlotte was missing and something was wrong.'

'Little early to jump to that conclusion, unless . . . '

'Unless what?'

He shook his head, unwilling to complete the sentence for her.

'There's more,' Munch said, thinking there was always more. 'Charlotte has diabetes. She's dependent on insulin and doesn't have any with her. I went to her school to get a picture and found out she was friends with that boy they found murdered in Venice last week. Steven Koon.'

St John listened without showing any signs of concern, but then he wasn't the type to reveal his every thought. 'What are you going to do now?' he asked.

'I'm getting some photos of Charlotte and Steven made from the negatives, although her hair is different now. The ends are dyed orange. We'll make up some posters, I guess. Check the hospitals and clinics. What should I do?'

'We'll put out a teletype to NCIC and the Missing Person Unit of the Department of Justice in Sacramento. We'll also contact the National Center for Missing and Exploited Children. That'll go out nationwide.'

'With the notices of all the other missing kids?'

He shrugged. 'It's what we do in a case like this.'

'What if there's foul play involved?'

'Somebody see her being forced into a car or hear her scream?'

'Not that I know of.'

'Find any blood at the house?'

'No.' She almost wished there were blood. At least it would get the police motivated.

St John spread his hands. 'Cops like things simple. If it looks like the kid is a good candidate to run away, they'll accept that. It's not illegal for her to run away. If the kid was taken against her will and doesn't surface within a day, it's probably too late to save her.'

'I really don't think Charlotte ran away. It doesn't add up. She's got all the freedom she could want now, a place to sleep, school isn't a problem.'

'The mother sounds like a jerk.'

'Yeah, but Lisa's not the kind of parent you run away from as much as rise above.'

The look St John gave her was a mix of sympathy and understanding. He probably thought she was talking about herself as a child, and maybe she was.

'Isn't there anything else we can do?' she asked.

'Wait.'

Maybe if he had a kid of his own or had seen the sadness in Charlotte's eyes, he would feel different.

'Well, thanks anyway,' she said. She followed him into the living room. Asia was sitting with Caroline and telling her all about Jasper. 'C'mon, honey,' Munch said, smiling at Caroline, 'time to go.'

As they drove away from the St Johns', there was an echo going off in Munch's head. It sounded like this: *Rico, Rico, Rico.* The internal clamor persisted until she wanted to roll down the window and shout his name.

She picked up the photographs on the way home. At least now she had a photo of Charlotte for the police. Once Asia got started on her homework, Munch made the call she'd talked herself out of for months. She still knew his number by heart, as if it were branded on the muscles of her fingertips.

'Hi,' she said when he answered on the first ring. 'It's me.' She paused, giving him time to recognize her voice and remember what he needed to remember. 'Got a minute?'

'Hi, sure,' Rico said back, his voice tenderly surprised, then concerned. 'Is everything all right?'

Everything. That's a tall order. 'I wanted to

ask you something.'

'Shoot.'

'Don't think I didn't consider it.'

'Things have changed.'

'I heard, but that's not what I'm calling about.'

'Kathy was never pregnant. I think she thought she was. I'm sure she did. She had all the symptoms — '

'You think that makes it better?'

'It makes it different.'

'Maybe, but it doesn't matter anymore,' Munch said. Too much time had passed, eight months. An aeon. He'd made his choice. If he really cared so much, he should have demanded a blood test before he chose Kathy over her and shredded her heart. And why hadn't he called as soon as he found out?

'This isn't a conversation we should have on the phone,' he said. 'Can I come over?'

'It's late.'

'Or we can meet somewhere, get some coffee.'

She pressed the heel of her hand against her forehead. She was having trouble breathing normally. His face with its crooked nose, quick smile, and soulful brown eyes flashed in her memory. His long, sinewy body also came to mind — the way he wrapped an arm protectively around her shoulders, how he made her feel when he took her face in his hands. She could almost feel him next to her, inside her.

You could at least hear him out, she thought.

No, she countered. *I promised not to set myself up like that again.*

Don't be a cold bitch.

Yeah, but don't be a chump doormat either.

'We've already talked about it,' she said.

'I mean with me in on the discussion, too.'

She heard the smile in his voice and surrendered ever so slightly to his charm. He knew, and more significantly, he remembered 'the committee' that raged between her ears. Points for that, for paying attention.

'I can't,' she began, trying to remember why it was so important to resist him. 'I can't tonight. I have a family emergency. My niece has disappeared. She's only fifteen, diabetic, and she was friends with Steven Koon.'

'What's her name?'

Munch heard the shift in his tone, away from the personal. His walls went up, walls that protected them both.

'Are you on the case?'

'Always,' he said.

She told him everything she'd discovered already, including what St John had said about Lisa leaving witness protection, and that Munch had a somewhat current photo of Charlotte.

'I've been working the burglary angle on the Steven Koon homicide,' Rico said. 'There appears to be a ring. The burglaries have been similar and haven't stopped. Homes are broken into when the occupants are away. The phone lines are cut, then the thieves steal jewelry, cash, and electronic equipment and drive away in the homeowner's car. These are two- and three-car families, so there's always a car in the garage. Steven Koon's body was found in one of those cars.'

Munch considered the intel that the victims were away when their homes were hit. Her past experiences on both sides of the law had turned her into something of an expert in criminal matters. 'Sounds like someone had inside information. How many, uh, incidents?'

'Seven, but so far the only thing I've found to connect them all is that the people all lived within a five-mile radius of each other.'

'Walking distance,' Munch said.

'That has occurred to us,' he said. 'I'd like to have one of the photographs of your niece. How about I stop by your work tomorrow morning?'

'I'll be there.' She hung up the phone gingerly, as if any sudden movements could upset the balance of the universe. Munch's was due to rock.

Overdue.

5

The following morning Munch and Asia arrived at the gas station in Brentwood together, as usual. Before and after school, Munch's boss, Lou, allowed Asia to share his office. Sometimes they warred over the small television. Lou kept it tuned to the local financial channel. Asia preferred cartoons. Lou gave in more often than not.

As soon as Asia's school bus departed, Munch told Lou about Charlotte and her emergency. She had come to work in her uniform in case he couldn't spare her.

'Go ahead and take off,' he said. 'I've got the work covered here.'

'Thanks, I'm waiting for Rico. I'll split as soon as he gets here.'

'He's back in the picture? Since when?'

'He's not exactly back.' She showed Lou the posters she'd had made of Charlotte.

'He wanted one of these.'

Lou raised an eyebrow. 'What's his wife think of him seeing you?'

'He doesn't have a wife.'

'But I thought — '

'Yeah, me, too. Just goes to show you where

69

thinking gets you.'

'Be careful,' Lou said, pulling on his lower lip the way he did when one of his stocks took a dive.

'I'm not looking to get hurt, you know,' Munch said. She saw Rico pull in. 'Speak of the devil.'

Lou grunted a response.

Rico was driving a black-and-white, which caused her heart to flutter with emotions that were too mixed to decipher. He was wearing a dark shirt and tie and looked improbably, unfairly, and exasperatingly good, although his forehead was creased with worry lines that Munch didn't remember being there before. Was homicide getting him down or was his near brush with matrimony the cause? She tucked in her gray uniform shirt, flicked her braid behind her, and went out to greet him.

His smile was full of relief, and she wondered what he had been expecting.

'Can we get that coffee?' he asked.

'I don't have time right now. I want to hit the streets and see what I can find out.'

His expression was blank, betraying nothing of what might be going on inside his man-brain. She hoped her face was as expressionless.

She handed him the photograph of Charlotte, explaining to him about the hair.

Caught in still life, the girl looked very young. Sometimes Munch forgot how young fifteen could be. She had been so old herself by then.

'There's some outreach programs in Hollywood,' Rico said. 'Covenant House, Passage to Hope, Paths. They might be a good place to start.'

'What about Venice?' she asked.

'You should try there, too, but Hollywood is the mecca of runaway teenagers. The woman who runs Passage to Hope is very savvy. She's helped the police before. In fact, she identified a rash of prostitute killings as serial.'

'Thanks, I'll keep that in mind.' It was odd not to touch him. She'd gotten more truly naked with him than with any man ever — had let him know her inside and out. Eight months of separation hadn't washed away all those memories. At times she worried that she'd never get over him.

Would his flesh still thrill her or was all that gone? The Rico of her imagination still took her breath away, robbed her of her free will. She visited him in her dreams, woke with the feel of his hand cupping her. The disappointment didn't set in until she was fully conscious. She reminded herself that she had phoned him. Time to snap out of it.

'Are you seeing anyone?' he asked.

She was tempted to tell him that she'd recently met a great guy named Jasper, but she wasn't going to lie.

'No. I've been busy.' *What was that?* she wondered. *Excuse or opening?*

'It's not that easy to make time for a love life when you're raising a kid,' he said.

'And it's not that easy to find a guy worth the hassle.'

He took a step closer, too close. 'Please don't count me out until you hear me out.'

'I'll be fair,' she said, finding it difficult to speak or even breathe.

'I'm sure of that.'

Kiss me, she thought. *Make your move.*

'You're right, though,' he said. 'This isn't the time.'

★ ★ ★

Munch went back to her house to change out of her uniform and check on Jasper. He greeted her with as much enthusiasm after she'd been gone for only a few hours as he had when they'd left him alone for the day. He'd also managed to open her closet door and bring out three and a half pairs of her shoes to the front room.

'You wanna go for a ride?' she asked as she

pulled on jeans, a thick white T-shirt, and clean tennis shoes.

His head tilted to one side, he sat taller and thrust out his chest to her in a gesture that seemed to say, 'Me? You want me? With you? Now?'

She had to laugh. 'Yeah, come on, baby boy.'

As he bounded joyfully after her, Munch felt the familiar tugging ache of missing Asia. At work, when she was busy, she was able to focus on what was in front of her, but as soon as things slowed down, memories of cute stuff Asia said and did filled her thoughts. It was scary, feeling so much love for another living being. It made her feel vulnerable to unbearable pain, yet she couldn't imagine her life being full without the little rug rat. Perhaps her love for Asia was so absolute that it left no room for anyone else. And now there was this dog. She loved him, too. If anything, her heart had expanded. She guessed that was what happened when people had multiple kids.

Lisa must be going out of her mind, the half she had left, anyway.

Part of Munch wanted to stop by the school and take Asia out for the day, though she knew that was foolish. Asia was smart enough to catch up after missing a day

— that wasn't it. But where Munch was going now wasn't an appropriate place to take a little kid.

Appropriate, Munch thought, hearing her own thoughts. When had that word snuck into her vocabulary? She felt the same when she heard herself refer to a woman as a *gal* instead of a *chick*. She was changing. No doubt about it.

Hooray for me, she thought as she headed east on Sunset Boulevard toward Hollyweird.

The air was scented by bus exhaust, carbon rich and sooty. Munch knew most people were repelled by those fumes, but to her it always smelled like money. When she'd started working on cars in the seventies, they all smelled like that. Catalytic converters had made a big difference. What came out of the newer cars' tailpipes now was cleaner, clearer, and slightly sulfuric. A lot of mechanics hadn't trusted or approved of the early smog equipment and were known to remove and/or modify it on occasion. The devices robbed engines of power and made them idle rough.

But, since Munch had been running smog checks with the infrared analyzer that measured carbon monoxide and hydrocarbons, she'd been sold on all the changes in the eighties' engines. So maybe the sunsets over the Pacific Ocean had fewer colors in them now, and cars lacked the muscle of previous decades, but Asia didn't miss days of play due to stage-three smog alerts.

Progress. Munch was learning not to fight it.

She stopped at the light on Highland and took in the sights. She'd gotten to know the streets of Hollywood pretty well in the last couple years. Most of the kids who rented her limousine for their proms wanted to cruise the Strip. Munch knew where all the clubs were, the big ones from the sixties like the Whiskey A Go-Go, Art Leboe's, The Roxy, Kaleidoscope, and the newer, hipper ones like The Stock Exchange downtown and Club One. The high school kids couldn't get into those places, but they insisted on at least driving by the outside. They ogled flamboyant transvestites, stared hard at the lingerie in the window of Frederick's, and sucked in, wide-eyed, all those siren promises of tawdry glamour and debauchery.

It was not the same in daylight. The cracks in the veneer showed. The red boas and black silk in the purple-framed windows of Frederick's appeared lurid, almost cartoon-ish; the nightclubs and porno parlors looked seedier without the neon.

Munch had looked up Passage to Hope in the phone book before leaving her house. The address was a storefront a few blocks off the main boulevard, in an area the cops and locals called Gower Gulch. The gulch was a mile east of the tourist draws of Mann's Chinese Theater and the newly restored Roosevelt Hotel.

The landmarks here included a Pep Boys franchise, the defunct and decrepit Henry Fonda Theater, a Korean-owned liquor store that accepted food stamps and sold lottery tickets, and First Continental Security Service, whose signs promised protection in four languages.

She had to park a short block away near St Augustine's Methodist Church. She clipped Jasper's leash to his collar and walked to the shelter.

Years spent as a barefoot hippie had given Munch the instinct to watch where she stepped. She often found money, tools, and other useful objects that most people passed right by. She noted that there were no stars on the sidewalks in Gower Gulch, just a lot of brown spatters that could be blood or chocolate, and quarter-size blots of black asphalt.

The Capitol Record building towered to the north. Its circular stories were each adorned with their own ring of green awning — it was built to resemble a stack of LPs on a turntable, complete with spindle. Munch thought it looked more like a huge mechanical, multilayered wedding cake. The builders must have been inspired by something they saw on that cartoon show *The Jetsons*. Or vice versa.

She was met at the front desk of the storefront headquarters of Passage to Hope by a woman who introduced herself as Dr Dianna Benét. The beginnings of tiny crow's-feet at the edge of Benét's eyes put her at thirty. At least. Munch was noticing a few of those things around her own hazel eyes. She figured she'd earned them.

'Have you lost someone?' Benét asked.

'My niece.' Munch showed Dr Benét the picture. 'She's diabetic and dependent on insulin. I thought maybe if she stopped in, you could give it to her and ask her to call me.'

'I can't do that,' Benét said. Behind her a phone rang, and a teenage boy answered it in a voice crackled by puberty. 'I'm not a medical doctor, I'm a sociologist. I founded this shelter.'

'Thank you,' Munch said, meaning it.

'We send kids to the free clinic if they need medicine, but your niece could also go to any pharmacy and get her insulin.'

'Without a prescription?'

'Insulin doesn't require a prescription.' Dr Benét paused to read a message that the boy who had answered the phone handed her. 'Tell her we need tennis shoes, size four and up.' Benét turned back to Munch. 'Where were we?'

'My niece's insulin?'

'Right. She could get it by telling the pharmacist how many units of what type of insulin she used and how often she took her shots. If she had the money, she could buy it on the spot. Syringes, too.'

'I didn't realize that,' Munch said, referring to the insulin. She knew about syringes, though.

'It's true.' Two different phone lines rang at once. The boy answered one of them, looking frazzled. 'Anything else?'

Munch pulled one of her flyers from her bag. 'Can I give you her picture and my number?' She placed the photo on the counter. Benét glanced at it briefly, showed no signs of recognition, but pulled it toward her.

'We rescue kids conned into prostitution and pornography. Do you have a reason to think your niece might be turning tricks?'

'I don't know her that well,' Munch said, 'but I have a feeling not. Her mom hasn't provided a very stable home for her, and a friend of hers died a little while ago. She might have felt she needed a break.'

'Let's hope she didn't come here to Hollywood for it.'

A young black girl emerged from the back. Her hair was wet. 'We're out of conditioner, Dr Di.'

Benét put a protective arm around the girl's narrow shoulders and gave her a motherly squeeze before releasing her. 'It's on our list. Maybe tomorrow.'

The street door opened and a man in a janitor's uniform brought in a large cardboard box full of used clothes and set it on the floor. He smiled at Dr Benét. 'Got some more donations for you.'

'Thank you, Larry,' she said. Munch liked her no-nonsense manner and that she seemed either unaware of her attractiveness or unwilling to use it to her advantage. Maybe she was trying to set an example.

A few more kids joined the two already in the anteroom, and together they fell on the donation as if it were treasure. Benét smiled and turned back to Munch. 'The runaways who flock to Hollywood are such easy targets. The pimps around here are expert predators and masters of manipulation. They prey on unhappy children who come from difficult homes.'

Munch considered that for a moment. 'I've never understood the whole pimp/prostitute thing. I mean, I know what the pimp gets out of it. But what about the girl?' When Munch had been strung out on drugs, she had worked the streets of Venice, making direct exchanges of sex for money with the mostly blue-collar johns who knew which streets to cruise. The world of the pimp was as alien as the world of high-class call girls who charged a thousand a night. She suspected the latter was just a fantasy anyway.

'I did my thesis on this relationship. Let me break it down for you.' Dr Benét gestured toward the world outside her front door. 'A kid such as your niece hits the street with no resources. She can't work or rent a room because she's underage. She does okay maybe during the day, but then night comes. It's dark and she's scared. The offers start getting weirder.'

'She's hungry and cold,' Munch added. Charlotte was already too thin.

'Right. And so she makes a compromise when some not-too-greasy old man invites her home.'

Munch shuddered, feeling again that walking-on-my-grave sensation. 'He feeds her, lets her sleep there, and all she has to do is screw him or jerk him off.'

'You sound like maybe you've had some experience,' Benét said gently.

'Yeah, it was some years ago. I used to be an intravenous drug user.' Munch looked at the good doctor sideways. 'They didn't give that heroin away.'

Benét laughed in the right place and Munch liked her even more.

'How long are you sober?'

'Eight and a half years.' Munch heard herself and smiled. She sounded like one of Asia's little friends, still counting her age with fractions.

'That's great,' Benét said.

'Yeah, I think so, too.'

Benét resumed her lecture. 'After that first compromise, she's ripe for the picking, and believe me, these pimps know how to spot their prey. He'll say, 'Why don't you buy those hundred-dollar shoes? Won't your daddy buy them for you?' The kid will say, 'My daddy drinks all the time,' or, 'I don't have a daddy.' The pimp will wine and dine her, giving her constant reinforcement and attention. 'You *need* a daddy,' he'll say, 'to give you all those fine things.''

''You and me against the world,'' Munch said, watching a brown-haired girl who couldn't be older than twelve admire a tie-dyed T-shirt that she pulled from one of

81

the donation boxes.

'Exactly. He tells her she's beautiful, that all these men want her.'

Munch thought of the Cat Stevens lyrics *It's hard to get by just upon a smile, girl.* She'd made her first break from home when that song came out. Those words had become a personal mantra.

Benét continued. 'He'll point out society's wrongs: 'If the president is a crook . . . ' or 'You know all those businessmen take advantage of the working man . . . ' She's just a kid, what does she know? And here's this grown man defining the universe for her. He says, 'Hey, the whole world is doing this, you better get hip.''

'And kids want to be hip,' Munch said, thinking she'd been cured of that aspiration when it had been drummed into her at Narcotics Anonymous meetings that the desire to be hip, slick, and cool was often a terminal condition for an addict.

Benét bent her head and dropped her voice. This woman had an intensity that demanded attention. Munch leaned closer so as not to miss a word.

'Then comes the degradation stage, when a pimp actually has the kid. If she tries to break loose, he threatens to expose what she's been doing. He tells her that no one would want her, not her family, certainly not a boy her own age, when they learn what she's been doing.'

Munch nodded. She still fought her own shame.

Benét loaded condoms and cards with the shelter's number into her shoulder bag as she spoke. 'He controls who she has contact with. The only people she meets are other prostitutes. Approval and affirmation go to the girls who bring in the most money. The pimp becomes her man, her father figure, her god. She'll do anything for him.'

'I never had a pimp,' Munch said, not counting Flower George, who wasn't much of a father figure either.

'No,' the good doctor said, 'heroin was your pimp.'

Munch exhaled in a sound that was half-recognition and half-shock as another puzzle piece of her past shifted into place, a Rubik's Cube moment. She wondered if she'd ever have her personal story all figured out. Would she live that long?

Dr Benét picked up Charlotte's picture and studied it. 'Runaway kids are divided into three subcultures. I just have to know two things about the kid. What does their hair look like and what kind of music do they listen to? Boys with short hair who are into disco, they're gay. That means West Hollywood, Santa Monica Boulevard. Kids into rap go hang out with gangs and pimps.'

'How about heavy metal, punk rock, and multicolored hair?'

'Then she's going to be with the squatters.'

'The squatters?'

'The kids into the punk scene live in groups, in abandoned buildings.'

'What abandoned buildings?'

'Here in Hollywood? There's the Gap Building and Max Factor. The businesses have moved out, but the power and water is still hooked up. Hotel Hell has been a real hotbed lately. Someone needs to go in there and root them all out.'

'Hotel Hell? Where's that?'

'A couple blocks east of here on Hollywood Boulevard. The windows are boarded up and there's a fence around it, but none of that stops the kids who take shelter there.'

'Charlotte, the girl I'm looking for, was friends with a boy who was killed about a week ago. The boy was involved with some home-burglary ring. I don't know if one has anything to do with the other, but it seems suspiciously coincidental.'

'Kids doing burglaries? Might have been one of Mouseman's crew.'

'Who's Mouseman?'

'A creep I've been hearing about for the last few months. I've never seen him.'

'Why do they call him Mouseman?'

'I'm not sure.' Benét looked at the kids nearby who were still going through the boxes. 'The kids say he isn't into sex or drugs.'

'What's he into?'

'Other people's houses when they aren't home. Or rather, getting underage kids to commit the burglaries.'

'Have you told the cops?' Munch asked.

'Oh, yes. I'm no friend of bad guys, but as I say, our focus is rescuing children victimized by prostitution. We're out there every day, walking the streets, letting these children know there's a place they can go.' She nodded toward the door leading to the sidewalk.

Munch was liking this woman more and more, already envisioning a continuing friendship where the two of them would take up the crusade together. 'I'd like to join you when you go out on patrol.'

'Today?'

'Sure.'

'Sorry, I can't do that. All our volunteers are fingerprinted, bonded, and have to be put on our insurance policy. Hollywood is the armpit of L.A. Anything could happen out there.'

'I understand,' Munch said, trying to hide her disappointment.

'But if I run across your niece, I'll try to get her to call you.'

'I just want to know if she's all right.'

'Then don't give up till you find her.'

Munch nodded, picked up her ice chest, and left.

6

Munch drove east on Hollywood Boulevard to the place Dr Benét had called Hotel Hell. It was eight floors of disaster on a corner lot. The roofline sagged and appeared caved in in places; the panes in the upper windows had been broken unevenly, leaving jagged teeth of glass. The gaping holes were punctuated by charred sashes. Green and blue patches of color spotted the inconsistent stucco like the lesions of some virulent disease. Clean, fresh plywood covered the lower window openings; black grating had been nailed across the doorway. Yards of chainlink ringed the ruined structure from the sidewalk to the back alley. Even in daylight, the building looked dangerous.

'We're not going in there without SWAT,' Munch told Jasper. Stubby tail wagging, he dug his forehead into her side and stayed there. He seemed happiest when they were touching.

Munch spent the next half hour taping posters to telephone poles and the walls of abandoned buildings. She returned to her car for another batch and to give Jasper some water.

She realized she was exhausted and took a moment to rest and consider her next move. She rolled her window halfway down for ventilation and studied the neighboring businesses. She was looking for a storefront with a counter that faced the street.

The next thing she was aware of was a white guy in a black leather coat rearing back from her window. Jasper had leaped across her, lunging at the guy. The dog had moved so quickly and with such quiet intensity that it took Munch a moment to realize what had happened.

The guy in the coat — she saw now that he was a teenager — must have gotten too close to the window and Jasper had protected his territory. She liked that and scratched his ears even as she apologized to the guy. She liked that a lot. She had Jasper's back, too.

'Hey.' The kid raised his hands in mock surrender. 'No offense.' He had the scraggly beginnings of a goatee and the slim build of no longer a boy, not quite yet a man.

'You live around here?' Munch asked, kissing the top of Jasper's head and moving him back to the passenger seat.

'Sometimes.'

Munch thought it was too warm to be

wearing leather, but it was probably the kid's prized possession. She pulled out one of her flyers and handed it to him through the window. 'Have you seen this girl around?'

He considered the picture for a minute. Munch could almost hear his wheels turning. 'You offering any kind of reward for information?'

Munch deliberated. She had a personal rule against giving druggies and drunks cash, and this kid looked like a little bit of both.

'If the family had any money, we'd hire an investigator to help us. Just tell me if you've seen her.'

'Why should I help you? How do I know your kid didn't have a good reason to split?'

'She's going to be in serious medical trouble if I don't find her soon. She has a disease.' Let this guy think that what Charlotte had was communicable and spread the word. At the very least it might prevent those coming into contact with Charlotte from making unwanted advances. 'She needs special medication and she needs it soon.'

'Yeah, you're breaking my heart,' he said. 'Life is tough all over.'

Munch fought the urge to open the car door into his face. Hard. She wondered what circumstances had led him to be on the street at his tender age and relented.

'Her father is dead, her mother isn't much help either. Kids your age deserve a shot at a future.'

'I never knew my dad,' he countered, 'and my mom is too busy with boyfriends to notice if I'm home or not. Like I said, we all got problems.'

'Don't you think it's time somebody broke the chain?' *Oh, God*, she realized, *now I'm quoting dumbfuck Lisa.* 'Just tell me if you think you might have seen her around.'

'Have you gone to the cops?'

'The cops? They don't give a shit. They'll take her name, send her picture out, and call the mom every thirty days to see if she's heard from the kid yet.'

'Tell you what I'm gonna do,' the boy said, sounding more like a carny rat as he sniffed an angle. 'Give me one of those flyers and your phone number and I'll ask around — see what I can do for you.'

'While you're asking,' Munch said, handing him a photo of Steven Koon, 'see what you can find out about this one also.'

'He split, too?'

'You bring me something useful, and I'll make it worth your time. My number's on the flyer.'

The guy nodded as he looked over the two pictures. 'I'll come up with something.'

'What's your name?'

'Painter Dave.'

As Munch drove away, she thought about how odd it was for a sidewalk commando like Painter Dave to ask her if she'd gone to the cops. Why would that matter to him? She also wondered if spray paint was his artistic medium of choice. His jeans shone with grime and his combat boots were worn and dusty. She watched him in her rearview mirror as he slipped into the alley behind Hotel Hell like so much smoke being pulled up a flue.

★   ★   ★

Munch considered the value of stopping at the free clinic on Sunset.

The people who volunteered at free clinics, mostly women, it seemed, had more heart, more love, than God usually gave to ten people. She didn't know how they did it, how they ministered to people who didn't even care about themselves for the most part. She had been one of those lost souls once. Driven to seek cures for the various itches and discharges that constantly plagued her.

It wasn't pretty remembering, but it was important not to forget.

Once she had gone in for an appointment

for yet another gynecologic ailment. On the way to the clinic she had turned a trick. She apologized to the woman doctor performing the pelvic exam when the woman commented on the amount of semen she was finding. The doctor — a white, middle-aged woman of unfathomable compassion — waved off Munch's apology as unnecessary and asked Munch if any other medical condition needed addressing.

'Well, I'm addicted to drugs,' Munch had said, showing the woman her scarred arms.

'Did you want some help with that today?' the woman asked. 'Or did you just want to wallow for now?'

'I think I'll wallow a bit more,' Munch said, not immune to irony even then.

The doctor continued with the exam and said something Munch would never forget. 'You're very pretty here.' She showed Munch the bunch of flesh at the opening of her vagina, her clitoris.

Munch looked down.

'It looks like a flower,' the woman said.

Munch had been pleased by the compliment. Only now, years later, did she realize what the woman had been trying to do for her, had in fact done for her. The woman had drawn Munch's attention to that part of her body she abused so readily, distanced herself from, and had no respect for. She had given her a small gift of pride and cursed her days of hooking.

God love her.

No, Munch decided, asking questions at the clinic would most likely yield nothing. Medical files were privileged information, and even if Charlotte had sought her medication at a free clinic, Munch had no way of knowing which one she'd go to.

She saw a pay phone, pulled over, and called Lisa.

'Have you heard from her?'

'You didn't find her?'

'Not yet, but we will. I have one more stop to make, then I'm coming over.'

There was an AA adage that included the words 'make sure your own house is in order.' Munch knew this was true both figuratively and literally. She drove to her work and borrowed Lou's powder-blue, vintage Chevy pickup truck, leaving her own car there and promising to be back by four-thirty when Asia's school bus dropped her off.

Lou relinquished his keys without hesitation and didn't even raise an eyebrow when Jasper bounded into the truck's cab.

'He doesn't shed,' Munch assured him.

'Hey, Munch,' Lou said, 'what do they call a Yugo at the top of a hill?'

93

She'd heard this one but said, 'I give.'

'A mirage.'

She smiled and said, 'Good one,' as she swung into the cab after Jasper.

Venice High School was not too far out of her way. Munch parked on Venice Boulevard, cracking the window for Jasper. As she made her way to the administration office, she noticed that she was already feeling a familiarity with the place. She walked up the concrete pathway with confidence. The clanging of the flagpole halyard caused her to look up. The flag was at half-mast and the wind was blowing hard across it. The sounds of young voices shouting, bouncing balls, and rubber shoes squeaking on concrete rose from the outdoor basketball courts. Fresh-cut grass cohered in fragrant piles under the classroom windows.

Munch pushed through the front doors and waited for the woman behind the counter to look up. 'Is Mr Lombardi available?'

'Do you have an appointment?'

'No, I was just hoping I could catch him.'

The woman stood. 'I'll see if he's free.'

Moments later, a slight, bearded man in a brown suit walked out of one of the side offices. His hair was gray, but seemed prematurely so. She guessed his age as late thirties, early forties. He was wearing a thick gold wedding band, so she skipped the other calculations she often entertained when meeting a guy for the first time.

'Can I help you?' he asked.

She offered her hand. 'I'm Munch Mancini. Charlotte Slokum's aunt.'

'Ah, yes. I saw your message. What can I do for you?'

'Do you have a minute?'

He ushered her into his office. It was cluttered with files and binders. A banner tacked to the wall read GO GONDOLIERS.

She sat across from him. 'What can you tell me about Charlotte?'

'What do you want to know?'

'Who are her friends? Was she any more troubled than most kids her age?'

He opened a filing cabinet and removed a folder with Charlotte's name on it. He read for a moment before looking up again. 'She scored almost fifteen hundred on her pre-SATs.'

Munch sighed. 'I'm sorry, but those numbers mean nothing to me.'

He blinked, but recovered quickly. 'That's very good. Sixteen hundred is a perfect score.'

'Her mom said she gets straight A's.'

'She was second in her class.' He delivered this information without having to consult the file.

'Was?' Munch asked.

'Currently,' he amended. He flipped back a few pages and found what he was looking for. 'Says here her top career choice was either an attorney or a psychologist.'

'Interesting spread.'

He nodded. 'She told me once she wanted to help people or make a lot of money.'

'I hope you told her it was possible to do both.'

'Of course,' he said, checking the clock on the wall.

'What about friends?'

'All I can tell you is what I see here. I'm sorry I can't be of any more assistance. If there's anything I can do for the family, please don't hesitate to call. In fact, call me as soon as you find out anything.'

Munch assured him she would. Although she would have had a better feeling for the guy if he had responded to her note or showed a little more proactive interest. Obviously, Charlotte wasn't his only charge or his first priority. They shook hands once more and Munch went on her way.

When Munch pulled up in front of Lisa's apartment, Lisa was standing on the sidewalk talking to a thin, fiftyish-looking woman. The woman held a full ashtray and a pack of Chesterfields in one hand and gestured with a smoldering half-smoked cigarette in her other. Both women turned as Munch parked and shut off the engine. Jasper also perked up when the truck stopped and stood on Munch's lap to look out the window.

The thin woman had painted a mask of rouge, thick black eyeliner, and dark red lipstick over her wrinkled face. Her sheer blouse showed cleavage, and her gold pants were cinched tight around her waspish waist. Munch thought she probably looked good in her own habitat, perhaps one of the many smoky dives on Lincoln Boulevard.

Munch shooed Jasper to the passenger side and got out of the truck.

'This is my neighbor, Bea,' Lisa said. Lisa offered nothing to Bea about Munch. Obviously they'd already covered that subject and Munch needed no further introduction.

Bea took a last drag of her filterless cigarette, added it to the other spent cancer sticks, and hacked out a hello.

Munch decided not to tell Lisa she'd been to the school and spoken to Charlotte's guidance counselor, or of Lombardi's disturbing use of the past tense when discussing the missing teen, as if he'd already written the kid off. 'When does Jill usually get home from school?' Munch asked.

'Three-thirty, unless she goes over to a

friend's house. Sometimes, I don't see her until dark. She knows to call if she has dinner at someone else's house.'

'Asia told me you had some stuff in storage. I thought it might be nice to get it now, as a welcome home for Charlotte.'

Lisa's eyes filled with tears and then shifted quickly sideways, as if she was nervous about something.

Munch was ready for her. 'I'll loan you the money for the back rental.' She didn't expect to be paid back, but she didn't want to rob Lisa of all her dignity, especially in front of her neighbor. Munch had known this reunion with Lisa was going to cost her since she'd heard Lisa's voice on that answering machine.

'I thought you wanted me to stay here by the phone,' Lisa said.

'Oh, honey,' Bea piped up with a whiskey growl, 'I can sit with your phone. You go get your stuff. I know you've been wanting to.'

Lisa hugged Bea, and the two exchanged sloppy vows of gratitude and mutual admiration.

Munch did a mental eye roll and promised to have Lisa back by happy hour.

'Bless your little heart,' Bea said.

The storage unit was on Beethoven Street in Culver City. It was a large, three-story, windowless warehouse in an industrial cul-de-sac. To gain access, they first had to stop at the front office and sign in.

Munch cracked open the truck windows a few inches. Jasper looked worried. She promised him she wouldn't be long.

The guy behind the desk had his feet up and was watching a soap opera. He was also barefoot. Judging from the layers of dirt on his soles, he'd been that way for years.

When the women reached his desk, he swung his feet down, ran a hand through his long, greasy hair, and asked, 'Can I help you?'

'Where's Micky?' Lisa asked.

'He's not here today.'

'I want to close out my space,' Lisa said.

'Number?'

'B thirty-six.'

The guy opened his ledger and ran a dirty finger down the page. Munch realized she knew him from AA meetings in Venice. He called himself Catfish. Munch's sponsor had warned her more than once that she'd meet people in AA she wouldn't have gotten drunk with. It was strange to see him here. Somehow, she'd never pictured Catfish as having a job.

'What's the damage?' Munch asked.

'It's all paid up,' Catfish said, sliding the book to Lisa. 'Sign here.'

Lisa and Munch looked at each other, a

look that said, *Hey, if this place can't keep their books straight, who are we to argue?* Lisa shrugged, picked up a pen, and signed her name.

Munch grabbed a flatbed, wheeled cart and let Lisa lead the way. The storage unit was on the ground floor. Lisa stopped at the combination padlock. Munch waited for her to open it, but Lisa was having trouble.

'What's the matter?' Munch asked.

'I don't know, I guess I forgot the combination. One of the kids usually does this part.'

Useless, Munch thought. 'Let me.'

'I don't know what you think you're gonna do,' Lisa said.

Munch inspected the padlock. It was a Master — impervious to picking because the casing clearances were so small, and case-hardened, so forget about cutting the shackle. She twisted the dial a few times to get a feel for how loose the inner mechanism was. She didn't see any rust, but sometimes dirt or spiderwebs got inside and gummed things up. This lock didn't seem old at all. In fact, it looked brand-new. She twisted the padlock up from the hasp so that the backside faced out. The serial number was legible, which meant they could write the company and have the combination mailed to them. If they wanted to wait that long.

She pulled down on the body of the lock, putting tension on the shackle.

'What are you doing?' Lisa asked.

'What does it look like? Shut up for a minute.'

Munch closed her eyes and dialed the number wheel to the right until she felt a sticking point. She stopped, noted the number, and then turned the face again. She felt a second sticking point. This was going to be a tough one.

'We're going to need some paper and a pencil,' she told Lisa.

'I'll ask the guy at the desk.'

Lisa returned a moment later. Munch recited twelve numbers, and Lisa wrote them down. Eliminating all the sticking point numbers ending in the same digit, and all the ones where the dial stuck between numbers, she was left with 38.

'That should be the last number,' she told Lisa. 'Sound familiar?'

'I think so.'

Munch took the paper and pencil from Lisa and did some simple calculations, which involved dividing thirty-eight by four, taking the remainder of two, and working up in increments of four. This gave her ten possibilities for the second number. There was a slightly different formula to figure out the first number. The guy who had taught her this process called it modulus operator mathematics. It was much simpler than it sounded. When she was done, she would also have ten possibilities for the first number and overall one hundred options for the correct combination. Chances were she'd hit on the winning series closer to her fiftieth attempt.

Lisa kept walking to the end of the hallway and looking both ways. Munch smiled as she worked. Knowing that she didn't need a lookout didn't change that it made her feel better. Plus, it kept Lisa busy and out of her light.

Munch worked the combinations in the order that was easiest for her to keep track of, remembering after each failed attempt to clear the tumblers with three full clockwise turns of the face dial. It was a good thing her fingertips were calloused from turning bolts, she thought, or this could get painful.

After ten minutes, the dial shifted an almost imperceptible millimeter inward as the last tumbler fell into place. Munch pulled the lock open.

'That was truly fucking elegant,' Lisa said, swinging the door open. 'You're handy to have around.'

'Yes, ma'am. Think of me first for your next B and E.'

Lisa pulled a thin overhead chain and a bare lightbulb snapped to life. 'What the fuck? Look at this mess. That motherfucker.'

'Who?' Munch asked, surveying the wreck before them. Boxes were upended and emptied on the floor. A mattress leaning against the wall had been slashed and its stuffing pulled out. An armchair and a small sofa had suffered the same fate.

Lisa picked up a green garbage bag and began stuffing clothes into it.

Pissed off, Munch noticed, but not surprised into inaction. Munch stooped down to pick up a book lying open and spine up. 'Who did this?'

'That's what I'd like to know. Son of a bitch.' Lisa kicked at the mattress.

'Let me see if the guy in the office has a broom we can borrow,' Munch said.

'What's the point?'

Something silver and shiny caught Munch's eye. It was a wad of duct tape. She bent down to examine it closer and instantly knew better than to touch it. A hank of human hair was still attached. The hair was long and black save for the last two inches, which were dyed orange.

Munch grabbed Lisa's arm and pointed.

Lisa said, 'Oh, God,' stared at it a moment, let the implications sink in, and then shouted, '*Oh! God!*'

Munch studied the mess before them, looking for blood or a white, lifeless limb extending from beneath a pile. There was the scent of mildew, of unwashed clothes, a trace of cat, but not the unforgettable rotten-meat smell of decay, of death. She noticed something red, but made of cloth. It was only a piece of red bandanna.

'When did Charlotte change her hair?' Munch asked.

Lisa only looked at her dumbly.

'When did she dye the ends orange? In the picture taken at school, her hair was streaked light.'

'Saturday. She changed it just before we met you at the park.'

Munch looked at the hair lying on the floor and the duct tape with its ominous implications. Rico couldn't ignore this.

She rushed back to the front desk and told Catfish there was an emergency and that they needed to use his phone.

'Employees only,' he said. 'Pay phone is on the corner.'

'We need to get the police here now,' Munch said.

'Why?'

'My kid is missing,' Lisa said, 'and we just found some of her hair in the storage unit. Besides that, someone's been going through my shit.'

'Are they there now?' he asked.

'No,' Munch said, wondering what it would take to raise this guy's adrenaline. She should have just come out yelling fire.

'This phone is for business only,' Catfish said, working a snooty tone of voice into his delivery. 'No exceptions.'

'I'm telling you — ' Munch started to say, but the guy cut her off.

'You don't tell me anything, woman.' He said *woman* as if it were some kind of insult, unplugged the phone, and dropped it into his desk drawer.

Munch left Lisa to tell the guy how many kinds of an asshole he was and called Rico from the pay phone outside. The storage facility was less than a mile from the Pacific Station. As luck would have it, Rico was at his desk.

She and Lisa were pacing ruts in the ground around Lou's truck when Rico arrived fifteen minutes later. He gave them a short wave. Munch answered by pointing toward the open door where Catfish sat.

Rico pulled into the NO PARKING zone in front of the office. Munch joined him as he

105

got out of his car. Rico brushed her cheek with his finger and asked, 'What's up?'

It took a second for her to get past the distraction of his touch. 'You need to see for yourself.'

'The guy behind the desk in there wouldn't let us call from his phone,' Lisa said.

Rico looked toward the office. Munch imagined his eyes narrowing behind his sunglasses.

'Yeah,' Lisa said, warming to her sense of being disrespected now that a champion had arrived, 'he said, 'Woman, you're not telling me what to do.'' She put the same emphasis on the words Catfish had.

Rico straightened to his full height of six feet. 'What did he call you?' he asked Munch, reading accurately what Catfish's tone had implied.

''Woman,'' Munch repeated, feeling a smile starting to curl her lips despite her anger. 'But that's not what's important.'

Rico took the steps two at a time. The women hustled to catch up.

'You!' Rico shouted as he pointed at Catfish.

The chair slipped out from beneath Catfish. Munch caught a vision of dirty toes clutching in midair.

'What is your major malfunction?' Rico

pressed, towering over the guy and not giving him room to untangle himself from the chair. 'These ladies needed your help, and you just sit on your fat ass? And put some shoes on. You're disgusting.'

Happy as Munch was to see Catfish get his due, she wanted Rico to see what she and Lisa had found in the storage room. She pulled on Rico's arm and then let it go. She didn't want to distract either of them from what was really important here.

Rico followed the women to the storage area and hunkered with a flashlight to inspect the evidence.

'Don't go back in there,' he said.

'I know,' Munch said. This wasn't her first crime scene.

'There's something wrong here.'

'You think?'

'I mean this isn't simple robbery or vandalism.'

'Don't forget abduction,' Munch added.

'No, I'm not. Obviously that is the priority here. I'm just saying' — he waved his hand behind him — 'destruction like this. This says rage.'

Rico returned to his car and got on his radio. Munch watched him work. He glanced over at her as if sensing her scrutiny and winked.

Did he think that was all it was going to take? she wondered. Hardly. She shook her head, and when she looked again, he was watching the street.

'What happens now?' Lisa asked.

'Let's go find out,' Munch said.

Rico emerged from his car. His expression was earnest as he addressed Lisa. 'I've got a crew of technicians coming. They'll dust the unit for prints and gather trace evidence. I'll need you both to come back to the station and make statements.'

'Now we're getting somewhere,' Lisa said, and headed back for the truck.

'I hope so,' Munch said. She didn't think she would feel overly encouraged if she were to find a lock of Asia's hair in a strip of duct tape. She turned to Rico, out of Lisa's earshot. 'This isn't all bad, right? A dead girl would not be brought into a locked room only to be removed again?'

'I wish I could tell you that was true,' he said. 'Who knows, Munch? Who knows?'

7

'What can you tell me about the dead boy, Steven Koon?' Munch asked. She was sitting across from Rico at his desk. She'd spent the last twenty minutes answering his questions, and now she had a few of her own.

'He had a history of truancy, running away, and one count of public drunkenness.'

'Was he on the run when he was killed?' Munch tried to act casual as she studied the framed pictures on Rico's desk.

Rico followed her gaze, which had come to rest on a framed photograph of his daughter on a beach. Looked like Baja. 'No. He'd been back home for almost a month. He was in school, and according to his parents and teachers he seemed happy and was responding well.'

'You spoke to the parents?'

'Yes.' Rico's hand rested next to his daughter's picture, a finger absently stroking the frame.

'That must have been rough. How are they doing?'

He shrugged. 'About what you'd expect. I had a grief counselor with me. The mother vacillated between hysterics and asking us if we wanted coffee. I'm told that's pretty normal given the situation.'

'How about the dad?'

'Man, he cried like a baby.'

Munch nodded. 'Sounds brutal.' It hurt her heart just to think about it. 'The paper said the boy had been questioned about a burglary?'

'He pawned a stolen VCR in Santa Monica about a month ago. The owner of the pawnshop checked the serial numbers against his hot sheet and called it into the Santa Monica PD when he found a match. The station was only a few blocks away and they picked the boy up at the Greyhound depot.'

'What did he say?'

'The usual bullshit. He was pawning it for a friend. He wouldn't give up the friend, but the detectives were working on him. His parents hired a lawyer and any interviews had to go through the attorney. Steve probably would have cooperated if the DA had been willing to deal.'

'Was the VCR part of the loot taken by the ring we were talking about?'

He paused before answering, then seemed to come to a conclusion to his inner debate. 'Yes.'

Had he decided she was trustworthy? she

wondered. Pretty fucking funny, considering. So funny she wanted to slam his face into his desk.

She wondered if the VCR Steve Koon had tried to pawn had been a Betamax or a VHS. She had given Garret Dimond a VCR for Christmas last year — he had wanted a Betamax. Garret was the man she was breaking up with when she met Rico. She had also given Garret a flügelhorn for his twenty-eighth birthday. It was a beautiful brass instrument and had come nestled in a blue velvet case. It had cost seven hundred dollars, a price she hadn't haggled over. Why was it that she always gave the most expensive gifts she could afford to the men she couldn't really love? She also had a bad habit of giving what she couldn't afford to the men who didn't/wouldn't/couldn't give her back what she needed most.

She looked at Rico again, shifting her mind to a puzzle that was solvable. 'So you've got a burglary ring hitting the homes of vacationing owners and the phone lines are always cut. The thieves wouldn't do that without reason. Mace St John told me once that MO was learned behavior, something bad guys per-fected and refined as they did their deeds.'

'That's still true,' Rico said. 'They don't want to get caught.'

'Sounds like they already knew nobody was home. So why cut the phone lines?'

'It's not that uncommon.'

Munch nodded as she continued to think out loud. 'We have a system at the garage that automatically phones the alarm company if the perimeter is breached. What I'm thinking is that this thief, or one of these thieves, got busted sometime by one of those silent alarms. Can we check who's been caught like that?'

'We can try, but it will take time. I have a bulletin out to other cop shops nationwide. If there have been similar burglaries and the detectives are paying attention, they'll contact us. The problem is most burglaries are investigated initially only by patrol officers. They *may* call for crime scene techs or request detectives to respond, but to have detectives in on the investigation from the get-go, the situation has to be extraordinary.'

'Like how?'

'Like a 'hot prowl' scenario where risk is increased to the victim because they were home when the burglar hit, or the loss is huge, or involves dangerous items being taken, such as guns.'

'Or a kid is found dead in a stolen car.'

He nodded. 'Yep, that would definitely be a red flag.'

'What about psychics?' she asked, thinking of the strands of Charlotte's hair stuck in the duct tape.

'What about them?'

'You ever use them?'

He snorted. 'If a psychic ever leads me to a body, I'm arresting the psychic.'

Munch laughed, then sobered quickly. Who was saying anything about a body? She was looking for a live kid.

'I have a name for you. Some guy called Mouseman. The lady who runs that shelter in Hollywood told me about him. He recruits kids to rob houses. I don't know anything more than that.'

Rico wrote the information in his notebook. 'What we're doing now is looking for the link that ties these victims. We've put together an extensive questionnaire and the victims are downstairs now in the roll-call room filling them out.'

The 'we' he spoke of, Munch realized, were his fellow cops.

Lisa emerged from the bathroom. Rico gestured toward her with his head. 'I want to talk to the mom alone for a minute. Do you mind?'

'I'll wait downstairs.' Munch took the stairs to the street level.

Several uniformed cops sat behind a

counter. Vending machines sold snack food and drinks. Munch bought a soda and noticed a stream of a dozen affluent-looking white people, mostly women, heading to the roll-call room in the basement, accepting forms from a cop she didn't recognize.

'You got one for me?' she asked the cop.

He handed Munch one of the forms. It was the questionnaire Rico had mentioned. These had to be the people who had been ripped off. She'd told Rico she would wait downstairs. But she didn't say how far, Munch thought as she merged into the flow of burglary victims heading for the basement.

Everyone took seats at the tables where the patrol cops got their morning briefings. The room looked like a community room where an AA meeting might be held. Chairs set in rows, a raised dais with lectern, a forty-cup coffee urn and all the fixings, plastic dispensers of 'literature', a blackboard. Only, instead of placards of the twelve steps, the bulletin boards held mug shots of men labeled 'Known Predators.' She was sure the literature had a much different theme, too.

Munch scanned the crowd, looking for a familiar face. They were all familiar: upper-class West Side folk, but none that she recognized. The two men who'd arrived with their wives had left the women to fill out the forms and were studying the photographs of bad guys. Munch sat with the women and read through the questions.

The people were being asked to list who insured them, where they shopped, who cleaned their house, which gardening service they used, and where the women got their hair done.

How about *Who does their babysitting?* she thought. That should be one of the questions. She saw a smudge on her T-shirt and wondered why she always managed to collect stains at breast level. Wearing white, she'd been asking for it. She also wondered if Rico had noticed.

Ten minutes passed before pens were laid down and the women started meeting each other's eyes and exchanging smiles. Munch connected with a woman in the front row and figured she was as good a place as any to begin. 'What a cute top. Where'd you get it?'

The woman smiled broadly. 'At Connie's in the Village Mart.'

'In Brentwood?' the woman sitting behind her wearing Nancy Reagan red asked.

'Yes.'

'Have you eaten at that deli lately?' the woman to their left with a European accent wanted to know.

Then they were off and Munch sat back

and observed. It was a little like watching round-table Ping-Pong, only it was verbal and anyone was free to hit a serve or return at any time in any direction. This was something Munch really dug about women in groups — how, even among strangers, they exchanged tips and health advice.

'I wouldn't trust their potato salad if I were you,' Nancy Reagan red said.

'The produce is fresh and organic,' a young, earnest woman in glasses responded.

'My daughter won't touch anything green,' a plump, volunteer-for-everything sort of matron offered with a smile.

'Do you all have kids at home?' Munch asked. Only four of the women said yes.

'They need a new streetlight at that intersection.' This from a woman in a business suit.

'My sister-in-law works the ER at UCLA and says the Wilshire on-ramp is the worst.' Volunteer lady.

'Tell me about it. Between the construction and detours we almost missed our plane last week.' Business suit.

'My mother always says that the kids won't starve to death, you just have to wait them out.' Nancy Reagan red.

'Bribing them gets too expensive.' Volunteer lady.

'Especially as they get older.' Young and earnest.

'Thank God school has started.' Business suit.

'I'm in my car eight hours a day.' Volunteer lady. 'Traffic seems to get worse every month.'

'Any store that delivers gets my vote. I even have my dog food brought to the door.' European accent.

'Mobile Pet Supply?' asked the lady whose top Munch had complimented. 'They stopped answering their phone. I think they went out of business. I'm not surprised. Their prices were entirely too reasonable, they had to be losing money.'

All eyes riveted on the last speaker and all mouths opened at once. Even the men stalled in their perusing to look over. The verbal free-for-all coalesced into one important question and Munch was there to ask it.

'Have you all used that service? Recently?'

The room grew quiet, not the quiet of silence, but that hushed reverence of breakthrough as one by one each of the women nodded affirmation.

'Let me go tell Detective Chacón.' Munch's cheeks almost hurt from her huge smile as she climbed the stairs. She felt like a kid running to show off to the teacher and slowed her gait so she wouldn't arrive at his desk out of breath.

When she got to the second floor, Lisa was sitting on the bench with her hands behind her back. A uniformed cop helped her to her feet and Munch saw that Lisa was in handcuffs.

'Can you believe this shit?' Lisa asked. 'Who's supposed to take care of my kids?'

'Don't worry about that,' Munch said. 'I'm on it. What's going on here?'

'They wanted me to take a lie detector test and I told them to blow it out their ass. I'm the victim here.'

Munch threw her hands in the air. 'Oh, for crying out loud.'

8

Munch stormed to Rico's desk. 'What's going on?' He acted unperturbed, but Munch knew to look at the small muscles on the sides of his jaws. They quivered when he was angry. They were quiet now, but Munch also knew that the flatness to his eyes meant he'd put up his shields. A fine film of sweat glistened on his forehead. She remembered how he seemed to run a few degrees hotter than most. She also remembered liking the moist warmth of his skin, once upon a time.

'She has warrants,' he said.

'Her kid is missing. Why would you even run a check?'

'She's not being completely truthful.'

'Imagine that.'

'I'm trying to help,' he said.

'How is busting her helping?'

'She left me no choice.'

His crooked nose that she once thought gave his face character now just looked damaged. 'Have you always been like this,' she asked, 'or did I just never notice before? Where is your heart?' Sometimes he was such a cop.

'If she were more cooperative, this would never have happened. It's out of my hands now.'

Munch shook her head in disgust and then remembered what she had come upstairs to tell him. 'Write this in your book: Mobile Pet Supply. All the victims used the service recently and now it seems to be out of business. Their prices were — get this — 'too good to be true.''

'How did they come to use it? Is it a storefront? Where is it located? What sort of vehicle was used for the deliveries? What's the owner's name?'

'That's your job to find out. What were Lisa's warrants for?'

'Traffic violations. Failure to appear.'

'Is there bail?'

'Eventually. That's up to the judge.'

Munch looked at the clock. It was close to three. She needed to get over to Lisa's house and be there when Jill got home. 'Am I free to go or did you want me to blow in a Breathalyzer?'

'You're free to do whatever you want. Thanks for calling me and all your help.'

She gathered up her purse and slung it over her shoulder. She had so many immediate decisions to make. Should she slam out of there in a huff or hold her head high and walk away with dignity? If he watched her butt retreating, did she want to swish it at him? And what message was she intending to send? All these thoughts came to her in the second it took to unhook her purse from the chair, then he laid them all to waste.

'My mom died.' The words sort of blurted from his mouth and he looked as surprised as she was at their utterance.

'When?'

'In June. June third.'

'I didn't know she was sick. I'm sorry.'

'It was sudden. A brain aneurysm. Anyway, that's part of the reason I didn't call. We took her back to Mexico to bury her. My dad has been taking it really hard. It never occurred to any of us that she might go first.'

Women, Munch had noticed, adapted easier to surviving. Men tended to react as if they had been cheated somehow.

'I wish I'd known,' she said.

She'd never met the woman but pictured her as a tough old matriarch. By American standards, Rico had once conceded, she would have been considered a child abuser. Rico's father had left her in Mexico with six sons and a daughter while he set up a new home for them in America. She had ruled the small house she built herself with humorless and violent proficiency.

'I didn't think you'd want to hear from me,' he said. 'You made yourself pretty clear on that point.'

'Well, yeah, you told me you were going to marry Kathy. I didn't think that left much room for us.' Besides, the issue of Rico having more kids had been raised, an arena in which she could never compete, having rendered herself infertile in the bad old days. Men wanted sons, at least one. It was better to leave things as they were. Whatever magic that had been between them had soured the day she found out Kathy was pregnant and engaged to Rico.

'Kathy has some problems.'

'We all have problems.' She didn't want to hear about Kathy, though it was funny to feel so much jealousy over someone Munch thought she had no intention of getting involved with again. 'I've got a kid coming home from school — two kids, now that I have to look after Lisa's other daughter. I need to be there for them. Then I'm going to find Charlotte and explain to her why her mom wasn't out on the street looking or home waiting for her. Why her mom was in jail on some traffic ticket.' Munch strode from the room. She stretched her hand toward the railing, not wanting her dramatic exit marred by a tumble down the stairs.

She didn't believe Lisa knew where Charlotte was. For one thing, if Lisa had done something to Charlotte, she wouldn't have wanted Munch to get involved in the search. Then again, she had to admit a few things weren't adding up.

In the parking lot, the woman in red caught up to Munch. 'Are you a policewoman?' she asked. A man came and stood next to her. Munch recognized him as one of the men who had been checking out the wanted posters in the roll-call room.

'No, I was just helping out. My niece is missing and her disappearance might be connected to the burglaries.'

'How so?'

'The boy who was found murdered in the stolen car was a friend of hers.'

The man and woman looked at each other with marital telepathy. 'Little Steven Koon,' the man said. 'A terrible business.' He had a slight Irish brogue, particularly noticeable in his *r*'s.

'How old is your niece?' the woman asked.

'Fifteen.'

'Let's exchange numbers,' the woman said, handing Munch a business card for an art gallery in Westwood. The name Meg Sullivan was written in gold script across the bottom opposite her phone and fax numbers and the phrase *By appointment only*. Munch liked that. It sounded classy. She made a note to add that line to her next batch of limo cards.

'Maybe we can help each other,' Meg Sullivan said. 'You seem to be making as much progress as the police.'

'I don't know about that. They're working on it and they're open to suggestions.' *When they're not being Nazis*, Munch added to herself. She gave the woman one of her A&M Limousine business cards. 'I'm Miranda Mancini. Everyone calls me Munch.'

'Who's the *A*?' Mr Sullivan asked.

'My daughter, Asia.' Having a business that started with A also put her first in the Yellow Pages' limousine section.

'How darling to include her,' Mrs Sullivan said.

'It's a side business. I'm a mechanic at the Texaco station in Brentwood.'

'How entrepreneurial,' Mrs Sullivan said. 'Is there no end to your talent?'

Munch felt a blush coming on. 'It's been nice meeting you. I have to run.' She wondered why she always felt the need to dodge compliments as if they were bullets. 'Good luck.'

'Keep in touch,' the Sullivans insisted, as Munch inched away from their intense eye contact. 'We'll make it worth your while.'

124

* ★ *

When Munch got back to Lou's truck, Jasper was standing on his hind legs, paws on the windowsill, watching for her. She wondered if he had been standing like that the whole time she was in the police station. Maybe it wasn't such a good idea to bring him along. At least at the house he had access to the yard, his water bowl, and the softer cushions of her furniture.

She stroked his head, and he flopped across her lap with a deep sigh.

★ ★ ★

When Munch got back to Lisa's house, Bea was sitting on the front porch with the telephone beside her. The twenty-foot cord was stretched to its limit. Munch watched her study the street, glance at her wristwatch, back inside the house, and then up the street again. A blue cloud of cigarette smoke hovered in the eaves above her head.

Munch pulled into the driveway and Bea stood. Bony fingers briefly touched each temple as if checking to see if her face was still attached.

'Any calls?' Munch asked.

'A few.' Bea thrust some envelopes into

125

Munch's hands with scribbling on the back. 'A man called a few times asking for Lisa. He wouldn't leave a name or number. Where is Lisa, by the way?' She delivered the question with a nervous giggle as if maybe a joke was in there somewhere and she was willing to get it.

'Lisa didn't make it back.' Munch glanced at the envelopes. They were unopened utility bills addressed to Jill Garillo and a phone bill addressed to Charlotte. Munch wondered if Lisa was intent on ruining the girls' credit. She also wondered why Bea had taken the trouble to write the non-messages down.

1:15, man called for Lisa.

1:40, man called again. No name. Same guy.

2:10, man again. Lisa still not here.

Bea delicately picked a fleck of tobacco from her lip, rolled it between her fingers, and let it drop to the floor. It seemed a practiced gesture.

Jasper, sitting at Munch's feet, leaned into her legs and looked up expectantly.

The phone rang. Bea reached for the receiver but Munch waved her off. On the second ring, Munch picked up and did her best imitation of Lisa's nervous whine. 'Hello?'

'Where have you been?' a man growled.

Whoever this was, Munch realized, he expected Lisa to recognize his voice. Munch kept her voice high and quavery — an upset mother near hysterics. 'Is she with you?'

'I'm only going to say this once.' His tone was menacing, almost a whisper, as if he had to keep it to a pitch where he wouldn't be overheard. 'Nobody has to get hurt. Do you have it or not?'

'Have what?'

'Who is this?' he demanded.

'You first,' Munch said in her normal voice. 'Put Lisa on.'

'She got busted. What do you want?'

'Who are you?'

'Family. If you want something from Lisa, you're either gonna have to wait or deal with me.'

'What did she get busted for?' he asked.

'Contempt of cop as far as I could tell. Who is this?'

'I heard her kid was sick.'

Munch knew that one of her gambits had paid off. How else would this guy know about Charlotte's health problems? 'Charlotte's diabetic. If she doesn't have insulin regularly, she could be in big trouble. Is she with you?'

'Like I said, this doesn't have to end badly. You tell her that.'

Munch wanted to suggest he tell her

himself, but he had hung up.

'Everything all right?' Bea asked.

Munch looked at the woman and thought that that was one of the dumbest questions she'd heard in recent history. Controlling her anger, she said, 'I'll wait for Jill. Thanks for your help.'

'Sure thing, honey. Anytime.'

Taking the phone with her, Munch went inside Lisa's house and closed the door. 'Fetch, boy,' she said. Jasper cocked his head sideways but made no other move.

'I know. It would help if we knew what we were looking for.'

She lifted the blankets in the corner of the front room, shook them open, then folded and stacked them with the pillows. She flipped through the pages of the paperbacks by the bedding. A receipt for groceries fluttered to the floor. She inspected it briefly, then stuck it back in the book it had fallen from.

The refrigerator held a carton of milk. Munch checked the date, smelled it, then poured the lumpy contents down the drain. There were also three wilted carrots, a shriveled tomato, and a small saucepan full of hardened white rice. The insulin was still there. Nine vials left, stacked neatly in their cardboard box like little glass soldiers.

128

The cabinets held a carton of white rice, a box of Cheerios, and packages of soy sauce and ketchup from fast food restaurants. Just to be thorough, she pulled back the cardboard tops of the dry goods and sifted through the contents with a long knife. Nothing.

She looked at Jill's room with its cheerful chaos. Stuffed animals filled her bed; pink and yellow and periwinkle-blue clothes overflowed from her closet. There were games and toys, some suited for infants and on closer inspection mostly broken. A bookshelf held a mishmash of titles and even a few movies on videotape. Munch decided that Jill shopped at the same curb as her mother.

The girl's name written in different mediums filled the walls: wooden plaques, brightly colored Styrofoam, dried beans, and macaroni spray-painted gold and glued to construction paper. JILL, JILL, JILL. Munch wondered if this was a show of pride or an affirmation of her identity. When children followed their parents into the witness protection program, were they allowed to keep their first names or did everything change?

She went into Charlotte's room. The contrast between the two girls struck her again. Charlotte was a minimalist, in color and mood. No toys, no books, few clothes. If Charlotte had more clothes, the tiny closet wouldn't have held them. Something was out of whack. Charlotte's closet shared a common wall with the bathroom on the other side. The bathroom was L-shaped to accommodate the bathtub, which left plenty of space for Charlotte's closet to be full-size.

Munch went into the bathroom and paced the distance from the hall door to the tub enclosure, then returned to Charlotte's room and did the same to the closet. She rapped what should have been the dividing wall between the two with her knuckles. It wasn't Sheetrock, it was plywood, painted to match the inside of the closet. The carpet pulled up easily to reveal a loop of cord. Munch tugged on it and the siding came loose.

Charlotte, it seemed, had her own storage unit. This one was filled with an odd assortment of booty. Brand-new clothing — shirts, socks, underpants — double-wrapped in plastic grocery bags with all the inventory tags intact. Looked like Charlotte indulged in a few five-finger discounts. There were also picture frames, again with price stickers and still filled with those generic, all-American-family pictures. Mom and dad, brother and sis, a golden retriever. Everyone smiling, everyone perfectly coiffed.

Munch found a stack of magazines: *Good Housekeeping, Country Home, Town & Country, Esquire.* And catalogs — thick, glossy publications with many dog-eared pages. Stuck between the pages of one of the catalogs was a newspaper clipping. Munch unfolded the yellowed paper and saw that it was a story about her and how she'd helped catch a murderer. The story had run in the *Times* back in January.

'Hi,' Jill's overly sweet, girlish voice greeted Munch from the hallway. 'What are you doing?'

She seemed unperturbed to find Munch in her sister's room. And if she noticed Munch hurriedly closing the closet door to disguise what she had been up to, she didn't let on.

'Your mom's not here,' Munch said, trying not to look too guilty. 'She wanted me to watch you.'

'Watch me what?'

'You know, take you home with me until she gets back.'

'Where did she go?'

'She's in jail.' Munch could think of no easy way to put it.

'Those warrants?' Jill asked.

'Yeah.'

'So probably just a few nights. I'll pack a bag.' Jill turned on her heel and left. Nothing,

131

apparently, was going to derail her sunny disposition.

Munch replaced the panel in Charlotte's closet. While Jill gathered her clothes and whatever else an eleven-year-old needed to spend a few nights away from home, Munch opened up the phone bill and was pleased to see which service options the family subscribed to. She punched the necessary symbols on Lisa's phone to activate the call forwarding, dialed her own number, and hung up on her answering machine. They made it back to the gas station in plenty of time to meet Asia's school bus.

'So how was school?' Munch took Asia's knapsack and put it on the passenger-seat floor.

'Fine.' Asia climbed into the backseat with Jill and buckled her seat belt. She was thrilled to see both Jill and Jasper.

'Who'd you eat lunch with?' Munch knew better than to ask yes-and-no questions if she hoped to get any information about Asia's day.

'Caitlin, Jessica, and Sarah.'

Best friends all. Sometimes Munch really missed being a kid — when the world was a safe and friendly place and her mother was still alive. 'How does Stroganoff sound for dinner?'

'Why don't we just swing by McDonald's?' Asia asked with casual sophistication.

'Oh, no, honey. You're powerless over Chicken McNuggets.'

'What does that mean?' Jill asked.

'It means she'd eat them for every meal if she had her choice, and that wouldn't be good for her.'

'So when you ask, 'How does Stroganoff sound?' you're not really asking so much as telling me what we're having,' Asia said.

'I was hoping you'd approve. Jill, do you like Stroganoff?'

'Sure, sounds great.'

'Should we take a vote?' Munch watched Asia's face in the rearview mirror.

'That won't be necessary, Mother,' Asia said.

Munch laughed. She loved it when Asia used her bigger words, even if it was for sarcasm. She wasn't raising a Stepford kid.

After they got home, Asia took Jill to her room and Munch brought Asia's knapsack into the kitchen. She unpacked it on the table looking for forgotten food, dirty laundry, and obvious garbage. Near the bottom she found what she first thought was trash. She straightened the torn and crumpled paper and read it. It was a permission slip for a field trip to Long Beach Harbor in November.

'Asia,' she called into the other room.

Asia emerged. 'What?'

'What's this?'

'Just some trip thing.'

'Don't you want to go? It sounds fun.'

'Boring,' Asia said, using her new expression. Munch wondered whom they had to thank for that.

'You're too young to be bored. Says here you get to go on a boat.'

'I'll probably get seasick.'

'You don't know that. You should try new things.'

'Why?'

Munch smiled. It was exactly the same question she had asked her sponsor, Ruby, when she was first sober and Ruby had been urging her to attend AA dances and picnics. Ruby had said Munch needed to learn how to socialize without dope and with her clothes on. Munch still remembered her first sober Fourth of July picnic. It was an AA and NA event with many of her newfound friends in the fellowship. They'd spent the day at a park in Reseda, ending with fireworks. It had been wonderful to realize that she was clearheaded as she walked to her car and that the following day she would be able to remember everything.

'If you don't try new things,' Munch told

her daughter, 'how do you know what you'll like?'

'I already know what I like,' Asia said.

'Bring me some tape.'

Asia slouched from the room with her eyes rolled to the top of her head and her shoulders slumped.

'Don't drag your feet,' Munch said. 'It's annoying.'

'You're annoying,' Asia mumbled.

'What?'

'Nothing.'

Munch stared after her daughter, trying to remember the exact point that this recent phase had begun. It couldn't be the dog. Jasper was equally devoted to both of them. Maybe some problem at school. Munch realized that Asia's life was filling up with experiences that she couldn't relay to her mother. Sometimes it was because Asia didn't feel it was Munch's business, and that was okay up to a point. But other times Asia kept bothersome things to herself because she either didn't understand them or didn't know how to verbalize them. None of that meant she had to go through them alone. Munch made a mental note to talk to Asia's teacher, Chrissy Hopp, the next day. She must try to get to the bottom of this latest phase of troubling behavior.

'Jill.'

'What?' the girl answered from the bedroom.

'Come out here for a minute. Have a seat. I want to talk to you.'

Jill settled herself primly on the kitchen chair and folded her hands in her lap. Munch had once helped Rico prep for an exam on interrogation techniques. Part of that test was the ability to read body language. According to social scientists, over half of communication between people was nonverbal. Hands clasped together in front of the body meant that the subject was holding back significant information or was in great fear and trying to protect.

'How are you doing?' The interrogator was also taught to be courteous and to build rapport with his or her subject.

'Good.'

Munch chopped up the mushrooms, garlic, onion, and beef. 'Anything you want to talk about? Any questions I can answer for you?'

'Not really.' Jill's hands remained firmly clasped.

Munch put the beef and vegetables into the frying pan. The mixture sizzled and released a plume of savory steam.

'Smells good,' Jill said.

Munch rinsed and dried her hands, then

squatted in front of the girl, at eye level. 'I'll take you to school in the morning and pick you up afterward. I want you to wait for me in the office, not out front.'

'Okay.'

'And if somebody else comes by and says I told them to pick you up, you ask them for our code word.'

Jill looked intrigued. 'What's our code word?'

'You pick it.'

'Ahh, *banana*.'

'Okay, *banana* it is. Don't tell anyone else. It's our secret word.' Munch patted Jill's knee, stood, and pointed an admonishing finger toward the girl. 'And don't go with anyone who doesn't know it. Okay?'

Jill nodded. 'Okay.'

Munch opened a can of cream of mushroom soup and dumped it over the cooking meat and vegetables. 'When's the last time you saw your sister?'

'She had a big fight with my mom so I shut my door. That was Sunday night. I didn't see her before I went to school Monday morning.'

'What was the fight about?'

'You'll have to ask my mother.'

Munch wasn't sure if this meant Jill didn't know or that she wasn't going to tell her mother's business. She suspected that Jill was probably a master at keeping her family's secrets.

Munch stayed silent.

Jill leaned forward, as if to share a confidence. 'Charlotte's kind of a freak.'

'Why do you say that?'

'She takes her temperature about a hundred times a day and she's always yelling at me, telling me what to do. Bossy.' Jill extended the syllables for emphasis. 'I tell her I already have a mother.'

'Are you worried about her?'

'Sure.' Her lips said *sure* but everything else shouted, 'Heigh-ho, the wicked witch is dead.'

'Try not to worry. I'm sure we'll find her soon.'

'Can we watch a movie?' Jill asked.

'What movie?'

'I brought my tapes from home.'

'Do you have any homework?'

'A little. I usually do it on the bus.'

'Do it now and maybe after dinner we'll check out your movie.'

Jill returned to Asia's room. Munch followed after a second and listened from the hallway.

'She said we had to do our homework first,' Jill reported to Asia.

'Told you,' Asia said.

Munch returned to the kitchen and smiled to herself as she stirred the Stroganoff mixture and turned down the fire. Then she went into her room and called Rico at home.

9

'Are you still mad?' Rico asked.

Munch checked her feelings. 'No.' She was, however, retaining the right to make him suffer at a future date. And since he was so into arresting first and asking questions later, there was no way she was going to tell him about Charlotte's shoplifting booty.

'Lisa Slokum was being belligerent,' he said, 'cussing us out and then not answering questions.'

'I know Lisa operates in a separate universe. Society's rules don't apply to her unless she wants them to. So fuck her. What I'm worried about is what's happening to Charlotte right now and that's what we have to focus on.'

'We are.'

'I took a call at her house. Some guy who thought he was talking to Lisa asked her if she had *it*.'

'What was the 'it'?'

'He wouldn't say.'

'Dope?'

'I don't think so. Dopers tend to use code. Something like 'Did the ship come in?' or 'Do you have any dresses?''

''Dresses'?' he asked.

She laughed at the memory, then explained, 'When I was hanging out with bikers, I had to use smack on the sly. One of the other biker chicks who chipped with me had an old man who worked for the phone company and could listen in on the line at will. So this woman and I devised a code. When she was looking for heroin, she would call me and ask if I had any dresses.'

'Did you ever wear dresses then?'

'Why do you think they call it dope?' That got a laugh out of him. She felt the pull of attraction again, their common ground. She wondered what he was wearing.

'So how did you leave it with this guy?' Rico asked.

'He said he heard Charlotte was sick and I mentioned that she needed insulin. I also told him that Lisa was in jail and that any business he had with her he could do with me.'

'Did you give him your name?'

'No. He hung up on me, but he didn't sound like the kind of guy who is going to go away easily.'

'What kind of guy is that?'

'The bad kind.'

Asia and Jill's laughter reached Munch from the bedroom. Homework had gotten

141

very amusing since she was in elementary school. 'Lisa has call forwarding on her phone.'

'And?'

'I activated it so that calls to her house will ring here.'

'Why'd you do that?' he asked.

'So I wouldn't have to sit in her skanky house, for one.'

'You really want to play cops-and-robbers again?'

'Is this where you lecture me and tell me not to get involved?'

'Hell no.'

She could feel his smile and decided he was wearing 501 Levi's with the button fly and no shirt.

'What's next?' she asked.

'We'll see who Lisa calls from custody and put a unit at the house. I'll touch base with my sergeant and tell him how we're handling this.'

'All right. I'll be waiting for your call.'

'Munch?'

'Yeah?'

'It feels really good to hear you say that.'

Munch decided this was an excellent place to end the conversation, so she hung up.

★　★　★

Next, Munch called Mace St John and brought him up to speed on the case. He wasn't thrilled with her involvement, but she expected that.

'Do you think you can turn me on to a psychiatrist?' she asked.

'For yourself?'

She laughed. 'No, I know what my problems are. It's about Charlotte. I'm trying to get a handle on her mental state. I found some weird stuff in her room and I was wondering what a shrink would make of it.'

'What sort of stuff?'

'Four thermometers, for starters. Her sister says she takes her temperature every few minutes. And something about the way she keeps her things seems to go way beyond normal teenage rebellion.'

'That does sound weird,' St John admitted.

'I don't want something for nothing. I'll pay the guy for his time. How much do they charge?'

'I'll put you in touch with Hy Miller. He does some consultation for the department and he's married to my ex-wife. He'll talk to you pro bono.'

White-collar professionals, Munch knew, needed Latin words to label their good deeds. 'I'd truly appreciate that. I'm really worried about my niece.'

'I'll call him right now,' St John said.

Munch checked the time. 'You've got his number at home?'

'Yeah, I'll call him first and pave the way. He knows a little bit about you. I first used him on the Ballona Butcher case.' The Ballona Butcher was a serial murderer plaguing Los Angeles when Munch had first met St John. In fact, it was her inadvertent connection to that case that had got St John so interested in her in the first place.

'You're all cool with each other?' she asked.

'Sure, why not?'

'Very evolved.' She didn't hate any of her exes, but that didn't mean she wanted contact with them. She wouldn't mind hearing how they were doing as long as she didn't have to talk to them. People put entirely too much weight on talking. Sometimes a person needed to shut up and move on.

She waited ten minutes and then called Dr Miller at the number St John had given her.

'Yes,' he answered, 'I was expecting your call. How can I help you?'

'Thank you for taking the time. I was hoping you could help me understand my niece. She's fifteen and missing.'

'Did she run away?'

'I wish that were the case. I believe she's being held somewhere against her will.

Something she was involved with or something she stole might have gotten her in trouble. She also might be a little' — Munch searched for the pop-psych word of the moment — 'disturbed.'

'Tell me about her.'

Munch described the items she'd found in Charlotte's secret hiding place, the condition of her room and work space at the school, the tract of worn carpet, also the blender, the unused birth control pills, the thermometers, and what Jill had said. 'I also have reason to believe she took my dog's tags when we met briefly on Saturday. Do you think she's a kleptomaniac or something?'

'Kleptomania is a rare and often misunderstood disorder,' he said. 'It falls in the compulsive-obsessive category. It's an anxiety disorder. The patient gets stuck in a panic loop; the triggers are increased in times of stress. What you've described — the hoarding, her obsession with symmetry, evidence of rituals — all falls under known criteria for diagnosis. In the case of kleptomania, the person is driven by an impulse to steal. The objects stolen are not needed for personal use or for their monetary worth.'

'Then why?'

'Some symbolic value. All disorders have

their own logic to them. You've heard of people who claim to have radios implanted in their molars? Perhaps by the CIA or even aliens from outer space?'

'Yeah.'

'These people are hearing voices in their heads and have come up with some means to explain them, hence the receivers in their teeth. We have a woman in therapy who is convinced her family is trying to poison her. She's seen them. Her claims were dismissed as delusional until last week when we learned that her mother and sister were putting her medication in her food. So you see, she had a real basis for her conclusions. We just couldn't see it.'

'What do you make of my niece's string of logic?'

'She might take her temperature constantly because she feels with absolute certainty that if she doesn't, those around her will get sick. It's a horrible existence governed by obsessions, rituals, and worries. Also, a deep-seated belief that her lack of action will bring horrible calamity to others. What's her home life like? The family unit.'

'Terrible.' Munch told him about the sisters having different fathers (both dead with no great loss to humanity), a stepfather who had disappeared, the mother's chronic flakiness. 'Both kids get straight A's in school.'

'Amazing, isn't it?' he said. 'The resiliency of the human spirit.'

'Tell me about it. I haven't had any contact with the kids since they were little. Charlotte saved my life when she was seven.'

'How so?'

'I was eight months sober and on slippery ground, wondering if I hadn't been a little hasty in jumping on this total abstinence thing. What I really was, was lonely. I hadn't seen the kids since I had gotten clean and was explaining to them how I didn't drink or use anymore. Charlotte chewed over the information for a few minutes and then said, 'Does this mean we won't have to wake you up in the bathtub anymore?' I'm telling you, it was like she was speaking with the voice of an angel.'

'You're still sober?'

'Yes, and clean.'

'From what sort of drugs?'

'All kinds, but heroin was my main poison.' God, it seemed as if she were telling the world lately.

'Congratulations.'

Munch wondered if she had been fishing for that response. Unconsciously or not, she realized she had let the conversation be about

147

her when she was supposed to be learning more about her niece. 'I had help.'

'I'm sure, but still. I don't know if Mace mentioned it, but I work two days a week at Metro Hospital in Norwalk.'

Munch had heard of the state-run facility. They took on the dregs of the dregs.

'Would you be willing, when you have some time, to come speak to the women in one of our jail wards?' he asked.

'I'd love to.'

'We have two units that might benefit. One is for our women who are too mentally ill to stand trial. The other is for women already sentenced but who are too sick to serve time in a normal jail. Many of these cases are drug abusers.'

Munch wondered if she'd see anyone she knew. Jasper trotted past her on his way to the dog door, head down, tail straight back. A man with a mission.

Dr Miller cleared his throat. A therapist once told Munch that people often did that when they had something to say and were having difficulty getting it out. Literally, the words were stuck in their throat. 'We are a state facility, and I'm afraid our budget is small.'

'I wouldn't take any money for it anyway,' she said.

'That's wonderful. I'll tell the staff. I'm sure they'll be very excited. I'm sorry, let's get back to the reason you called.'

Yeah, Munch thought, *why don't we?* 'Do you think my niece, after hearing what I've told you, would be attracted to a father figure?'

'Almost certainly, the sister as well. Keep in mind that the compulsive-obsessive personality is guided by emotional forces they have no control over. In their acts, they are making up for something that is missing, trying to keep away the pain and depression.'

'Aren't we all.'

'Indeed, and if she does suffer from an impulse-control disorder, she most likely will have additional manifestations such as trichotillomania, bulimia nervosa, pathological gambling, pyromania — although this is more prevalent in males . . . '

'What was the first one?' Munch heard scratching, followed by a deep bark at the back door, and wondered why Jasper wasn't coming back in the same way he'd gone out.

'Trichotillomania. It's the recurrent pulling of one's own hair that often results in noticeable hair loss.'

Munch thought of Charlotte's odd fashion choices, her partially shaved head, the drawn-on eyebrows. 'Even eyebrows?' she asked.

'Yes, eyebrows, eyelashes, scalp.'

'What's the treatment?' She figured it was like alcoholism, incurable but not hopeless.

'Therapy, education, family support. There's a lot of progress being made with SSRI drugs, serotonin reuptake inhibitors, such as Prozac. If we can get a patient on the correct medication, it relieves their anxiety and gives them some room to make choices.'

'Thank you.' A small part of her brain wondered if Prozac might be the answer for her. She told herself not to consider it. She'd made it this long without chemical support. And yet . . .

'I hope I've helped,' he said, interrupting her speculations.

'Yeah, you have. You've given me a lot to think about.' *Too much, probably.* Jasper's barks were growing frantic. 'Maybe we could talk again about all this. Right now I've got a hound in distress here and I don't want to take up too much of your time.' She also didn't want to tie up the phone. 'Let me know when you set something up at Metro.' She gave him her phone number, put the frozen peas to boiling, then went to see what had Jasper so upset.

He was sitting on the back porch waiting

for her. She closed the door behind her and bent to demonstrate to him that the dog door flap pushed both ways. When she pushed on it with her hand, it resisted her effort. She pushed harder, then saw the problem: the frame had twisted, causing the door to bind. Jasper rose to his hind legs and gently landed against her, like a baby seeking a hug.

'You've got all the moves, don't you?' she said, taking a moment to stroke his fur and massage his shoulder muscles.

He gave her a look that was pure love and swiped her face twice with his tongue.

'Our first kiss.'

She went back into the kitchen and got a claw hammer out of the drawer by the sink. The noodle water was boiling. She dumped in the pasta and turned off the peas.

'Ten minutes to dinner, girls,' she yelled.

The frame straightened with three sharp strikes of the hammer. As she tested the flap, making sure it swung both ways, she thought about Charlotte's hair in the duct tape and what Dr Miller had said and wasn't sure what anything meant anymore.

10

The phone rang halfway through dinner. Munch left the kids to finish eating and took the call in her bedroom. It was Meg Sullivan, the woman Munch had spoken to outside the police station.

'Have you found your niece?' she asked.

'No, I was hoping this call would be her or news about her.'

'I'm sorry to disappoint you then. What's her name?'

'Charlotte.'

'I'll say a prayer for her. Have you made any progress?'

Jill popped her head into the room and pointed to the phone in Munch's hand. 'My mom?'

Munch covered the mouthpiece and shook her head. 'No, sorry, honey. Finish eating. I'll be in there in a minute.'

'Oh, dear,' Meg Sullivan said, 'have I interrupted your dinner?'

'We were almost through.'

'Then I'll be brief. My husband and I are offering a private reward for the return of some jewelry we lost in the burglary. It has sentimental value. We'll pay you for any information that leads to its recovery.'

'My main concern is getting Charlotte, my niece, back safely.'

'Of course, as it should be. But I don't think we're on very different tracks here. As you pointed out, her disappearance and our burglary may be related.'

'Can you describe your missing jewelry?'

'I can do better than that. I have photographs.'

More than Lisa had of her own kid. 'If you bring them to your gallery tomorrow, I can swing by there after I take the kids to school. Look for me around nine.'

'I'll look forward to it. You know, I met Steven Koon.'

'You did? When? How?'

'His mother brought him by to apologize after he was arrested for trying to pawn my VCR.'

'Did you ask him where your other stuff was?'

'He said he didn't know.'

'Did you believe him?'

'I have no idea how to read a fifteen-year-old boy. Now I feel sorry for the mother. I've expressed my condolences. Are the police close to catching his killer?'

'They wouldn't say.'

'Frustrating, isn't it? You like to think they're trying, but when they never tell you anything, what are you supposed to believe? That's why we thought, my husband and I, that we should pool our resources. Maybe then we could get something going.'

'Yeah, I hate it when I have to depend on someone else,' Munch said.

'Listen, hon, I'll let you go and I hope Charlotte comes home soon. We were impressed with you today. Keep up the good work. Keeping the heat on might even help catch the killer of that poor boy.'

Meg Sullivan didn't say, 'Before they kill again,' but Munch heard the words as clearly as if she had. She also thought Mrs Sullivan was a little too free with her compliments, but maybe it was condescension that she was detecting, or her own distrust of people who seemed too nice.

★　★　★

After dinner, Jill brought out her movies from home. Munch looked at the boxes. One was an animated Disney flick, the other a Benji movie. She opened the box for the Benji movie, but the tape inside was an unlabeled Beta. 'This one won't work on our VCR,' she told Jill.

'Oh,' Jill said, 'that's okay, I haven't seen the other one.'

Munch put the Disney tape in the machine. 'I have to make a call, and I'm expecting a call, so if the phone rings, I'll get it.'

'No problemo,' Asia said.

'Is your homework done?'

'Yes, Mommy dearest.'

Jill watched their exchange with unblinking concentration as if she were committing it to memory. Munch could always tell with a kid when the recorder was on. Asia did it at odd times, such as once when Munch paused to close the freezer door at the market that someone had carelessly left open. Asia, at five, had said solemnly, 'That was nice of you.'

Another time when Munch had backed into a pole that had dented her GTO's bumper, she had let loose with an involuntary 'Shit!' She had gotten the impression from the look on Asia's face that her daughter would remember the moment forever.

Munch turned to her niece. 'Jill, did you finish your homework?'

'Yes.'

'Good girl.'

'Auntie Munch?'

'What?'

'If my mom calls and I'm asleep, will you wake me up?'

'Sure, honey. But remember, she might not get a chance to call.'

'I know, but if she does.'

'I'll get you up. Don't worry.'

★   ★   ★

The following morning, Munch took the canvas cover off the limo — her fleet of one. Asia came outside as Munch was screwing in the mobile-phone antenna.

'Do we have a limo run?' she asked.

'No, I'm expecting some important calls so I need to be in a vehicle with a phone.'

'Cool.' Asia's legs were bare and she'd be leaving her navy blue uniform cardigan at home today. Munch had on black cotton slacks and a white shirt, looking the part of a chauffeuse. She had already called Lou and told him not to expect her today.

The Santa Anas were blowing the hot desert air to the ocean. It was earthquake weather, disaster weather. Small brush fires burned all across Southern California, having awaited such a wind. The warmer temperatures also meant more business at the gas station, overheats and air-conditioning recharges. Munch hoped Lou wasn't too overwhelmed.

Before leaving the house, Munch set her

home phone to forward to the Cadillac's mobile unit, which meant the calls to Lisa's house would also ring in the limo. She made sure Jasper had plenty of water and promised him she would be home as soon as possible. She also gave him a pair of old tennis shoes and jammed a chair against the closet knob to keep him out of there. Feeling very bourgeois and high-tech, she let the kids ride in the back and watch cartoons.

Jill rolled down the back window as they got close to her school and called loud hellos to every kid she knew.

Munch opened the back door with a flourish. 'Remember what I said about after school.'

'Banana,' Jill said in a whisper. 'I won't forget.'

Munch kissed her cheek, thinking that Jill's ability to adapt to the good as well as the bad was going to serve her well in this life.

As Munch headed for St Teresa's, the *Mark-and-Brian Show* was on the radio. She listened to the pair every morning and sometimes dreamed they were in her living room, hanging out. They even had positions on her internal committee. She wondered how 'the guys' would feel about her giving Rico another chance. Then she wondered how far she was from receiving communications through her teeth and decided that if she had been destined to go crazy, it would have struck in her teenage years.

'What's a boner?' Asia asked.

Oh, Lord, it's starting already. Munch turned down the volume. 'Who's talking about boners?'

'I don't know. Just something I heard. What is it?'

'When a boy's penis gets hard, they say he has a boner. There are other ways to say it, too. The correct word is *erection*.'

'Wouldn't his pee shoot up in the air?'

'It causes them all kinds of problems.' Munch tried to remember how old she had been when she'd learned about these things. 'It's what happens to a man's penis when he's going to have sex.'

'Sex?' Asia hooted, half-horrified, half-intrigued. She hid her face in her hands. 'I don't want to know. Yucko. I'm never *doing it*.'

'Works for me,' Munch said.

They arrived at St Teresa's just as the first bell sounded. Munch clipped on the name tag that identified her as a volunteer and parked in the school lot. Asia looked surprised when she turned off the engine.

'I'm coming in for a minute,' she explained.

'Why?'

'I want to talk to Miss Hopp.'

'Am I in trouble for something?'

'Any reason you should be?'

'I don't think so.' Asia sighed, as if resigning herself to the many eccentricities of the adults in her life. 'But you never know.'

Munch laughed. 'I just want to ask her about something.' They stopped first in the office at the entrance to the school grounds so Munch could sign in. This was a new policy at the school, instituted by the principal, Mrs Frowein, after the horror of last October when Munch had found a threatening note pinned to Asia's jacket.

It read, *If I needed to hurt you, I could*, and had been left by a crazy rapist who perceived Munch as a threat to his happiness. Now, the only way into the school was through one narrow gate that was guarded by fierce nuns.

Munch spent every Thursday afternoon from twelve-thirty to two in Asia's classroom, reading with the kids one-on-one. She liked the teacher, Ms Hopp, a lot. Her first name was Chrissy, and although she was in her mid to late twenties, Munch felt more comfortable addressing her as her students did.

This was the woman's first class of her own, and she was a natural — combining just the right measures of sternness and compassion to make the kids adore her *and* behave.

When Munch arrived at the classroom, Ms Hopp was calling the class to order and passing out a spelling test.

'Sorry we're late,' Munch said. 'My fault.'

There was a low table in one corner with two little chairs where Munch sat when she tutored. Today that chair was occupied by a TA, a thin, young woman with acne who looked as if she weren't out of high school yet.

Munch greeted the kids she knew, starting with Brittany, a little girl with long eyelashes and a deep voice for a nine-year-old. Brittany had a way of screwing up her face and making a fist of frustration whenever she got a word wrong, even if it was the first time she'd ever come across the word. Munch felt a deep empathy and affection for Brittany. Actually, each kid in the class was special: hyperactive Miles, who couldn't stop squirming, but loved books about animals; serious little Adam, who never missed a word and listened with rapt attention when Munch explained what he was reading about; Lindsey Ramsey, whose little white blouses always needed ironing and who read at a maddening rate of a word a second, pronouncing each syllable in the same monotone, without ever pausing to distinguish the end of the sentence. Sometimes it was all Munch could do to keep her eyes open.

Her job as a reading mentor wasn't to help the kids decode the words. If they couldn't read a word, Munch counted to four silently and then just said it for them. Her job was to make sure they understood that all those words added up to a story, and that the story was what made the reading fun and worthwhile. The boys seemed to go more for nonfiction, and last year, Munch had been fascinated to learn anew how bees pollinated flowers, why the moon wasn't always full, and how planets could be distinguished from stars because they didn't twinkle. Boy penguins had a built-in storage space and flap for keeping the couple's egg safe and warm. Always nice to see the male of the species contributing.

Munch credited her extensive vocabulary and a command of the language that belied her lack of formal education to her love of reading. Although it was also true that she was much more secure thinking a word than she was saying it out loud. Until recently, she had thought *banal* rhymed with *anal*. Then she'd heard some guy on one of those highbrow talk shows say it and learned that the word actually rhymed with *cabal*.

'Did we have an appointment I forgot about?' Ms Hopp asked.

'No,' Munch said. 'I wanted to talk to you about something if you have a minute.'

'Sure.' The teacher turned to her assistant. 'Ms Gunter, would you please watch the class for a few minutes while I go talk to Ms Mancini?'

Munch looked at the young girl with true sympathy. She knew how quickly Ms Hopp's well-trained students would turn into an unruly mob when their teacher stepped out.

Munch showed Asia's teacher the crumbled and ripped permission slip. 'Have you noticed a change in Asia's behavior?'

Chrissy Hopp thought a moment. 'She has been clingy lately.'

'Exactly, and she's been snarly at home. Did something happen here? Did she have a falling-out with her friends? Is she having trouble with any assignments?'

'Not that I'm aware of.'

'What would have happened if she didn't turn in this permission slip for the trip to the harbor?'

'She would have had to stay in the office all day.'

'Now why would she prefer that?'

'I don't know. Come to think of it, she spent a lot of the field trip to the petting zoo sitting by herself on the bus. She said she was tired.'

Munch looked over Ms Hopp's shoulder and saw that all the students had left their seats and had descended on the TA. 'You'd better get back in there. They're starting to riot.'

'It only takes a minute. See you Thursday, uh, tomorrow.' Ms Hopp grinned and returned to her charges.

Munch passed a pregnant woman on the way to her car. The woman was getting out of a Buick station wagon. Her purse was no doubt filled with credit cards and her list of housewife chores for the day. Munch smiled automatically albeit falsely, feeling old Mr Jealousy lifting his ugly head. She loved her life well enough, but sometimes utopia looked a lot like what other women had: the husband, the 2.5 kids, the family car, the house in the suburbs.

She doubted such women lost a wink of sleep knowing they couldn't reseal their own power steering pumps.

★   ★   ★

On her way to Meg Sullivan's studio, the car phone rang. Rico.

'I sent a unit to Lisa Slokum's house. Did you leave the door open?'

'No, why?'

'It was open when they got there.'

'Did they go in?' A fire truck with siren blaring turned the corner and Munch pulled over.

'What's going on?' he asked.

'I'm in the limo.'

'Where are you now?'

'San Vicente, heading east. I just left Asia's school and I have an errand in Westwood.'

'What kind of an errand?'

'My ship came in and I'm picking up some dresses.'

'Very funny.'

'Actually, I'm meeting with Meg Sullivan — one of the burglary victims I met at the police station. She's hoping I can help get some of her stuff back.'

'Good luck,' Rico said.

'So you didn't finish telling me, did they go in Lisa's house?'

'Yes. No one was there. I was hoping you could meet me over there this morning and tell me if anything is missing or disturbed.'

Munch checked the clock on the dashboard. 'Give me an hour. I'm stuck in going-to-work traffic.'

'All right. If you get there first, don't go in, wait for me. Be careful.'

'I pity the fool that messes with me,' she said in her best Mr T voice.

'Yeah, I know,' he said. 'I'm one of them.'

11

Meg Sullivan's art gallery was in a Tudor-style house with a peaked, shingled roof, dark timber support beams, and mullioned windows. Creeping fig clung to the aged brick walls. The trim front lawn sported a statue that looked Grecian. It reminded Munch of the mortuary in the Valley where she had driven a funeral party last month.

The funeral had been an easy charter. Four billable hours and most of that time was spent waiting at the mortuary and then the cemetery. She'd even provided a box of tissues for the grieving family members who rode with her. She always tried to distinguish her service with those extra touches.

For weddings she had a banner that she put on the limo's bumper. On the way to the service it read ALMOST MARRIED. She then flipped it over after the ceremony to proclaim JUST MARRIED.

She had joked with the hearse's driver about getting him a similar arrangement. Only his would read ALMOST BURIED on the way to the funeral and . . .

He said he got the idea. He hadn't even

smiled and she suspected he threw away her card at his earliest opportunity. Couldn't win them all.

Munch parked in the art gallery's delivery lane and knocked on the back door.

Meg Sullivan answered after a minute. 'Right on time.'

'I love your shop. Do you have those pictures of the jewelry?'

'Yes, let me get them. Come in.'

Munch stepped into another world. Treasures abounded. Glass display cases held an array of snuffboxes, antique jewelry, and detailed miniatures of all sorts of household items: tiny, black, pedal-operated Singer sewing machines, washboards, a full set of copper pots and pans. 'My kid would love this. Where do you get all this stuff?'

'Estate auctions, private sales. My husband and I have a few choice spots that we hit every year. Look around, browse.'

'I'd love to, but actually I'm in a hurry.'

'Has something new happened?'

'Maybe. I need to meet the police over at my niece's apartment. There might have been a break-in there and they want me to help them determine if anything is missing.' Munch wondered why she was telling Meg Sullivan all this. They hadn't agreed that Munch would share everything she knew, and she didn't like it when she caught herself bragging.

A miniature collie stuck his pointed nose out from behind a counter, took one look at Munch, then yapped in a high-pitched bark that set Munch's teeth on edge. She stuck out her hand toward the dog in that stupid way humans have when they want to show a dog they're friendly.

'Queenie, hush,' Meg Sullivan commanded.

The dog gave Munch one last malevolent look and then slunk back.

'Sorry about that,' Meg Sullivan said.

'Cute dog,' Munch said, thinking how lucky she was to have gotten a non-neurotic purebred in Jasper.

Mrs Sullivan handed Munch an envelope of photographs and a piece of paper with a phone number written on it. 'I talked to Cheryl Koon, Steven's mother. She'd like to meet with you.'

'She would?' Speaking to the mother of one of Charlotte's friends might provide valuable information. Munch's gut reaction was to avoid the experience. She didn't want to spend time with a grieving mother. Lisa, she could handle because most of the time Munch was pissed off at her and that blocked her feelings of sympathy. Lisa's histrionics could also always be traced directly back to

Lisa's actions and attitudes, so Munch didn't feel vulnerable around her. Cheryl Koon might be the rare 'innocent victim' — a term in police parlance that was almost an oxymoron.

Munch wondered if Asia would agree to be fitted with a LoJack — one of those tracking devices buried deep in a vehicle's wiring to facilitate recovery if it was ever stolen — when she turned thirteen.

'Cheryl's expecting to hear from you,' Sullivan said.

'I just hope I don't say something stupid that makes her feel worse.'

'Let her do the talking, then.'

Munch smiled at the obvious, but good, advice. 'I'll be in touch.'

★　★　★

Rico was waiting for her when she pulled up in front of Lisa's apartment.

'You look nice,' he said.

'Lisa didn't call.'

He opened his trunk and pulled out a large flashlight even though it was daytime. She figured it was because he didn't want to miss anything. 'She was arraigned this morning. Normally, they'd probably kick her out Friday.'

169

'Yeah, Jill didn't think she'd be gone for more than a few days. The kid has experience.' Munch looked in his trunk. You could read a lot about a person by how he kept his trunk. His held a gym bag, a box labeled CSI, and a shotgun.

He turned to her. 'How's she doing?' he asked, adopting an intimate tone.

'Breezing right through, from all appearances. I took her to school this morning and told her not to leave with anyone but me.'

'That was smart. She's lucky to have you.'

Munch noticed that her breathing changed around him, as if suddenly she needed more oxygen. She also had an absurd worry about how her hair looked and tried to remember the last time she'd brushed it. 'What do you mean 'normally' they would kick Lisa out in a few days?'

He opened the CSI box and she saw that it was filled with rolls of yellow perimeter tape, a camera, and an assortment of evidence collecting bags. 'If this is a kidnapping for exchange ransom, the Feds aren't going to want to let Lisa go until they're convinced she's not withholding any information.'

'Anything pan out with that Mobile Pet Supply?'

'The phone is disconnected. We're tracing the account, but if the guy paid cash . . . '

Rico shrugged, turned back to his trunk, and dug beneath the evidence bags.

Munch sneaked a look at herself in the car window's reflection. It was as helpful as a fun-house mirror. 'Are we going in or not?' she asked.

'Relax.' He handed her a pair of paper bootees and latex gloves. 'Put these on.' Rico shut the trunk, blew into his own gloves to inflate them before slipping them over his large fingers.

'We're really taking this seriously now, aren't we?' Munch asked as she mimicked his moves.

'You bet.' He switched on his Maglite. 'Follow me.'

They entered the apartment. Rico stopped her at the doorway. 'Anything look different?'

'Not yet.'

They walked into Jill's bedroom. 'How about here?'

'I'm not sure. A few things might have been moved, but I didn't watch Jill collect her stuff.' Munch noticed for the first time a collage of photographs pinned to a cork-board. Jill with a large chipmunk, or rather a Disneyland employee in a chipmunk suit. There were also photos of Jill at Sea World, Knott's Berry Farm, and Universal Studios. The kid was bound and determined to have a happy, fun-filled childhood. Good for her.

They entered Charlotte's room. 'Her boom box is gone.' Munch had Rico shine his light toward the closet. The secret panel was intact. 'Her clothes are still here, it looks like.' She debated again whether to show Rico Charlotte's hiding place, torn between protecting the girl and withholding from the police — from Rico. She could always pretend to discover it later.

'We should check the refrigerator,' she said.

'Hungry?' he asked.

'She keeps her insulin in there. There were nine bottles last time I checked.'

They walked into the kitchen. Rico opened the latch carefully, so as not to disturb any fingerprints. The shelf that had held the insulin was empty.

'And now there are none,' he said.

'Yep,' Munch said.

'What are you so happy about?'

'You don't need insulin for a dead diabetic.'

'So you're encouraged?'

'I think they want something she has and they're going to keep her alive till they get it.'

'I hope she's smart enough not to give it to them.'

'I have a feeling she is.'

They were still standing in the kitchen.

Rico took her arm to guide her outside again. She felt his body behind her as if a charge of electricity connected them.

'I sent our evidence from the storage unit to the DOJ lab,' he said.

'The tape and hair?' Munch asked, thinking now that 'our' included her and liking the feeling of that inclusion.

'Yes. We should get some results soon.'

They were standing on the front porch now. Munch thought of Charlotte out there somewhere, probably bound and gagged, scared and alone. 'We're going to get her back, aren't we?' It wasn't really a question because she was only going to accept one answer.

'I'm not quitting till we do.' He drew her to him for a quick hug and she let him, savoring the moment of comfort. She hoped she'd done the right thing, not showing Rico Charlotte's hidey-hole or mentioning what the shrink had told her. If it did come to light that Charlotte pulled out her own hair, the police end of the investigation might lose some serious steam.

The phone rang once, startling them both. Munch looked at it a second, then ran out to the limo. She turned on the ignition key and was rewarded by the ringing of the limo's mobile phone as the call was forwarded.

'Hello?' She gestured for Rico to listen in.

'You still offering that reward?'

Rico's cheek was pressed against hers. She cupped her hand around the mouthpiece so the sound of his breathing wouldn't give him away. Rico pointed to the receiver and mouthed, *Who is it?* Munch held up a finger to shush him.

'Who is this?'

'I met you in Hollywood. You're looking for that chick, right? I think I have something for you.'

Rico made a rolling gesture with his hand, urging Munch to keep the guy talking. She shut her eyes, not needing his distraction or obvious advice.

'I'm listening. Dave, right? Painter Dave.'

'Not over the phone.'

'Don't waste my time,' she said.

'My time is valuable, too.'

Munch smiled at his audacity. He wasn't that much different from the wannabe con artists she'd hung out with in her teens. In fact, he reminded her a lot of Sleaze John.

'And, hey, it's your kid,' Dave said, pushing the obvious.

'When and where?'

'One o'clock. Where we met before.'

A minute later, the limo phone rang again,

only they didn't hear it ring in Lisa's apartment first, which meant it was being forwarded from Munch's home line. The woman caller identified herself as Cheryl Koon.

'Can you come see me?'

'Well, uh . . . ' Munch heard the desperation in the woman's voice. The appeal was so naked — the woman sounded so low; Munch knew she'd feel worse if she refused or made some excuse. Rico was watching her with narrowed eyes. She knew that look. He was jealous.

'I'm not driving right now,' Cheryl said. 'I don't really trust myself behind the wheel of a car.'

'I can come now, if you want.' She wrote down the directions and hung up. 'That was Cheryl Koon.'

'You didn't say you knew her.'

'I don't. She wanted to meet me. I guess 'cause she heard about Charlotte. Look, anything I can bring you might help, right?'

'Just be careful,' he said. 'It's not unheard of for guilty persons to insinuate themselves into an investigation to keep track of what's going on.'

She promised Rico that she would call him later and left him waiting for the forensic team.

Cheryl Koon lived in Venice Beach, in one of those incongruous sleek, modern houses sandwiched between two run-down World War II-vintage bungalows. Overgrown banana trees shadowed the neighbors' homes, which looked like the kind of places where the bodies of dead movie starlets might be discovered. The Koons' house had meticulous, if minimal, landscaping. A Jaguar was in the driveway and a basketball hoop was over the garage door.

Steven Koon's mother greeted Munch at her front door. The woman had long hair that she'd allowed to go gray, and a coarse complexion, no doubt made rougher from grief. Garlands of dangling turquoise and silver jewelry hung from her ears and around her throat. A belt of leather studded with silver conchas cinched her tight jeans, which were fashionably distressed. She tugged at the open collar of her gypsy blouse as she motioned Munch inside. The lacy front and billowing sleeves covered more flaws than they revealed, but none of that detracted attention from the dark bags under the woman's eyes and the tremble of her hands.

'Can I offer you a drink?' she asked, raising her own glass. Her breath was foul and bitter, a drinker's breath. It was only eleven in the morning, but Munch wasn't there to judge her.

They settled in the living room. Pictures of Steve in all stages of development adorned the mantel. He had been a slight boy who never seemed to look directly into the camera.

One of the photos showed a Christmas tree in the background. Young Steve was wearing a black cape and top hat. A flag draped from the wand in his hand read YOUNG HOUDINI. Next to him a good-looking man smiled broadly with perfect white teeth. He could easily have graced the cover of *Gentlemen's Quarterly* or modeled chic sportswear in one of Charlotte's catalogs.

Munch felt a stab of guilt, remembering what she had concealed from Rico. How could he make a fully informed investigation if she was choosing what he should know?

Munch pointed at the photo. 'Your husband?' She was pretty sure it was. Her reasons for asking were twofold. She wanted to stop thinking about Rico, and she needed to see how Cheryl responded when she answered questions truthfully.

'He's been so upset. He's known Steve longer than he's known me.'

Munch must have looked confused.

'Michael is not Steve's father, not by blood anyway, but in every other way that's important. He adopted him after we got married.'

Munch nodded, wondering why people even needed to make the distinction. She remembered Rico telling her that the father had cried when he got the news.

'Steve met him through the Big Brother program. They made up for lost time. Michael took Steve everywhere with him.' Her voice turned husky. 'Then Steve went into his teenage angst and started pulling away, rebelling. I thought it was natural, but still, Steve's rejection hurt Michael after all he'd done for him.'

'I worry about that, too. My kid is eight, but I already see the signs.'

'Steve was so darling at eight. Always small for his age, but so earnest.' She stood, crossing the room to stand before a huge entertainment center. One shelf was devoted entirely to videotapes with handwritten labels. Judging by those labels, most were home movies. *Christmas, 1980. Anniversary, 1983. Mom's Surprise, 1984.*

Cheryl selected a tape at random and slid it into the player. 'Little Houdini' did a card trick for the camera. She touched the screen when Steve broke into uncontrollable giggles at his mark's amazement when he announced which card the mark was holding. 'So anxious to please. He seemed to change overnight. Clothes, attitude, hair.'

'Drugs?'

Cheryl waved a dismissive hand through the air in front of her face, as if dispersing smoke. 'I put it off to hormones. Michael wanted him tested. He's always been anti-drugs. I said no. I didn't want to invade Steve's privacy. Maybe I was wrong. You never know which is the right way to go. More or less. Then, when he started running away . . . ' She shut off the television. Little Houdini collapsed into a thin bluish line that became a tiny white dot, then disappeared into the dark void. The blackened screen cast a muted reflection of the room.

'Is your husband at work?'

'He keeps busy.' Tears leaked from Cheryl's eyes. She dabbed them with a moist tissue. 'I never knew I could cry so much. Just when I think I'm completely wrung out, I start again.'

Munch didn't think the booze helped. She showed the woman Charlotte's picture. 'Steve was friends with my niece Charlotte Slokum. Have you met her?'

'I want to. I should have. I should have known all his friends.'

'They were in school together.'

'She works on the school paper, doesn't she?'

'The yearbook, I think, maybe the paper, too.'

'He doesn't . . . didn't bring many friends home. Michael was always the social director. We thought Steve was happy this time and would stay, finish high school. We thought we could finally put the bad times behind us.' The tears trickled unchecked down her ruddy cheeks. 'I want to know what happened. I need to know what happened.'

'I'll do my best,' Munch said, thinking Cheryl Koon's desire for involvement was coming a tad late. Absolution, apparently, was still an issue. A black Range Rover pulled into the driveway. Cheryl looked at the door with a guilty start and slid her glass behind what appeared to be her wedding photo.

Cheryl glanced at the clock on the mantel and then back to the door.

Munch thought the woman should chew on a few breath mints if she really hoped to disguise her bad habits. Maybe she was new to the alcoholism thing.

'Your husband?' Munch asked, finding Cheryl's unease contagious.

'I wasn't expecting him. I hope nothing's wrong.'

Munch had to wonder how Cheryl defined wrong. It seemed to her that nothing here was right. Outside, a car door slammed. Cheryl flinched slightly, plucked at her blouse, and ran a finger under her lower lip to clean up the lipstick line.

Munch watched the doorknob, waiting for it to turn.

'I'm glad he's here,' Cheryl said.

You should tell your face, Munch thought.

'You'll see when you meet him. He's a wonderful man. Hardworking, attentive. And handsome.'

'I noticed,' Munch said, nodding toward the picture.

'I used to wonder' — Cheryl briefly touched her husband's photograph — 'why he picked me. All the women he could have had.'

The door opened and Cheryl's private paragon entered.

He smiled with his perfect white teeth, although his forehead was grooved with worry lines. Finding his wife with company obviously surprised him, but he recovered quickly. 'Hi,' he said in a radio-announcer voice, 'I'm Michael Koon.'

Munch had to admit the guy had presence. One of those types who expected to be noticed when he entered a room. Noticed and remembered. He was a little slick for her taste.

Cheryl introduced her. 'Her niece is Charlotte Slokum. Charlotte was one of Steven's friends from school.'

Munch nodded to confirm that this information was correct. She stuck out her hand. 'Glad to meet you.'

Koon's handshake was firm and dry. Nothing less than what she expected.

Cheryl said quickly, 'Her niece is missing and she's been working with the police.'

Munch felt a little annoyed at having her business reduced to those few terse sentences. Cheryl made it sound as if Munch were the intruder rather than being here reluctantly at Cheryl's own request. Maybe Cheryl hoped to deflect attention from herself.

He walked over to the couch and kissed his wife's cheek. His eyes passed over the highball glass, but he didn't react.

Mourning had its own protocol. It was also paradoxical, leaving you delicate and invulnerable at the same time. Priorities shifted. To be linked with someone in shared pain was a special relationship.

'Is there something we can help you with?' he asked, turning to Munch.

'I don't know,' Munch said, wishing she

hadn't come. 'I guess I'm just on a fact-finding mission at this point.'

Cheryl looked up, her rheumy eyes clearing for a moment of unexpected intensity. 'I'm sure you think something like this could never happen to you. I hope it never does. I pray that your niece returns home safely.'

Munch tried to make her mind go blank. It was as if Cheryl Koon had read her thoughts.

'I don't mean to scare you. I'm only saying I thought I was safe, too.'

Michael Koon patted his wife's shoulder and she fell silent.

Munch had seen odder couples. Obviously Michael saw a different woman from the one Cheryl Koon viewed in the mirror. She wondered if Cheryl was the bank. It sounded pretty cynical, she knew, but Munch had an instinctive distrust of guys with clean hands, movie star smiles, and deep tans.

She edged toward the door. 'I really should be going.'

Michael Koon picked up a cardboard box by the door. 'I'll walk you out.'

He lifted the tailgate of the Rover and set the box next to several other cartons filled with Nintendo games, boy's clothes, and several brands of expensive tennis shoes: New Balance, Nike, and L.A. Gear high-tops. He followed her gaze. 'I thought it would be easier if I got these out of the house.'

Munch wondered why the Koons felt they needed to explain their every action. 'You look familiar,' she said. 'Have we met?'

'I've done some work on television, some commercials, a little modeling.'

'That must be it.' She pointed to the boxes. 'I know a shelter in Hollywood that would love to get this stuff.'

'I've already promised it to the Boys and Girls Club on Lincoln.'

'That's good, too.'

'Can I get your number?' he asked.

'Your wife has it.'

He nodded, but didn't look particularly happy. 'I'd like to be kept informed. If you find out anything . . . '

'I can't make you any promises.'

He slammed the tailgate. 'In the future, I would appreciate you speaking to me first.'

As he spoke, he put his hand on her shoulder. She didn't think he was hitting on her. It was more as if he felt he were doing her a favor touching her. She stared at his hand until he removed it.

She did her best to think charitable thoughts of him as she drove away. He had lost a son. Grief had many faces. Of course, so did guilt.

12

Munch was heading for her rendezvous in Hollywood when Rico called. He asked how it had gone with Cheryl Koon and she filled him in.

'I got some results from the DOJ,' he said.

'And?'

'They analyzed residue on the duct tape. There was definitely saliva on the sticky side.'

'So she was gagged.'

'They also found saline traces on the outside surface.'

'Tears?'

'That would be one interpretation. I was more interested in what it didn't show.'

The light ahead changed to yellow. Munch decided not to try to make it. She was going faster than she realized and had to brake hard. The *Thomas Guide* map on the seat beside her slid to the floor. 'What do you mean?'

'Charlotte is not diabetic.'

Lisa had lied. Not a huge shock. 'But the insulin?'

'The mother's. She came clean when she went into custody. An hour ago she confessed that the insulin was hers.'

Munch couldn't blame her. Lisa had just done what she could to bring heat to the investigation. Munch would lie in a heartbeat if Asia was in trouble.

'There's more.' Rico sounded tired, even sad. 'The hair in the tape also had some odd characteristics.'

'Besides the color?'

'The follicles showed signs of trauma, the outer root sheaths were wrinkled.'

'Meaning what?' she asked, but already suspecting.

'I asked that, too. The tech said it was an indication that the hair was constantly yanked.'

'Like loose threads curl when you pull them,' Munch said. 'Are you saying she was abused?' She tried to inject a wide-eyed guileless quality to her voice. Rico had no doubt heard the tone before of a guilty person doing her best to sound innocent.

'We found a secret panel in Charlotte's closet,' he said.

'What was in there?'

'In where?'

'Behind the panel.' He hadn't said there was a compartment behind the panel, but wasn't that a logical assumption, er, uh, Your Honor, sir?

'Is there anything you want to tell me?' he asked.

Munch knew a setup when she heard it. 'Wait a minute. The light changed.'

'Before you go any further, you should know we pulled fingerprints from the picture frames and I put in my own call to the department's psychiatric consult. I believe you know him. Dr Miller. He's married to St John's ex-wife.'

Lights were changing all over. Go. Caution. Stop. It was time to choose. 'All right. I searched her room and found her stash. If I thought it was important — '

'You should have told me. The Feds don't believe we're looking at a kidnapping now. They think Charlotte got scared and pulled a rabbit.'

'Even so — '

Rico didn't let her finish. 'Withholding or providing false, misleading information in a criminal investigation is a chargeable offense.'

'How much trouble is Lisa in?'

'Lisa? She never told us her kid was diabetic. In fact, there is no record that she ever reported her missing.'

'No, she left that to me. Un-fucking-believable.' Munch made a turn. She hoped it wasn't a wrong one. The big car swung wide through the intersection. Highball glasses

187

tinkled together in the back bar. She caught a whiff of bourbon from one of the crystal decanters.

Rico sighed. 'I need you to come in and talk.'

Cops always wanted you to come to them. It was all about home court advantage and taking the subject being interviewed away from her comfort zone, not to mention the shorter distance to custody, if it came to that.

'I can't now.' Somebody honked. She realized she had cut the other driver off and waved an apology.

'Make the time, before this gets any uglier.'

There he went, going all cop on her again. She made a left and pulled to the curb under power lines. The connection filled with static. 'I'm losing you.' She switched the power off. 'You're lost.'

★ ★ ★

Parking was tight in Hollywood and Munch had to circle the block several times before finding a slot that would accommodate the limo.

Painter Dave was not on the sidewalk. After ten minutes, Munch walked around back to the alley where she'd seen him disappear before. A rental Dumpster decorated with graffiti emitted foul odors of rotting food and old cement. She thought about Little Houdini and innocence lost.

At fourteen, she had been learning how to panhandle and had stayed a few nights in an abandoned building with some of her new wino friends. Hotel Hell reminded her of those times. Some alcoholics ended up in alleys drinking cheap wine from brown paper sacks. She had begun there.

When she was a teenager, she rarely had the sense to be scared. That came later as she learned what the stakes were. Not caring whether she lived or died gave her an edge until she found out how many bad places existed in between. Jail. Pain. Heartbreak. Humiliation.

She heard a loud noise of wood tearing inside the abandoned hotel. This was followed seconds later by a terrified yelp and a crashing thump. Traffic continued on the street unaware. She ducked under a flap of chin-link. The back door hung open. The smell of urine was overpowering. A mist of fine dust escaped into the sunlight. The walls creaked as if giving voice to a sigh.

She kicked aside debris, pulled the door all the way open, and listened. The stink was stronger, definitely of human origin. It reminded her of one of those horrible nursing homes. She picked up a length of steel pipe.

'Are you all right?' she called into the darkness. The walls cracked, like old bones settling. She wondered what the odds were of the building taking this moment to collapse.

'Dave?'

She took another step.

'Over here, Officer,' she said loudly, adding impersonating backup to her growing list of sins.

Something small and furry ran over her feet.

She screamed. The rush of adrenaline gave her impetus. She used the pipe to rip a sheet of plywood from one of the windows and daylight flooded in. The dust was thick, but the sickening putrid stench had diminished. She suspected it was still there and that her sense of smell had shut down in self-defense.

Judging from the center counter, double sinks, and gaps where large appliances had once stood, she figured she was standing in what must have been the hotel's kitchen.

There was a large gap in the ceiling overhead and beneath it a pile of clothing. No, not clothing, but a clothed body. She knelt beside the still form of Painter Dave and pressed two fingers to the side of his neck. The skin was warm, but there was no pulse. She turned him on his back, trying to remember the CPR mnemonic.

'Two and five keep them alive.'

But was that two chest compressions and five breaths or the other way around? She tilted his head back and blew air into his mouth. His thin chest rose in response, which meant his airway was clear. She found the spot on his sternum and pumped the heel of her hand against his heart muscle. Blood spurted from the jagged crevice slashed across his neck below his left ear, and she realized she was not going to be able to make a difference. Painter Dave had one more thing in common with Sleaze John. They were both dead way too young.

She lifted his hand, still clenched tight. Wiping tears from her cheeks with the sleeve of her shirt, she pried his fingers open to see what was so precious. It was a dog tag. Jasper's tag, the loop at the top gapped open as if it had been pulled violently from its ring.

Upstairs, a door slammed.

Munch pocketed the thin metal token and rose cautiously.

'Charlotte?'

She heard whispered exclamations and running feet. The sounds echoed weirdly through the building, the voices muted and urgent. Something large slammed against the floor above her. The sound was sharp, something hard slapping against an equally hard surface. Not the cushioned thud of flesh, but furniture or a fixture.

'Get out,' a voice yelled down to her.

'I need help,' she called back. 'This boy is hurt.'

Above her, someone giggled. It sounded feminine, and it creeped her out royally.

'I'm not kidding.' She heard a touch of hysteria in her voice.

Now several voices added to the giggle, coming from different angles above her. Mocking jungle calls, like monkeys laughing, hooting, taunting. They grew bolder and closer. A shadowy form jumped across the hole above her. Chunks of plaster and dust sifted down around her, landing in her hair and on her shoulders. Grit filled her eyes. She could taste the powder in the back of her mouth. The walls started chiming. It took her a moment to make sense of the sound. The pipes. They were beating on the water pipes.

How many there were, where they were, she had no way of knowing. She did know that she was outnumbered by the little bastards and seriously out of her element. She backed out of the ringing building and ran to the limo to use the phone.

Rico was wrong about one thing. It had already gotten uglier.

She called 911. The operator was suspicious. Her system showed that Munch was on a mobile phone, which meant the operator's locator system was ineffective. Munch had to repeat herself several times, spell out her name, and provide the limo's license plate.

When the police got there, the body was still as she'd left it. She told the officers that she had come looking for her runaway niece, that she'd heard some of the kids took refuge in the old building. Finding Dave had been happenstance. The larger of the two patrol cops — Officer A. North, according to his nameplate — took Munch aside.

'His name was David?'

'Painter Dave. That's what he told me the other day, anyhow.'

'So which time that you found him are you chalking up to chance?' Officer North was one of those sarcastic types. Dave's blood had yet to dry on her blouse. The last thing she needed was this cop giving her attitude.

'I just meant that I didn't know him from Adam yesterday. He came up to me in my car and started talking to me.'

'And you were looking for your niece, you say?' North's tone and expression suggested that he thought she was making up that part, that she didn't have a niece, that she was in his town just to get in his way.

She handed him one of the flyers she had made of Charlotte. North rested a hand on the butt of his revolver as he perused the handout. She almost laughed out loud. It was going to take more than the revolver to intimidate her.

'I'm gonna need to see some photo ID,' he said.

She handed him her driver's license without looking at him.

'Your attitude isn't helping,' he said.

'This has been pretty fucking traumatic all around, you know?' She didn't usually swear in front of people she didn't know, but, hey, kids didn't die in her arms every day either. 'How long is this going to take? I've got to pick my children up from school. I'd like to go home and change first.'

'You're not going anywhere until I say so.'

Several responses came to mind, suggestions involving parts of his anatomy and members of his immediate family. She held her tongue. The way this day was going, he would probably arrest her.

A fire truck and paramedic arrived. The various uniformed personnel went inside the building to look at the body, wrote things on clipboards, spoke on their radios, and conferred with one another. Munch met the patrol sergeant and retold her story. He thanked her.

Officer North returned her driver's license.

'In your expert opinion,' she said, striving for the proper balance of deference without giving ground, without groveling, 'was this an accident or a murder?'

He looked back at the building. 'I don't know. Maybe it was suicide. We get a lot of that around here.'

'Sad, isn't it? Kids so young think they're already out of options?'

'People get trapped in narrow lives.'

'How's that?' she asked, surprised at his use of metaphor.

'Their world is what they see day in and day out. Mean existence has a way of shrinking, choking the life out.'

She felt a stirring of empathy for this guy. She didn't know why he'd chosen to be a cop, why anyone would choose to be a cop, but the reality of the work had to hold its share of disappointments. She took off her sunglasses so he could see her eyes. 'I have a friend who's a cop in West L.A. Mace St John.'

'Sure. I know who that is.' North's face relaxed, started to look human.

She didn't tell him that they had met when

he came to arrest her. That was a long time ago, and beside the point.

'He told me once about the first murder he ever came across. He was on patrol and they got a call to investigate a shooting. Two brothers. One was dead on the kitchen floor, the other was sitting at the table — gun in front of him. Mace said the first thing they did was secure the weapon.'

The cop nodded in agreement. That's what he would have done also.

'Mace asks the guy, 'What happened?'

'The brother goes, 'I shot the son of a bitch.''

Officer North was still wearing his sunglasses. They picked up the reflection of the coroner's wagon arriving.

'Mace thinks, 'Cool, we solved the case.' His partner asks the guy, 'Why'd you do it?'

''Look at that.' The brother points at the fried hamburgers still on their plates and says, 'He always took the biggest one. Always.''

North smiled. 'Exactly. An ounce of ground beef finally tipped the scales.'

Munch noticed that her sunglass lenses were smeared. She fogged them with her breath and wiped them clean with her shirt-tail. 'You ever hear of a guy around here they call Mouseman? He has kids steal for him, commit home burglaries.'

'Is your niece hooked up with this guy?'

She put her shades back on. 'There's some connection.'

'Why do they call the guy Mouseman? He pay the kids in cheese?'

She smiled at his lame joke to show him that they were all being friendly here. 'I don't know. He must be giving them something good.'

The cop looked up and down the boulevard, then spit in the curb. 'Around here, that could be anything.'

Munch nodded.

Then North surprised her again by asking, 'What did you want more than anything when you were a kid?' The question was personal, but not offensive. She wished she'd thought to ask it herself.

'Love, acceptance. I didn't know it then.' She shook her head and chuckled. God or the universe or whatever had a way of sending her the most unexpected messengers. 'How about you?'

'I wanted to play pro ball.'

'Well, yeah, if you'd let me finish. Fame and fortune were on my short list, too.'

'You've got cop connections,' North said. 'You might want to check with the narcs, they got guys working undercover at the high schools, look about fifteen. If anyone's heard of your Mouseman, it'd be one of them.'

13

Munch left Hollywood and headed for West L.A. It was already almost three. The kids would be out of school soon. Rico was probably good and pissed off. She called his direct line. He answered as he always did.

'Chacón.'

'Mancini,' she echoed.

'What?' he said flatly. No sense of humor. He was really ticked.

'I found a body.'

'Who? Where?'

'That kid I was meeting in Hollywood. He fell or was pushed or jumped. We're not sure which. There was a nasty gash in his throat.'

'Who's we?'

'Officer North, the coroner, just about everybody who was there.' She fingered the dog tag in her pocket.

'You couldn't call me?'

A childish point. She was calling him now, wasn't she? 'I have something to show you. Dave had it in his hand. I forgot about it in all the excitement.'

'You forget a lot of things.'

He was one to talk. She mentally counted

to five, resisting the urge to hang up. That wouldn't help Charlotte.

'This cop I talked to had a good idea.'

'What was that?' Rico asked, sounding as if he was doing some mental counting of his own.

'He said I should talk to undercover narcs who work the high schools, that they might have heard something more about this Mouseman guy. Can you introduce me to one of them?'

'Let me tell you why that's *not* going to happen. We're working the case. I'm giving it top priority. It's a dangerous situation and more complications are not what we need. In other words, I don't want you sticking your nose in or your neck out.'

'What you want and what I want hasn't always been the same thing. Charlotte is still out there somewhere. She needs help. Her disease might not be physical like I first thought, but her mental health is every bit as critical.'

'I've made up my mind,' Rico said. 'I don't want you starting shit with this guy Mouseman or whoever the hell.'

'What are you talking about?'

'We've rerouted the call forwarding. Stop asking questions. You're going to piss off the wrong guy.'

'First of all, you got it all backward. The guy on the phone started the shit with me. I'm the one who's pissed off now.'

'I'm not introducing you to any narcs.'

'Fine. I never counted on you in the first place,' she lied. This time she did hang up, which on the mobile phone involved pushing a button. Slamming down the handset would have been much more satisfying. She was deferring gratification a lot lately, it seemed. Maybe she would be a better person as a result. All she knew was that there god-damned better be a heaven at the end of all this.

She stopped at a gas station and changed into a clean shirt. She always kept one in her trunk. As she drove toward Jill's school, she decided to have some more posters made of Charlotte and have Jill and Asia help her post them throughout the neighborhood. Rico wasn't the boss of her.

The final bell was ringing as Munch parked on the street opposite Jill's school and walked to the administration office. Jill was at the drinking fountain, bent over for a slurp. What was it about schools and water pressure? Two girls her age idled nearby. Munch considered the eleven-year-olds carefully. They were already experimenting with lip gloss and jewelry, no doubt jazzed about getting that first bra, starting to notice boys in a different way. Their eleven-year-old male counterparts tromping by seemed big-footed and loud. Some had the bleached-blond, tanned surfer look. Noses in a permanent state of peel and sunburn. Others were going for the urban-gang look: pressed pants, white T-shirts, hair slicked back.

The boys jostled and pushed, unconcerned with their dirty faces and untied shoes. The girls leaned against the wall, trying too hard to pretend they hadn't seen or heard their classmates, covering their noses with cupped hands as they passed their secrets. Alien observers would think they had stumbled on to two separate species of Earth beasts.

'Auntie Munch,' Jill called.

Munch caught up to the girls and gave Jill a welcoming hug. 'All ready?'

'Did you bring the limo?'

Munch smiled to herself, wondering if she had helped raise Jill's status. 'Yep, we need to go. Asia will be getting home soon.'

'Bye, guys,' Jill told her friends. The girls' heads converged for one last giggle and whisper.

'We do have a little extra time,' Munch said. 'Do any of your friends need a ride home?'

The girls looked at one another and

squealed. Munch smiled.

'Wait out front, I'll bring the car.' The curb was full of mothers picking up children. It would take a little longer this way, but Jill might as well enjoy her prestige.

Jill and her two friends were waiting on the curb with barely contained enthusiasm, casting protracted glances over their shoulders, hoping for witnesses. A woman who must have been a teacher or perhaps the principal stood at the school's entrance.

'Good-bye, Mrs Hansen,' Jill's blonde friend yelled.

'Good-bye, Rachel.' Mrs Hansen waved back.

This went on for another minute or so. The performance was repeated with every adult and child, until Munch sensed the impatience of the other parents waiting to pick up their kids. She loaded the three girls in the back and followed their directions to their various homes.

After the last friend was deposited safely at her door, Jill leaned across the seat separating her and Munch.

'When I was in first grade, I used to think only movie stars rode in limos.'

'I wish a few of them would hire mine,' Munch said, although she'd had her share of so-called producers. It was L.A., after all.

Wannabe moviemakers were as common as palm trees.

'Auntie Munch?'

'Honey, you're going to have to put your seat belt on.'

'I will. I was just wondering . . . '

Munch found the eleven-year-old's face in the rearview mirror. 'What?'

'Did you know my dad?'

Munch wished she had some story to give the girl, an anecdote that she could share. 'No, honey. I'm sorry. I wish I had.'

Jill shrugged as if to say *Worth a try*. Munch knew it mattered, but there was nothing she could do. She was tempted to make up a little history, but that wasn't the answer to the child's wish to know her father.

Two blocks from the gas station, the mobile phone rang.

'Will you accept a collect call from Los Angeles County jail?' the operator asked.

'Yeah,' Munch said, 'put her on.'

'Can you believe this shit?' Lisa asked. 'How's Jill? I tried calling your work, but nobody would accept a collect call.'

'Jill is with me. I just picked her up from school.' Jill sat up higher in her seat upon hearing her name. Munch held up a finger and mouthed to her, *One moment.* Then she lowered her voice to ask Lisa, 'You know a

203

guy called Mouseman?'

'I don't know.'

'You don't know?' Munch knew there was no privacy in custody. The walls had eyes and all communication made by prisoners was closely monitored. A lawyer had told her that. Lisa would probably be oblique anyway, just out of habit.

'I mean, no, I don't. Why?'

'Does Charlotte spend time with any older guys? A father-figure type who maybe does things for her, takes her places?' Munch glanced in the rearview mirror. Jill had disappeared. 'Hang on a minute,' Munch said into the phone. She pulled over to the curb, put the car in park, and stuck her head into the rear passenger compartment. Jill was kneeling on the rear-facing seat, obviously having jockeyed herself into the best eaves-dropping position available to her.

'You want to say hi to your mom?' Munch asked.

Jill reached for the phone. As soon as the receiver touched her ear, she began crying. 'Mommy? When are you coming home? I miss you.'

Munch couldn't help feeling a little hurt. She thought she was showing Jill a pretty good time. Then again, Munch knew that when you were down to one parent, that

204

parent became all the more precious. Her dead father, Flower George, used to say that the same was true about his one good eye. Speaking of messed-up parents. Even he had had to screw Munch over repeatedly and royally before she had finally severed the relationship, and then it had been by emptying the full clip of a .22 automatic into his face.

'Okay,' Jill was saying to her mother, 'I won't. Bye.' She handed the phone back to Munch.

'What?' Munch asked, realizing she had adopted the same tone Rico had used with her when last they spoke. She wanted to ask Lisa what she and Charlotte had argued about the night before Charlotte disappeared. She didn't for two reasons. Jill was listening and might feel Munch was betraying her. And two, it would probably be a waste of breath anyway. Lisa's interpretation of reality wasn't reliable.

'You gotta get me outta here,' Lisa said.

'Why don't you just sit tight? Rico says you'll go to court Friday and probably get kicked out for time served.'

'I know what *he* wants,' Lisa mumbled, running her words together, speaking quickly to slip her message past the cops.

Munch didn't ask who or why, but picked

up the conversation as if there had been no break in continuity. So Lisa did know why Charlotte had been snatched. 'I don't see why we should spend the money on bail.'

'I'll pay you back. But I got to get out of here to make things right.'

'All I can do is all I can do,' Munch said. Let whoever was listening take that any way they wanted. 'Thanks for the snake job, by the way.'

'Whadda you mean?'

'Charlotte's not the diabetic, you are.' Might as well get this little tidbit on the record.

'And if I told you I knew she was in trouble because she hadn't made her bed, I'm sure you would have believed me.'

'God forbid you try the truth first,' Munch said, matching Lisa's sarcasm.

'I'm sorry, all right? I love my kids, no matter what anyone thinks. What I do is for them. I can't do anything for them from in here, but you do what you think you have to do.'

'I will,' Munch said as she pulled into her gas station. 'I won't let these kids down.'

14

Asia was in Lou's office, watching his little black-and-white television as usual. Munch sent Jill in to join her. The two hoists were tied up with a Thunderbird and a Mercedes. The Thunderbird's rear axle had been pulled, and all four tires were off the Mercedes. The accumulation of black asbestos dust on the rims told Munch that the Mercedes was probably in for brakes. Carlos was up to his elbows in grease and bent over a Chrysler New Yorker. Even Stephano had managed to work up a sweat.

Lou held a clipboard and was writing up a young girl while the tow truck dropped her overheated Toyota Supra in the lot. From the looks on both their faces, he was delivering bad news and she wasn't happy about it. Though in this neighborhood, she was probably more put out by the inconvenience than the expense.

All in all, the world of Bel Air Texaco seemed to be going on all right without her. She silently calculated all the money she wasn't making and tried not to feel too jealous.

'Any luck?' Lou asked, having let the young Toyota owner use his phone to call whomever. Her daddy probably.

'Lots of it,' Munch said. 'Just none of it good.'

'No news on your niece?' Lou asked as if he really cared. She appreciated that.

He and she had come a long way together. He hadn't seemed to like her much when he'd first met her. Truth be told, the feeling had been mutual.

He explained to her later that once he'd heard she'd been on drugs, he'd expected her to go back on them. Somewhere in her first year clean and sober, he'd been convinced otherwise. He'd asked her once how smart she'd thought she'd have been if she hadn't destroyed so many brain cells. She'd explained to him that heroin didn't really fry your brain as much as put it to sleep. He'd said he thought she was waking up nicely.

'Have you eaten?' he asked now.

'Not since breakfast.' As soon as he said the words, she realized she was starving.

'Give me your keys,' he said. 'I'll fill your tank. You need any money?'

'No, I'm good.' She handed him her keys, and he whistled for Miguel to come fetch them.

'There's an apple in the office and one of

208

those muffin things you like.'

She kissed him on the cheek, at least she meant to, but at the last moment he turned his face and their lips pressed together. She put her hands on his shoulders and pushed him away, laughing as she said, 'Hey, watch it.'

She hoped to God that Lou and his wife never split up. Then she'd really have to set him straight. She was never very good at saying no or hurting feelings, but she knew how to do so when she had to.

'Asia, Jill, c'mon, we need to get going.'

'You got a call,' Lou said, reaching into his shirt pocket. 'She left a number.' He handed Munch a slip of paper with the name Kathy Pascoe on it and a phone number.

'What did she want?' The words came out in a snarl.

'She didn't say. Who is she?'

'The broad Rico was going to marry. The one who said she was pregnant and wasn't.'

'You going to call her?'

'I guess so. Christ, this is all I need.'

'Maybe she wants to give you her blessing.'

'Like I need it.' Munch watched the office door, but the girls hadn't appeared.

Lou wiped at a spot on his shirt with a grease rag. 'So, you two getting back together?'

'I don't know.' It wasn't as if Rico could ever hurt her again. Deeply anyway. She was pretty well inoculated after last winter's bombshell. She'd been so into him before, so worried what he thought and felt, now it wasn't like that. The playing field was much more even. Who believed in perfect soul mates in any case? Even Mace and Caroline St John had once spent months apart. Honeymoons only lasted so long. Expectations were made to be lowered.

You spend enough time with anyone, Caroline once confided, and there comes a day when you hate the way he chews.

Munch hoped she'd get the relationship thing right soon, so Asia would have a good example. She already knew there were some good men in the world. Men worthy of respect, capable of love, willing to contribute. What hope did Jill and Charlotte have with the information they'd been provided by Lisa? Munch hoped they'd rebel by becoming debutantes, joining country clubs, and learning how to play bridge and golf. Couldn't get much further away from Lisa than shrimp cocktails at the club.

Munch headed for Lou's office, stepping over reels of air hose, noticing the graveled wear on the Mercedes brake rotors. They would have to be replaced. She resisted the urge to lift the calipers and see if the seals were seeping hydraulic fluid. It wasn't her job, why sully her hands, not to mention lungs, with someone else's brake dust?

She grabbed the apple and muffin on Lou's desk. Jill and Asia were sitting side by side in the padded desk chair. Thick as . . . cousins.

'Your coach awaits, mesdames.'

'All right then,' Asia said in an arch tone. 'Home, James.'

'At your service, milady,' Munch said, relieved that Asia had decided to be eight again. Lou stood in the doorway, his wiry arms crossed over his flat chest. His uniform shirt was uncharacteristically dirty. A smear of grease was under one eye and he looked tired. She was letting him down. 'I'll be here tomorrow,' she told him, 'unless something happens.'

'What are you going to do now?' he asked.

'This lady I met is offering a reward for some missing jewelry. I thought I'd take a run over to Santa Monica and check out the pawn shops.'

Lou followed them to the car. 'Couldn't she do that herself? And don't the cops do that regularly anyhow?'

Munch opened the back door and gestured for the kids to get in. 'I know a guy who runs a private operation.'

'A fence?'

Munch made sure the girls strapped on their seat belts. 'Something like that.' Actually Benny Harper was exactly that. 'I'll see you tomorrow.'

'Yeah, sure.'

Munch didn't respond to his disbelief. She didn't like to make promises she wasn't sure she could keep.

* * *

She'd met Benny when he was the bartender at the Venture Inn. The bar, a dive really, was on Venice Boulevard, close to the boardwalk. It was one of Munch's old watering holes. Benny had had some battles with cocaine, which he felt helped him to keep up with the frenetic pace of the bikers ordering drinks.

When the Venture Inn closed, Benny got a job at an uptown establishment in the Marina. He also got sober, or what passed for sober as far as he was concerned. He no longer snorted cocaine or drank, but he considered weed medicinal. He also kept his hand in the brokering of expensive trinkets of dubious pedigree. He liked to think of his suppliers as modern Robin Hoods. Munch warned him of the bad karma associated with stolen items, how they had a habit of keeping moving, but Benny fancied the action. In a weird way, Munch kind of liked that about him. He was also fair in his dealings, never low-balling selling customers, no matter how desperate they were. Maybe those small acts of kindness balanced out his karma.

Munch knew he didn't approve of violence. Once, years ago, on a slow Monday morning, an ex-Mongol (and she stressed the word *ex*) named Grinch had knocked her off a barstool for refusing to remove a cutoff vest he felt too closely resembled biker club colors. Benny had vaulted the bar, bad leg and all, and pushed the guy back with the sawed-off base-ball bat he kept under the counter.

Munch might have removed the vest, but she wasn't wearing anything underneath it. And what was the big deal anyway? She'd earned every patch sewn on the thing. Broken Harley wings, signifying she'd been in a wreck. A guy in a Quaker hat flipping the bird and saying FUCK THEE. A coiled snake with the legend DON'T TREAD ON ME.

She'd considered herself quite a threat back then. An alligator attitude attached to a canary ass was more like it. Though, to be fair, attitude often carried a person a lot farther than ability.

What Grinch had objected to was the banner across the bottom, drawn on with

Marks-A-Lot, that read VENICE. Seems the Hells Angels or some other bunch of macho, he-men assholes once used that as part of their colors.

Munch was born and raised in Venice. She had a right, she felt, and told him so.

She was also nursing a black eye, and she'd just spent a hellish weekend trying to get away from a band of Satan's Slaves who'd kidnapped her. The kidnapping was her own fault. She had stupidly and drunkenly proclaimed on a meeting night that she was nineteen and wanted it nineteen times. Some celebration *that* birthday had turned into. After sobering quickly in the back of a windowless van, she had talked most of the guys out of doing her. Then she'd spent the rest of the weekend in bum-fuck-she-didn't-know-where, trying to get their old ladies to help her escape or at least point her to the bus that would take her back to Venice and out of that nightmare.

Those pleas had fallen on deaf ears. The women looked right through her, as if she were the one trespassing and in the wrong. Self-righteous cunts. Munch had vowed then to support her sisters. Shit, the guys were already rough on them, why give it to one another as well? How about a little compassion?

So when the dude in the bar told her to take off her colors, Munch was in no mood to acquiesce. Fuck him.

Grinch was a surly son of a bitch. He didn't get his name for nothing. She knew for a fact he hadn't had a bike for a year, so who was he to push her around, tell her the law? Who died and made him King Kong anyhow? she asked him. Then Grinch slapped her off the stool and Benny did his jack-in-the-box broad jump over the bar before the punk had an opportunity to kick her.

Benny took a chance doing that, and she'd never forgotten it. Later he had given her a ride home in his convertible Coupe de Ville, spotted her a twenty, and suggested she lie low for a little while.

Two years ago, Munch had seen Grinch again. He was at an AA picnic, missing his front teeth, and looking pretty humble. She had grinned at him until he asked, 'What?'

She just shook her head and hadn't let him in on the joke. Life had a funny way of balancing out.

The bar where Benny hung his shingle now serviced an upscale restaurant with a view of the Marina. There was also a coffee shop in front for the family crowd. Munch parked the limo, got her and the kids a booth in the G-rated section, and caught Benny's eye.

Benny had gone completely gray and now used a cane. He limped over to their table with a big smile on his face.

Munch rose to greet him with a hug. There had never been a sexual side to their relationship. Benny went for big-titted, tall blondes with red fingernails that went on for miles. His affection for Munch had always been fraternal. Her very own Uncle Bad.

'Don't order the crab cakes,' he warned in his gravelly voice.

'I never do,' Munch said. 'I like to know what I'm getting.'

'That's my girl.'

He held out his palm to Asia and she slapped him five. He rewarded her by seemingly pulling a fifty-cent piece out from behind her ear. He always knew the way to a little girl's heart.

'Who's this?' he asked, smiling at Jill.

'My cousin,' Asia said. 'You might want to check her ear, too.'

Benny laughed and pulled the fifty-cent trick again. Jill had it in her pocket before her hair had a chance to settle.

'What do you say?' Munch prompted.

'Thank you,' the girls chorused.

'You guys go ahead and order. Get me a turkey sandwich. I want to show Benny the limo.'

Benny flipped his bar towel over his shoulder and followed Munch outside. He spread his arms to encompass it all — the sleek silver Caddy limo with the boomerang antennae, the parking lot full of Mercedes, red Porsches, and Rolls-Royces, the yachts dipping on their moorings. He laughed and said, 'Look at us now.'

Munch unlocked the driver's door and grabbed the photos she'd stashed in the visor. They were the pictures of Meg Sullivan's stolen jewelry. She looked more closely at them as she passed them to Benny. The first showed three rings with stones. Going by their colors, the stones were probably ruby, emerald, and sapphire respectively. The next photo was of a cameo brooch. The cameo had a peach background and a raised scene of a bare-shouldered lady draped in an old-fashioned lacy gown sitting on a bench next to a lamb. She had a gentle smile on her face and was pouring fluid from a goblet into a fountain.

'Bucolic,' Munch said, handing it over.

This brought a strange grunt from Benny as he reached for the third picture, showing a heart-shaped locket that seemed to be made of gold and inlaid with tiny diamonds. As he sifted through the stack, his face gave little away.

'You doing a little early Christmas shopping?' he asked.

'The lady who lost these is offering a reward.'

'Sentimental value?'

Munch shrugged. 'So she said.'

'Wasn't she insured? You know she was. She go to the trouble of photographing the stuff, she probably wants to double-dip.' He shook his head in seeming disgust. 'The world is full of crooks.'

'I'm looking for just one of them. Guy named Mouseman.'

Benny thrust the pictures back to her. 'Can't help you, doll.'

'Let me give you the whole story.'

'You never get the full story,' he said, looking wistfully back at the door to the restaurant. 'Remember I said that. People only tell you the parts they want you to know.'

'My niece has disappeared. Jill's older sister. She was tied up in some burglary ring led by this Mouseman dude. I don't care about anything except getting her back safe. Two kids are already dead.' She told him about Steve Koon and Painter Dave. He looked pained, even as he shook his head.

She gave him all her numbers. 'These kids never had a chance. Anything you can tell me, anyplace you can lead me, would be appreciated. I believe this jewelry was snatched by Mouseman's crew. I'm hoping it can lead me back to him.'

'The cameo,' he said, tapping the photographs. 'It looks old. I know a guy who's into that kind of thing, a collector, like. It's a long shot and I'm not promising anything, but I'll drop a dime, see what I come up with.'

'That's all I ask. I won't make any trouble for anybody. I just want Charlotte home safe.'

When they got back inside the restaurant, Asia was telling the waitress she wanted french fries and a chocolate shake. Munch cleared her throat.

'Just kidding,' Asia said, making a little laugh to prove it. 'Spaghetti, please.'

'And milk,' Munch added. 'Jill?'

'Can I have a hamburger?'

'Sure, you want cheese on it?'

'Yes, please. Thank you.'

Munch reached over to pat her hand. Jill quickly balled her fist, but not before Munch caught a glimpse of silver on the little girl's finger. When that hand reappeared to lift her sandwich, whatever had glinted earlier was no longer there. Munch shrugged it off. Growing up with Lisa, living in the witness protection program, the girl was bound to pick up some sneaky ways. Heck, most kids had a sneaky side. Even Asia.

Jill ate everything on her plate; Munch wondered where she put it all. Munch saved a quarter of her own turkey sandwich as a treat for Jasper, an apology for being gone so long. She laughed at herself. She couldn't get just any dog. No, she had to find one with abandonment issues. She couldn't fall in love with some regular guy. No, he had to have crazy exes or some other kink.

'That's what I like about you,' her old boss Happy Jack once said. 'Nothing's ever simple, there's always all these — whatchacallit? — extenuating circumstances.'

Wasn't that the truth. She didn't think she went looking for trouble. Complications had a way of falling in her lap.

15

When they got home, Jasper virtually cried with happiness. He grabbed at their hands with his teeth, not so hard as to bite them, more as if he wanted to hurry them inside to show them what he'd been up to. The chair Munch had wedged against her closet door was on its side. The closet door was missing a few stripes of paint and hanging open.

Jasper waved his tail with pride at the pile of shoes by the front window.

Munch smiled as she scratched his ears and then picked up the footwear. 'You think you done good, huh?' She opened a can of dog food and mixed it with the turkey from her sandwich. Jasper would only eat if she stayed with him in the kitchen.

Munch sent Jill to do her homework and asked Asia to come help her in the front yard. The roses were in full bloom, but thirsty. Jasper came out to keep them company as they watered, weeded, and checked for bugs. Daylight saving time would be coming soon. Fall back. The time change meant that it would be dark when they got home after work. What annoyed her was that the change took place just in time for trick-or-treating. Couldn't the powers-that-be wait until November so working mothers wouldn't have to scramble home ahead of traffic?

'Have you decided what you want to be for Halloween?' Munch asked.

'Either Elvira, Mistress of the Dark, or Michael Jackson.'

Close call, Munch thought, but you needed cleavage to pull off a convincing Elvira. 'You've got the moonwalk down. What else do you need?'

'The glove, for sure.'

'With sequins? We can do that.' Munch moved the hose to another rosebush — a two-tone beauty called Peace. The petals were a buttery yellow in the center and edged in pink. They were her favorites. Jasper chomped on blades of grass as they worked. 'You know when you went to that petting zoo?'

Asia suddenly busied herself studying the large red blossom of a Mr Lincoln. 'Yeah,' she barely mumbled.

'Did something bad happen? Somebody hurt your feelings or something?'

Asia exhaled. 'Well, there was this man.'

Munch felt a cold, deadly chill. 'What man?'

'He was like following me around. He started out nice. He had a daughter.'

'Was she with him?'

'No, he just told me her name was Taffy, like the candy.'

Munch tried to keep her voice very calm. She wanted to crush something. 'Did he touch you?'

'On the arm.' Asia looked scared and stared at her arm as if expecting to see worms emerge.

'Nowhere else?'

'No, he wanted me to ride on a horse with him.'

Munch knew her heart had stopped beating. The world surrounding her and Asia felt preternaturally still and unimportant. 'Where were the other grown-ups?'

Asia's eyes filled with tears. 'I was by myself.'

The berm beneath Munch flooded over. She flung the hose to another plant, not caring when a branch snapped. Jasper's body went into a hunter's pose: head up, tail pointed straight back. 'What did you do when the man asked you to get on the horse?'

Asia's voice was unnaturally high and the tears were flowing freely. 'I ran away.'

Munch scooped her in her arms and held her. 'You did right. You did exactly right. I'm so proud of you.'

'But, I' — the words came out as hiccups

223

— 'shouldn't . . . have . . . wandered . . . off.'

'Honey, baby, don't cry. Shhh.' Munch buried her face in Asia's hair. Her arms encircled the little girl. She willed her anger away, lest Asia think that the emotion was directed at her. 'Come on. It's okay now. Next time you'll stay with the group. You're a good kid. You're the best. You did the exact right thing. You trusted your instincts. A stranger is a stranger, no matter what he says or looks like. If you don't know him or her, he or she shouldn't ask you to go someplace with them.'

Jasper nosed his way into their circle, offering whimpers of concern. They both laughed and petted him.

'Is that what happened to Charlotte?' Asia asked. 'Did some bad person take her away? Is she dead? Will she go to heaven anyway?'

'Whoa, let's not bury her yet. I think she's okay, but she needs us to find her. And of course she's going to heaven when she dies. We all are.' Munch watched a stream of water snake toward the sidewalk. 'Well, probably not bad men who scare little girls.' She stopped at that. She didn't want to fuel Asia's imagination with any specifics.

'I'm sorry, Mommy.'

'You don't have anything to be sorry about. Just tell me next time if something happens that makes you feel weird. I think we should tell the police about this guy.'

'He didn't really do anything. It was just a feeling I had.' ·

'That's enough for me.' Munch lifted Asia's chin and looked into her clear brown eyes. 'Maybe this guy was okay, but in case he isn't, we should go on record with this. Maybe the next little kid won't be as smart as you.'

Asia nodded, seeming to think that this was a likely probability. 'Are you going to call Rico?'

'Him or Mace. Maybe both. They'll want you to describe the man. Can you do that?'

'He had hair on the back of his fingers.'

Munch turned off the hose. The roses could wait. She had a lynching posse to assemble. And the neck wasn't what she wanted to hang this creep by.

'Let's go see Mace right now,' she said. 'Go tell Jill we're all going to visit your godparents.'

When they got to the St Johns', Caroline answered the door. 'I'd hug you, but I'm running at a hundred and twenty degrees today.' She fanned her face.

'You catching a bug?' Munch asked.

'It's either that or some kind of early hot flash. My doctor's been adjusting my hormones. Either way, this weather isn't helping.'

225

'Drink lots of fluids.'

'I have been. Just to replace what I'm losing. Look at this, I've drenched my blouse.'

She had indeed. Her throat was damp and red. 'Trippy,' Munch said. 'Hormones, huh? I've never been on the pill. I haven't needed it.'

'You're lucky.'

Munch shrugged. That was a matter of perspective. 'Where's Mace?'

'Training. He should be home soon. Cops have to keep taking continuing education courses.'

'That's comforting.'

Caroline seemed to consider that for a moment. 'Yes, it is.'

St John arrived home within ten minutes. 'Hi, honey, how are you feeling?' he said, seeing only Caroline as he came through the door. He was carrying a grocery store bouquet, a mixed bunch of daisies and carnations. Some of the carnations were an impossible shade of blue, and two of the daisy blossoms dangled from wilted stalks. The leaves toward the bottom were mushy, having been too long in water. Munch felt an envy so palatable she had to push it away with her hands.

St John noticed Munch, started to smile, then asked the question with his eyes: *What's up?*

Caroline took the flowers and kissed her husband on his cheek.

'Not too close,' he said. 'I don't want to catch anything.'

Caroline pushed a hand against his chest. 'A little late for that.' They exchanged sly smiles and then she opened a cabinet and retrieved a vase.

'And I brought you this.' He extracted a Japanese-style accordion fan from his suit pocket.

'What a guy,' Caroline said, putting it to use immediately.

Munch watched the exchange. She realized she was staring, but she couldn't seem to stop herself. What had she just been thinking about perfect soul mates? Maybe there was some middle ground after all.

St John turned to Munch. 'Is something wrong?' He loosened his tie. 'Is it your niece?'

'Something else. Can we talk?'

'Sure. You mind if I get comfortable first?' He already had his jacket off. His badge holder was flipped open, showing off his shield. He hooked a thumb under his shoulder holster, pulling the leather strap away from his shoulder.

Munch held up her hands in mock surrender. 'No problem.'

He touched her arm. 'I'll just be a minute.'

When he came back out of the bedroom, he was barefoot and wearing black fleece sweatpants and a red sweatshirt. His day's white shirt and black socks were balled in his hands. Munch wondered if he was still armed.

'You got a load of laundry going?' he called to Caroline.

'Done. It needs to go in the dryer.'

St John motioned for Munch to follow him to the laundry room. He lifted the washer lid.

'Wow, look at this, all whites.' He said it as if he were discovering an unforeseen harmonic convergence.

'Ace detective,' Caroline said, coming up behind him and taking over the task of transferring the load. She also relieved him of the clothes he carried.

'They never do get the separating-the-colors thing, do they?' Munch asked out of the corner of her mouth.

Caroline looked at the two kids. 'Maybe in the next generation.'

Mace slipped an arm around his wife's waist and kissed her cheek. 'What about their generation?'

'They'll be seeing lots of changes.' Caroline addressed the kids, 'You guys want some cookies?'

'Okay,' Asia said.

'We'll have to make them.'

Munch gave her a grateful smile and followed St John to his backyard. Jasper had found one of Nicky's old tennis balls and was wagging his stubby tail. Munch told Mace what Asia had said.

'Son of a bitch,' St John said.

'Yeah,' Munch said. 'It's always something, isn't it?'

'Did you tell the school?'

'I will tomorrow. I just found out about an hour ago.'

'I'll make a report. We'll send a sex crimes unit to the petting zoo when they open. Can Asia describe the guy?'

'Probably just generalities. He was a grown-up. She remembers what he was wearing, what the backs of his fingers looked like. It's already been almost a week. Didn't you tell me that a witness's reliability was all but useless after forty-eight hours?'

'Sometimes less than that.' Samantha walked over to Mace and he ruffled the dog's ears, let her lick his face. Brownie barked. St John laughed. 'Jealous little bitch.'

'Anyhow,' Munch said.

'Yeah, what about Charlotte? Did she come home yet? Have you heard from her?'

'No. I've got a bad feeling. Her mom is in jail. Rico busted her for warrants. He thinks she knows more than she's saying. I'm sure he's right — not that that's putting us any closer to getting Charlotte back. He says he's working on it, but it doesn't look good.'

'It's a big city. All he can do is go after the leads he has. That starts with the family.'

She told him about the phone call she had intercepted at Lisa's house, the insulin that had gone missing from Lisa's refrigerator, and Painter Dave's fate. 'Rico told me the Feds don't think it's kidnapping.'

'Why?'

Reluctantly, she also told him about the hair they had found at the storage unit. Evidence that was later negated by the signs of Charlotte's strange hair-pulling compulsions.

St John shook his head and threw the ball for Jasper again. 'Chacón's right. I hate to say it. You need to keep leaning on the mother.'

'He's working the burglary angle. All the victims used the same pet food delivery service. It's since gone out of business, but there might be some kind of paper trail.' Brownie brought Munch a knotted rope and let her know that she wanted to play tug-of-war. It was a game Munch understood well.

St John watched for a minute. 'What did Rico think about the guy at the petting zoo?'

'I didn't tell him yet. He's already not

helping me enough.'

St John seemed to like that, if she was reading his smug smile right. 'You know one thing you have to feel good about.'

'What's that?'

'Asia passed the test. God knows sometimes horrible things happen to kids. There are a few monsters out there, and no amount of preventive training protects us from them. We're not helpless, though. I always say there are lots of things a good parent can do to protect their children. The foremost thing is communication.'

'I try.'

'You do more than that. You always know where Asia is, what she's doing, who her friends are. She knows she can confide in you.'

'I hope so.' Munch was trying to act modest. The truth was he couldn't compliment her more highly. If he didn't shut up soon, she was going to cry.

'You done good,' he added.

She laughed.

'What?'

'I knew there was a reason I came here. An hour ago I was as angry as I've ever been. Now you've made me feel really good. I'm getting dizzy.'

'You'll survive.'

They went back into the house. The first batch of Toll House cookies was already in the oven. Munch glanced at her watch. 'I hate to cut this short, guys, but we should get home.'

'Ten minutes?' Asia asked.

'Sure. I want a cookie, too. But it's a school night.'

Asia wrapped her arms around Munch's waist. 'I love you, Mommy.'

Munch hugged her back, then reached out and included Jill.

★   ★   ★

Benny called at ten. 'You asleep?'

Munch yawned, looked at the clock, and shook herself awake. 'Yeah, that's all right. What did you find out?'

'I talked to that guy about that thing. He'd like to look at the pictures. Should I send him to your work tomorrow?'

'Yeah. I'll be there around nine. What's his name?'

'Mr Big.'

'Shut up.' Munch grinned in the dark.

'Colin Webster. Kind of a funny old guy. Real sweetheart, though.'

'I'll look out for him. Thanks.' Munch hung up the phone and went through her nightly ritual of prayers. She gave thanks for all that she had to be grateful for. She didn't ask for anything else. Some nights, she wasn't even convinced that there was a God. The point was to remember how good she had it. That worked whether someone was listening on the other end or not.

As she waited for sleep, she remembered she hadn't called Kathy. She didn't know if her memory would improve any by tomorrow.

16

Munch got the kids off to school. She kissed Asia and told her she would see her in the afternoon. It was Thursday — Munch's day for helping out in the classroom. She planned to get to St Teresa's early and have a little chat with the staff about where they took their kids on field trips.

After Asia's school bus picked her up, Munch told Lou about the incident at the petting zoo. He voted for trying to find the guy on their own. Munch assured him she was keeping that option open.

Carlos took Jill to Palm Elementary. He had parts to pick up at a dealership nearby. Jill had a swimming class at the YMCA after school, and one of her friends' parents promised to deliver her back at the gas station afterward.

Munch threw herself into the work, dividing the jobs among the mechanics, calling customers with estimates, ordering parts, checking on delivery times. She lifted the phone several times to call Rico, but each time decided against it. The third time she lifted the receiver there was no dial tone.

She waited a second and then said, 'Hello?'

'It didn't even ring,' the man said.

'Who is this?'

'Chet Lombardi.'

Munch looked at the work orders on the desk, trying to place the name.

'Ms Mancini?'

'Yes?'

'You came to see me on Tuesday. At Venice High. I'm the guidance counselor.'

'Oh, right. Mr Lombardi. Sorry. I couldn't, uh, so much has happened. Never mind. Have you heard something?'

'No, I'm actually trying to track down Lisa Slokum. I've called her house, but whoever answers her phone won't tell me anything.'

That would be the cops, Munch knew. 'She's sort of unavailable until tomorrow.' Munch didn't want this guy to think Lisa had taken off or gone on some vacation with her kid missing. The truth wasn't so hot either, but it was what it was. 'Lisa is in jail. She had some traffic warrants. She should be out by tomorrow.'

'Who's taking care of Jill? I seem to remember that there isn't a father in the picture.'

'No, he's dead. Jill's staying with me. She's fine.'

'And still no word from Charlotte? Are there other relatives she might have gone to?'

'No, I'm it.' Munch watched Stephano talk to one of his customers. The gas pumps were crowded with the morning rush. 'I meant to ask you the other day. Were you Steve Koon's counselor, too?'

'Sadly, yes. Steven was one of mine. There are three guidance counselors here at the school. We divide the students alphabetically. I have *I* thru *P*, for the most part, but sometimes I take some of the others to even the distribution.'

'Ms Lubell said Charlotte and Steve ate lunch together sometimes. That they were part of a small group. Do you know who any of the other kids in their group were? Maybe one of them might know something.'

'I'm sure they've all been spoken to. I don't know anything about a clique. They were both loners, as far as I know. Steve missed a lot of school this quarter and Charlotte spends most of her free time in the humanities lab. She helps publish the school paper and she's on the yearbook committee. But rest assured, we'll continue to ask a lot of questions.'

Munch was glad to hear Lombardi refer to Charlotte in the present tense. 'Maybe we'll get some answers soon.'

'I understand that you've been distributing some flyers about Charlotte.'

'Yes, I put some up in Hollywood.'

'Do you have any more? Even one? I could make some more copies and have my kids distribute them at their hang-outs.'

'That would be a big help.' Munch hung up the phone smiling. One thing about bad situations, they often brought out a lot of unexpected good in people.

* * *

At nine-thirty, a red Ford Galaxy that Munch didn't recognize pulled in front of the office. An old guy with white hair, cane, and big gut wrestled out from behind the steering wheel.

Munch was on her way to change a fan belt on a Chevy pickup that had been towed in earlier. She had a large, yellow-handled screwdriver in one hand that she used as a pry bar, the new belt in the other, and a box-end $9/16$-$1/2$-inch combination wrench in her back pocket.

She stopped to greet the guy, giving him time and room to stand. 'Can I help you?'

He looked her up and down with a bemused expression. Munch was used to that. People didn't expect to see a woman in a Texaco uniform, especially one with grease embedded in her fingernails and tools jammed in her back pocket.

'I believe we have a mutual friend,' he said, pausing to cough into a large white handkerchief.

'Mr Webster?'

'At your service.'

'Just give me one minute.' Munch jogged back to her workbench. She set the fan belt and large screwdriver on the counter next to her toolbox. The envelope containing the photos of Meg Sullivan's missing jewelry was tucked in the open top of her Snap-on rollaway, next to the manuals of torque specs and timing mark guides.

She brought the photos back to the guy. He was leaning heavily on his fender, mopping his brow with the same white handkerchief. Munch wondered if she should get him a chair.

'You want some water?'

'I'll be fine.' He stared first at the picture of the cameo. 'Very nice.'

'Is it valuable?'

'Possibly. Although, to appraise this with any accuracy, I would need to touch it and examine the workmanship under magnification. That would allow me to determine if the carving was man- or machine-made. Also if the cameo has been carved from one piece or assembled from different materials and glued together.'

'What can you tell from this?'

'Every decade had its trends. The woman's long Roman nose dates this piece as pre-Victorian. Cameos have been around for many centuries. They've been discovered in archaeological sites in Italy and Egypt, often depicting mythological motifs such as this bacchante maiden with the grape leaves in her hair.'

Munch looked again. 'Is that what those are? I thought they were flowers. What does *bacchante* mean?'

'The Bacchae were the female revelers of Bacchus, an ancient Greek and Roman fertility god associated especially with the vine and grapes.'

'Kind of a party dude then.'

'Yes, I can send you some literature if you're interested.'

'I could write a book on the subject myself.'

Mr Webster smiled. 'Benny said as much.'

Munch grinned and blushed at the same time, hoping Benny had kept a few of their stories private. 'Ancient history,' she said. 'Speaking of which, if this cameo was hundreds of years old, what would it be worth?'

'Depends on the provenance, but I've paid as much as fifteen hundred dollars for a museum-quality piece once owned by Catherine the Great.'

Munch nodded, keeping her true feelings to herself. She could see paying that much for a car or putting the money toward a savings bond, but a piece of jewelry?

As if reading her thoughts, Mr Webster said, 'It's not just the ornamental value. This might very well be a piece of history. Queens Elizabeth and Victoria loved cameos. So did Josephine. In fact . . .'

Webster studied the picture again, then flipped to the other photos. He gave the picture of the gold locket no more than a cursory glance before he dismissed it. She was getting ready to apologize for wasting his time when Mr Webster made a startled noise. He had come to the third photo, the one of the rings with the colored stones. Munch noticed the tremble in his hands.

'I thought this one might be a sapphire,' she said, pointing to the blue. 'But it's too big.'

'Were these pieces all in the same lot?' Webster's voice had become younger somehow, and he no longer leaned against his car.

'They were all stolen from the same lady.'

'This woman is offering a reward?' Webster's eyes were bright. Munch wondered what had gotten him so excited all of a sudden.

'She said they had sentimental value.' Munch suddenly felt foolish, as if she were

240

passing on a bogus story she had been gullible enough to swallow. Two kids had died, and another was missing. Was something they had stolen that valuable?

'Have you ever heard of the Hope diamond?' Webster asked.

'Yeah. It's a really big diamond, right?'

He spread his thumb and forefinger a few inches apart. 'Forty-six carats. It's last private owner was Harry Winston. He donated it to the Smithsonian in 1958.'

'Must have been a very rich man.' She wondered briefly if he had anything to do with Winston tires or Winston cigarettes. Great, now she was going to have that jingle in her head all day. *Winston tastes good like a (eh eh) cigarette should.*

'Some say he did it to rid himself of the curse.'

'The diamond was cursed? Like King Tut's tomb?'

Webster shrugged. 'There are supporters of both sides of the theory.'

Munch stole a look at the pickup waiting for its new alternator belt. 'Excuse me a minute,' she said. Carlos was walking back from the bakery with a white bag in his hand. 'Carlos, would you do me a favor and hook up the charger to that truck?'

'Sure,' he said, changing direction toward

the corner of the shop where they stored the extension cord and battery charger.

She turned back to Webster. 'Sorry, you were saying?'

'The legend begins with a theft. Three and a half centuries ago, a Frenchman named Tavernier traveled to India looking for artifacts. While there he discovered a large statue of the Hindu goddess Sita. The deity had a large blue diamond in her forehead, which Tavernier purportedly stole.'

'How large?'

'One hundred and sixteen carats.'

'How big is that?'

'Slightly smaller than a man's fist.' He closed his hand to demonstrate.

'But the Hope diamond is less than half that.'

Webster smiled. 'You're getting ahead of the story.'

'Sorry.'

'No, actually, this is an important distinction. Tavernier, incidentally, was reputed to have been torn apart by a pack of wild dogs in Russia, but not before he traveled back to France and sold the stone to King Louis XIV. King Louis decided to recut the diamond to enhance its brilliance. The newly cut gem was now a little over sixty-seven carats and officially named the Blue Diamond of the

Crown. Sometimes referred to as the French Blue.'

'Did something bad happen to Louis XIV?' Munch wasn't exactly up on her French history.

'He died of gangrene. Some say in disgrace with his kingdom. Then, in the eighteenth century, the diamond was passed on to Louis XVI and his wife, Marie Antoinette.'

'And we all know what happened to them,' Munch said, drawing a finger across her throat. 'Of course, a lot of people were beheaded in the French Revolution. You can't blame the diamond for that.'

'Quite so. But then during the French Revolution, the story takes another twist. The crown jewels, including the French Blue, were stolen. Though most of the crown jewels were recovered, the Blue Diamond was not.'

Munch looked at the picture of Meg Sullivan's stolen ring. 'You think this is a diamond?'

'The shade of blue is certainly, ah, thought provoking.'

'How big is this stone, do you think?'

'Hard to say without a reference to its dimensions. If this were a typical lady's ring, I would guess three, perhaps four carats.'

'Worth?'

'Whatever someone is willing to pay,' he said. 'It doesn't appear to be an expert cut.

However, if it could be sourced to the Hope or French Blue, it would be very precious indeed.' He winked. 'Or not. Depending on how much credence you give to the curse.'

Munch studied the picture. Could something so little, this tiny freak of heat and pressure, have cost both Steven Koon and maybe Painter Dave their lives? 'So what you're saying is the Hope diamond is the French Blue and they're both cursed.'

'There is some evidence of this. A stone surfaced in England in the early 1800s. No one is quite sure if it was the same diamond that disappeared in France. There is a portrait of George IV of England wearing the insignia of the Royal Order of the Golden Fleece set with a large blue stone. The cut was different and it was smaller, now an estimated forty-six carats.'

Royal Order of the Golden Fleece sounded like an award they should give to a few of the mechanics she'd worked with over the years. 'What happened to old George?' she asked.

'He died in 1830, his estate encumbered by great debt.'

Well, yeah, Munch thought, *if he wasted his money on big shiny rocks.* 'Where does Hope come in?'

'A decade later, a large blue diamond appeared in Henry Phillip Hope's gem catalog. No history of the stone was given and there was no proven method to verify pedigree. Not that he was required to provide any proof. The size and beauty of the rock spoke for itself.' Webster raised an index finger as if he were a professor making an important point. 'Now we know that under exposure to ultraviolet light, and in a dark room, the Hope diamond phosphoresces red. Most other blue diamonds phosphoresce light blue.'

'Cool,' Munch said.

'Quite.'

'And the curse?'

'There is a long history of owners of the stone losing their fortunes, their sanity, their lives.'

'People's fortunes reverse all the time,' Munch said, thinking that stolen items also had an energy, a karma of their own, and that they often kept moving.

'Yes, and some even say Cartier created the myth to increase the stone's value.'

'Did it work?'

'Perhaps too well.'

'There's also another twenty-some carats unaccounted for. Or am I wrong? What happens to the chips left over when they cut a diamond?'

'Depends on the size of them. Some are

used for accent pieces. The powder is used for a variety of things, mostly industrial.'

'How about a really big diamond?'

'Ah' — he smiled — 'you're catching the bug.'

'It is a good story.'

'I've always thought the missing pieces of the blue diamond would probably turn up someday in some obscure little antique shop.' He lifted his walking stick. 'Perhaps stuck in the head of a cane or something like that.' He smiled. 'You never know. I do look very carefully at all gemstones . . . especially the blue ones.'

Munch felt a little thrill at his words and touched the picture with the tip of her finger. 'Look, I don't care who ends up with what. My niece has been missing since Monday. I just want to get her home safe. She's tied up in this mess in some kind of way. Benny will vouch for me. I'm not looking to get anyone in trouble. I just want Charlotte home. So if you hear anything, if some of this jewelry surfaces, I'd appreciate a heads-up.'

'I'll keep that in mind. If you locate this cameo, I would be interested in appraising it. No charge.'

'I'll pass that along to the owner if she gets it back. Maybe we'll get a chance to shine a black light on this blue stone.'

'Yes, that would be fun. Just think of it. A piece of history.'

He could have the past. Munch was much more interested in the future.

17

Munch shifted her knees. They were balanced on the top of a hot radiator of an Oldsmobile Toronado that was giving her fits. Its quadra-jet carburetor that she had rebuilt kept flooding. She set her plastic-wrapped sandwich on the broad fender of the Olds in between bites and removed the top of the carburetor to reset the float. The lunch meat was beginning to taste like gasoline, and the dangling secondary rods kept working loose and dropping in the wrong ports. She knew she needed to take a deep breath and step back. Some jobs, most jobs, didn't respond well to rushing.

A black 450 SL Mercedes coupe limped in on a flat tire. A handsome man in a snowy white dress shirt and red 'power' tie got out of the driver's seat. He looked around him at the busy workers, stroked his tie as if to assure himself it was still attached, then looked at his watch. No one came out to greet him. Munch thought he looked familiar and then realized who he was. Meg Sullivan's husband, the Irish-man. She set aside the carburetor parts, gave up on the sandwich, and climbed down out of the engine compartment.

'Mr Sullivan, can I help you?'

He smiled in relief and pointed to his tire. 'I was hoping to find you here. Looks like I need your help again.' The reason for the flat was obvious. The hooked end of a bungee cord had pierced the sidewall.

'It's not repairable,' she said. 'I can put your spare on, but I'd have to order the tire.'

'That would be great,' he said. 'I'm in a bit of a hurry. I bet everyone tells you that.'

'No problem. I'll have you out of here in a jiff.'

She fetched her air gun and a seventeen-millimeter impact socket from her toolbox. Tucking the tools under her arm, she rolled out the floor jack. The man opened his trunk. The carpet inside was spotless and still had that new-car smell. He started to reach for his spare, but Munch stopped him.

'I'll get it.'

He backed away and let her work. She felt his eyes on her and made every effort to move as gracefully as possible.

It took less than three minutes to jack up his car, zip off the lug bolts, and install his fifth wheel. While sitting on the concrete, she balanced the spare tire on her legs, lined up the holes, and hand-threaded the bolts before tightening them.

He crouched beside her, poking at the hole

in the ruined tire now lying on its side. If he didn't watch out, he was going to get his hands dirty.

'You want me to order you a new one?' She lowered the jack and whipped the air hose out of the way. 'Same brand? These run about a hundred and thirty dollars, mounted and balanced.'

'That's not a problem.'

He didn't look as if it would be a problem.

'Any luck on locating your niece or our missing jewelry?' he asked.

'I put the word out as best I could. I might even have found a customer for you if you retrieve the pieces. He's a collector of old cameos, but he also expressed an interest in the rings.'

'The rings aren't for sale, but we probably could be persuaded to part with the cameo.'

'He offered to appraise it for free.'

'What's this gentleman's name?'

'Colin Webster.'

'Oh, sure, he has a good reputation.' Sullivan pronounced sure with a soft Gaelic roll. He handed her a twenty and his card. Sullivan Development.

Probably into real estate deals, she thought, or maybe he was one of those savings-and-loan guys. These were boom times and no one saw them ending anytime soon. Even her little house had almost doubled in value since she'd bought it. Most of her well-to-do customers wanted to canonize Reagan. She wasn't whining. Lord knew, enough of the boom economy trickled down to her.

She started to refuse the twenty. 'You can pay me all at once.'

He patted her shoulder. 'Keep it. I appreciate you taking care of this so quickly.'

She pocketed the bill and rolled the damaged tire over to the tire machine. 'My pleasure.'

He flashed her a last smile before getting in his car. 'What's a nice girl like you doing in a place like this?'

'Some of that famous Irish charm!' she asked, thinking blarney was more like it. Still, she laughed. No one had ever said that to her before. If only he knew what a twenty-dollar tip used to entitle a man to do with her. She wrote the brand and size of his tire on the back of his card, attached it to a clipboard, and went back to the Olds.

The carburetor went together smoothly. Munch had to run the car around the block to clean the carbon buildup off the spark plugs. By the time she wrote up the work order, ordered the Mercedes tire, and put away her tools, it was eleven-thirty.

'What you got next?' Lou asked, coming out of the office.

'I'm going to the school,' she said.

'Oh, yeah, right. I forgot for a second.'

'I'll come back after.'

'Nah, go on. Might as well call it a day.'

'Jill is getting dropped off here later. I'll be back.'

He rocked back on his heels and squinted out across the islands to the street beyond. Munch had a feeling he wasn't seeing the traffic. 'I keep thinking about that guy with Asia. Sick motherfucker.'

'We don't know for sure. I'm just glad nothing more happened.'

'Remember what I said.'

'I will, thanks.'

Rico called as she was almost to her car. She came back to the shop in answer to the page.

'I'm waiting,' he said.

'I was just about to leave.'

'You coming here?'

'Wasn't planning on it. This is my day to go to Asia's school. I need to get there early. Asia told me last night that some man accosted her on her last field trip.'

'Accosted her how?'

She pictured Rico sitting up suddenly at his desk. 'He tried to get her to ride on a horse with him when no one else was around. Asia ran away. She only just told me about it.'

'You're lucky she told you at all. So many of these things go unreported.'

'That's what St John said.' She knew the words would hurt Rico as they left her mouth. She was playing on his jealousy and it was small of her. 'I was going to call you.'

'Where was the field trip? You want me to take a run over there?'

'Lou wants to round up a posse and pay the guy a visit.'

'Works for me,' Rico said, surprising her. She didn't think cops were supposed to go in for the vigilante thing. Though they were probably just as tired as the rest of the world of bad guys getting away with their crimes.

'Maybe you, me, and Asia can all go together. I know she feels safe with you.'

'Let me know and I'm there.'

She smiled into the phone. He would know that she was smiling. She was sure he knew precisely all the effects he had on her.

'I talked to Hollywood PD,' he said. 'They haven't ruled on David Limitz's death yet, but they're investigating.'

Limitz had to be Painter Dave's last name. 'Thanks.' He didn't have to keep her in the loop.

'They've gone in and cleaned out the building. The conditions were incredibly bad, I hear. Kids with staph infections, one even had gangrene. You die from that shit.'

'Gangrene? No kidding?'

'That's right.'

Funny, Munch thought, how the same subjects have a habit of coming up in clusters. 'How many kids were holed up there?'

'At least a dozen. Those that could cleared out when the Limitz kid fell.'

'Or jumped or was pushed. I hope to God he didn't die because he was meeting me.'

'You really think he knew something about Charlotte?'

'He was holding my dog's tag in his hand when I found him. The same tag that went missing last Saturday when I first saw Charlotte. He knew something.'

'It's still not your fault. Although you might have mentioned the dog tag a little sooner.'

'I know.' That was as close to an apology as she could manage. Sometimes she had trouble getting words out with all that was going on in her head.

'Munch?'

'I'm still here.' She twisted the cord around her hand. Lou was looking at her, probably wondering what was keeping her from leaving. 'Your friend called me.'

'My . . . ?' Then he got it. Rico was always quick on the uptake. She wouldn't like him if he were dumb. 'What did she say?'

254

'I didn't talk to her. I wasn't here. She left her number so I could call her back.'

'Are you going to?'

'Any reason why I should? Or shouldn't?'

He laughed without mirth. 'I'm not stepping into that one. You'll do what you want. I've got nothing to hide.'

'I don't really have anything to say to her. I can't see that anything she thinks she has to say to me will make me feel any better or different.'

'Go on to Asia's school now. I've got to go, too. We're serving a warrant and I need to be there.' He paused. 'I'll be home tonight. Call me and let me know how it went at the school.'

★   ★   ★

The staff at St Teresa's was appalled when Munch told them what Asia had said. Mrs Frowein, the principal, paled visibly and then urged Munch into her office. She looked both ways down the hall before closing her door.

Munch repeated her story.

Mrs Frowein rubbed her temples. She tapped her pencil against her desk blotter, making a constellation of graphite dots, but no notes.

Munch noticed that she avoided touching

last Friday's calendar square, the day of the field trip.

Mrs Frowein seemed to become aware of her jiggling pencil and put it down. 'So nothing actually happened?'

Munch crossed her arms over her chest and leaned back in her chair. 'I wouldn't exactly put it that way.'

'I'll call a special staff meeting.' Mrs Frowein moved on to her eyebrows, massaging each simultaneously with a thumb and forefinger. Her right hand gripped the pencil again. Her left effectively covered her eyes. 'We need to reemphasize to everyone proper behavior when out in the world.' She looked up then, as an idea occurred to her. 'Does Asia wander off on her own often? Our other problem with her happened this time last year, didn't it?'

Munch felt her eyes fill with blood, then realized what was going on. The McMartin Preschool trial was constantly in the news. It had become a circus, a witch-hunt. Kids were telling bizarre stories about playing naked movie stars games and traveling through secret underground tunnels to partake in satanic rituals. To Munch, it all sounded like hooey. If any part of the kids' stories was true, there would be mounds of evidence. So far, the case was built solely on the preschoolers' testimony. Kids lied. Hell, for that matter, parents lied to kids at that age. Santa Claus, the tooth fairy, the Easter bunny. Munch had seen the older lady who ran the school on TV. Peggy McMartin was confined to a wheelchair. She wore a teddy bear pinned to her dress. Something about the way she carried her head didn't indicate that she was anybody other than who she claimed to be.

The paper quoted the elderly lady as saying she would never harm a child, that she loved children. Munch believed her. But even if every child recanted his or her story, the damage was done. Her school, the life she had known, her reputation — all were ruined. Six nearby schools and one church had also closed. No wonder Mrs Frowein blanched at the hint of sexual misconduct on a school-sponsored outing.

'I'm not blaming anyone,' Munch assured her. 'Not the school.' She paused to make herself absolutely clear. 'Not Asia.'

'No, I didn't mean to suggest that. I'm sorry. I'm so glad that she kept her head and didn't go off with this man, whoever or whatever he was. I'm just thinking, hoping, that we can keep this in-house. I really don't think we need to involve child services.'

'I already told the police,' Munch said.

Mrs Frowein looked as if she were going to be ill. 'Was that necessary?'

'Asia's godfather is a cop. I went to his house last night. He's going to send a unit to the petting zoo. They'll probably try to determine if the man works there or what. Believe me, I wish this hadn't happened.'

Mrs Frowein folded her hands in front of her and took a long time studying her nails. Munch almost apologized, but then decided that of her many regrets, going to St John wasn't one of them. She was sorry if it put this woman in some kind of bind, but every job had its bad moments. That's why they called it work.

Mrs Frowein shook her head and looked at Munch as if she had failed to complete an important assignment. 'Maybe St Teresa's and your daughter are not a good fit.'

Munch blinked, not quite sure she had heard correctly. 'What are you saying?'

'I have four hundred students. We have enough problems with normal issues. You and your daughter have managed to embroil the school twice — '

'Four hundred students and we're the only ones ever to give you problems?' Munch's eyebrows were almost in her hairline. The smile on her face was not to be mistaken as one of amusement.

Mrs Frowein's return smile was equally strained. 'I have to look at what's best for the school.'

Munch gripped the armrests on her chair until the tendons in her wrists bulged. 'I can't believe you're making this political. I'm inclined to agree with you. This school and my daughter are not the fit I thought they were. Now let me tell you what's *not* going to happen. I'm not going to pull Asia out of this school in the middle of the year, take her away from all her friends, and try to explain to her that she isn't being punished for confiding in me. And you' — Munch pointed at the principal — 'are not going to kick her out.'

'I never suggested — '

Munch didn't let the woman finish. She held up a hand and said, 'Don't.' Maybe they could find a way back to civility on another day. If the woman started lying to her now, that would make this damage all the harder to repair.

Munch stood. 'This conversation is over.' She wanted to tell the woman, *Good fucking day*, before she stormed out the door. But that wouldn't help either. She'd probably only draw another one of those disappointed looks.

18

Munch had a difficult time concentrating on the words as the child read to her. She took a deep breath and tried to focus on the large print, forcing herself to put aside her anger and concentrate on the task at hand.

Sahara was reading to her. Sahara was black. Her mom was white, very blonde, and German. Munch suspected that Sahara was adopted, but never asked. Sahara was one of those talky, open kids who was always on top of her classwork, anxious to learn, the first to raise her hand, and usually cheerful.

When Ms Hopp asked for a two-page story, Sahara gave her ten. For today's reading, she had selected a book about the Underground Railroad. The whole concept of slavery seemed new to her, and Munch felt an awkwardness with the subject matter. Sahara was completely absorbed. In the story, white people were kind to the runaways and the escaped slaves made it safely to sanctuary in the North.

Sahara read quickly, giving animated voice to the dialogue, complete with proper inflections and facial expressions.

Inside the front cover of the book was a map of the continental United States as it existed before the Civil War. The slave states were shaded red, the free states green. Most of the states west of the Carolinas were a neutral white. Munch didn't know if that meant they weren't part of the Union or had merely been undecided on the slave issue. Sahara pointed to California, one of the few shaded states on the Western coast. It was green.

'Whew,' she said with a smile that broke Munch's heart.

'Yeah,' Munch agreed. 'Lucky thing.' Sahara reached the end of her book. Munch looked at her list for the next child's name. 'Would you tell Brittany to come over?'

'Okay.' Sahara bounced back to her table and informed her classmate.

Brittany brought a book about the neighborhood inventor. He was an eccentric guy who built a submarine in his backyard and then invited the kid in the story to go exploring with him. As Brittany stumbled over the words, Munch thought about the guy at the petting zoo.

'What would you do if this guy wanted to take you in his submarine?' she asked.

Brittany looked up, unsure how to answer. 'If any grown-up wanted to take you somewhere, you'd make sure your parents knew and said it was okay, right?'

Brittany flipped back a page, wondering if she'd missed something. 'The parents aren't in this book. The mom must be at work.'

Munch sometimes despaired at all the things these kids had to learn. How did you teach them to think beyond their parameters? 'Even so,' she said, 'if this were you, you'd check before going off with anyone, right?'

Brittany shrugged. 'I guess. A submarine would be pretty cool, though.' She looked around the room, obviously growing restless.

Munch pointed to mid-paragraph. 'You were here.' The inventor had found an old inner tube, which he used to waterproof the hatch. The undersea world they explored was full of brightly colored fish, octopuses, and seashells. They also found a cave and pirate's treasure. Brittany stumbled over the word *doubloon*.

'They're gold coins,' Munch said.

Brittany studied the illustrations, clearly more interested in the pictures than the text. Munch once again directed the child's attention to the story and its dubious message.

Two kids later, Munch's tour of duty was up.

Asia was immersed in an art project.

Munch stood over her for a bit, admiring. 'This is coming out nice.'

'Thanks,' Asia said. 'I'm going to use glitter on the sky part.'

'That'll be pretty. What's the house made out of? Papier-mâché?'

Asia gave her an arch look. 'It's mixed media.'

'Right. I knew that.'

'Uh-huh,' Asia said, sounding unconvinced.

'So I'll see you later?'

Asia twisted her face for a kiss. Munch obliged her.

'I love you, honey.'

'I love you, too, Mommy.'

* * *

'I'm glad you came back,' Lou said when Munch pulled into the Texaco station. 'We got swamped after you left. I've got five smog checks lined up and three AC charges.'

All gravy jobs. Lou had a smog license, but he was slow. 'Sounds good to me. Let me make a quick call and then I'll get right on them.'

Lou looked at his watch.

'Five minutes,' Munch said, thinking how quickly he forgot that he had urged her to take the rest of the afternoon off. She went into his office and called Rico.

'Hey,' he said. 'You just caught me.'

'Did I?' She told him about the principal's reaction.

'So she was more interested in covering her ass, huh?'

'Seems to be an epidemic of that.'

'I'm thinking of giving up coaching for the same reason.'

'That would be a shame.' His daughter, Angelica, played softball. When he and Munch had been dating, Munch had spent one Saturday at the park watching him. Loving him for it. The team's battle cry was 'KP.' Munch later learned that it stood for 'Kick pussy.' The teenage girls all thought that was hilarious.

'I worry now that I might pat some girl on the butt and have it taken wrong,' Rico said. 'I don't need that shit. Bad enough the parents taking me aside and telling me what position their daughter should play.'

'Like it's a democracy,' Munch said.

'Right. I'm the coach. There is no voting.'

She smiled, thinking any misguided yuppie parents who thought they could tell Rico what to do were in for a shock. 'How's *your* day going?'

'I've been looking into Mobile Pet Supply. They paid the phone bill with cashier's checks and they never applied for a business license. I have a composite sketch of the delivery driver.'

'I'd like to see it.'

'I'd like to show it to you.'

For a second, Munch wasn't sure what she and Rico were talking about anymore. After a pause, she changed her tone. 'How about the storage unit?'

'We gathered a lot of evidence, but it's not doing us much good yet. Unfortunately, we're at the wait-and-see phase. Maybe one of the kids from the building in Hollywood will tell us something.'

Munch sifted through the work orders on Lou's desk, balancing the phone against her ear. A lady who had gotten a new camshaft on her Caddy was complaining that her trunk light hadn't worked since. Kind of like getting a new roof and blaming the contractor for a running toilet. 'You still think Lisa will get out tomorrow?' she asked.

'Probably mid-morning.'

'Oh, joy.' Munch noticed that Lou's desk clock was an hour slow. While she watched, the second hand fell back one tick for every two. The collet had probably come loose. She pried off the glass cover and used her pocket screwdriver to cinch the brass clamp, then reset the mechanism to show the proper time.

'Jill will be happy anyway. She's missing her mom.'

'You don't sound thrilled. I thought you wanted her free. You were pissed at me for taking her into custody.'

'Okay, I think you were right all along. Lisa is somehow involved with Charlotte's disappearance. And given the fact that all Lisa touches turns to shit, I don't see any advantage to her being back on the street.'

'I don't have a good enough reason to hold her anymore.'

Munch set the clock back down. 'Ah, screw it. Maybe she'll even make herself useful and lead us somewhere.'

Munch rubbed her neck, feeling the strain of the last week. Her confrontation with Mrs Frowein had left her feeling nauseated now that her adrenaline had drained. She needed to get active, to work it off.

'When am I going to see you again?' he asked.

She grinned into the phone. 'Soon, real soon.' The nausea had passed into a yearning. Another excellent way to relieve tension occurred to her. 'Let's get together later, but not at the police station.'

'When you say get together . . . '

'I mean it in the biblical way.'

Too late she heard the creak at the door.

Lou stood with his arms folded across his chest, shaking his head in mock disgust. 'You little hornball.'

Munch covered the mouthpiece. 'Do you mind?'

Lou held up his hands. 'Not at all. I can see this is important business. I don't mean to interfere with your social life. I'll just go explain the situation to your customers.'

Munch spoke back into the phone, 'I've got to go. My boss is listening. Yes, I know there are laws against that, but what are you going to do?'

Lou stuck his tongue out at her.

'I don't even want to tell you what he's doing now.'

'I'm holding you to your word,' Rico said.

'Promises, promises.'

Munch scooped the work orders off the desk and returned to work, doing her best to ignore Lou's smirks. Hey, she never claimed to be a nun.

The work continued to stream in. Asia and Jill were delivered before long, and Munch told them to amuse themselves in the office, where they could do their homework and watch television. In that order.

At five, Munch ordered them a pizza from the trattoria next door. It was dark by the time they arrived home to be greeted by an eager Jasper.

Munch took a hot bubble bath, scrubbing her hands until the water turned tepid. The kids took their turns next. By nine o'clock they were all in bed. Munch read less than a chapter of her book before her eyes grew too heavy to stay open. She rested the hardcover against her chest and closed her eyes. A minute later, she rolled over and turned off the light.

A rustling noise in her closet woke Munch from a deep sleep. Her heart sped, then she realized Jasper wasn't beside her. He had developed a habit of using her second pillow.

The clock next to her bed read 11:07.

She swung her feet out of bed, thinking she'd check on the kids as long as she was up.

'I'll be back,' she said to the closet.

Jasper barked twice. Munch looked at the closet, feeling more surprised than scared. Jasper's barks originated from outside the house.

Rats?

There was a small reddish glow at the bottom of the closet door. Rats didn't generally carry flashlights or use their hands to mute the light. She looked at the phone, then back at the closet. The chair she had used so ineffectively to keep Jasper out of the closet was standing by the door. She slid it under the knob just as the door pushed outward. The chair jammed it shut, but she didn't know for how long.

She lifted the handset. No dial tone. She ran to the kids' room. They were sound asleep. She put her face close to Asia and nudged her awake.

Asia blinked away her dreams. Her breath was warm on Munch's cheek. 'Mom?'

'Listen to me,' Munch whispered. 'Someone's in the house. Take Jill and go out the window. I'll be right behind you.'

A loud cracking thump, followed by a man's muffled curse, emanated from Munch's bedroom. Jasper's barking was furious now, punctuated by sharp yelps of distress. The back door rattled as the dog frantically scratched to get back inside.

Jill sat up, her eyes wide. 'Are they here?'

Munch grabbed the kids' tennis shoes and pushed them into their hands. 'Let's go.'

She pulled Asia's dresser across the door, surprised at how light it seemed. Jill didn't ask any more questions. She pulled on her shoes, grabbed her schoolbag, which she had hung on the bedpost, and headed for the window.

Munch raised the window sash and lifted Asia to the ground. She followed with Jill, then climbed out after them.

'Jasper,' Munch called, 'come on, boy.'

Jasper came bounding around the side of the house. Munch guided the kids in front of her, toward the street. There was enough light from the streetlamps to help them avoid the various shrubs and flowers. Munch picked up a stone the size of a softball, then discarded it for a length of two-by-four left over from a gardening project, an arbor she had built to hold a wisteria vine. She was barefoot, dressed only in a T-shirt and panties. The kids were in pajamas. She guided them to the gate in the eight-foot chain-link fence that separated the front and back yards. The gate was padlocked and she didn't have the key. Asia clung to the hem of Munch's T-shirt. Her eyes were wide and alert, the whites glowing in the mercury light coming from the street.

Jasper growled low in his throat. Munch grabbed his collar and pulled him close.

'Shh, boy. It's okay. Hush.'

'He's protecting us,' Asia whispered. Munch looked down and noticed that Asia had an egg-size rock in her hand.

That's my girl, she thought. Jill still clutched her book bag. Munch wondered what she had in there that was so precious to her.

'I don't want him hurt either,' Munch said. 'We'll be okay. We'll go over to a neighbor's house and use their phone.'

'Let's call Rico,' Asia said. 'He'll get here really fast.'

'You read my mind, honey.'

★ ★ ★

Munch crouched low and led the kids to the pittosporum hedge lining the western property line. The guy who lived on the other side collected old Nash cars. He didn't have a dog, but Munch wondered if he was the kind of guy who shot trespassers in the dark. She had a nodding acquaintance with him, but they'd never exchanged names. She regretted that now. She also regretted that she didn't own a gun.

She'd learned on the street that owning a gun was a good way to get yourself shot. She had a girlfriend, Middy, who carried a gun in her purse. One time at a bar, Middy dropped her bag, the gun went off, and the bullet ricocheted inside Middy's guts. Munch would never forget kneeling beside the woman, Middy drunk and bleeding, not yet feeling any pain, and saying, 'I seen it go in, but did any of y'all see it come back out?'

Actually, at the time, it had been kind of funny.

271

They heard a car start in the street and drive off.

'You think he's gone?' Asia asked.

'Let's not take any chances,' Munch said.

Munch guided the kids to a low point in the fence. 'Time to make like monkeys,' she said. Jill started scrambling with no further encouragement.

'What about Jasper?' Asia asked.

'We're not leaving him behind. Go on.' Munch lifted Asia and helped her turn around at the top. She followed. Jasper whined until Munch pried an opening for him underneath. He wedged himself through, and together they ran up the neighbor's driveway. Munch knocked on the door.

'Who is it?' a voice called from inside.

'Munch, from next door. I need to use your phone.'

The guy with the Nashes opened his door and stared at them. 'What's the matter?'

'There's a burglar in our house,' Asia said.

The guy, whose name turned out to be Ralph, brought them inside.

'Can I use your phone?' Munch asked. Asia was practically glued to her legs, her bare legs. Jill clung to Munch's other side, holding her schoolbag in a death grip. 'I'm gonna need one of my arms,' she told the kids.

Asia laughed. That her daughter always got

her humor was another in a long list of things Munch appreciated about Asia. Rico was at home.

'Someone broke into our house.'

'Are you okay?' he asked.

'We climbed out the window and I think he left. I'm at the neighbor's.'

'Okay. Sit tight. I'll be right over.'

'I haven't called anyone else yet.'

'I'll take care of the rest. Can you see the street from where you are?'

Munch looked around her. Neighbor Ralph wasn't much of a housekeeper, but he did have a window with a view of the street. 'Yeah, I'll watch for you.'

'You want a beer?' Ralph asked, after she'd hung up the phone. He scooped dirty laundry off his couch and threw it in a corner.

'No, thanks.'

Jill leaned over and whispered into Munch's ear, 'I have to go to the bathroom.'

Munch hugged her. 'Can we use your bathroom?'

'Sure, just a minute.' He went through a door off his hallway and emerged a moment later, his arms full of towels and magazines. 'Go ahead.'

Munch took Jill's book bag and gave her a little push.

With Jill gone, Munch glanced inside the

bag. Videos, school supplies, a few books. Munch read the title of a well-thumbed tome: *The Diary of Anne Frank*. Munch wondered if Jill felt a special kinship with the young girl who had spent years in hiding. She had to know how poor Anne ended up.

19

The first patrol car arrived five minutes later. The officers had been at a nearby coffee shop, they explained, when they got the call.

'Thank God for doughnuts,' Munch said. Ralph had lent her a bathrobe, but she found herself shivering. It wasn't that cold out. The chill she felt was internal.

The cops had her wait while they searched her house. She saw the beams from their flashlights bouncing off the walls. A moment later Rico arrived. Munch met him on the sidewalk, her small family in tow.

He put a hand on Munch's cheek. She wanted to step into his warmth.

'Is everyone all right?' he asked.

'A little shook up. But physically we're all fine.'

He bent down and picked up Asia, who rested her head on his shoulder. Munch wanted to cry. There was no sweeter sight than a good man holding a child. He looked at Jill and extended his hand.

'Hi. You must be Jill. I'm Rico.'

Asia lifted her head. 'He's a policeman.'

'I thought so,' Jill said.

Rico and Munch exchanged smiles. After a moment, Rico set Asia down.

'This is Jasper,' Asia said. 'He wanted to bite the bad guy, but we made him stay with us.'

'Probably best,' Rico said. 'The guy probably would have given him indigestion.'

Asia giggled.

Rico tweaked her nose. 'I'm going to go talk with the other officers and see what's going on.'

'We'll be here,' Munch said.

Rico huddled with the Santa Monica cops. They directed his attention to the junction box and shined their flashlights along the ground outside Munch's windows. Rico did a lot of nodding.

After ten minutes or so, he returned. 'You can go back in the house now. I'll stay if you want me to.'

Munch didn't need to put it to a vote. 'Thanks.'

They got the kids back to bed. Rico showed her where the prowler had removed a front screen and climbed inside. They locked all the windows and doors. Munch noticed that the prowler had blocked Jasper's dog door from the inside. She shuddered to think how long he'd been in the house, creeping through the rooms as they slept.

'Were the phone lines cut?' she asked.

'Yes.'

'So, like the burglaries.'

'Let's do a walk-through and see if anything's missing,' he said.

The stereo was untouched as was the television in the front room.

'How about jewelry?' Rico asked.

Munch laughed. 'I have about four pairs of earrings. I keep them in a box on my dresser. My gem collection is probably safe. What I don't get is why the guy broke in at night. I mean, we're gone all day. Wouldn't it make more sense then?'

'Maybe the dog deterred him before. Experienced cat burglars hit at dinnertime, when alarms are off, purses left out, the family busy in the kitchen and making noise. Eight minutes is all they need. If they haven't found what they're after by then, they go somewhere else.'

'The guy was in my closet. I think he was looking for something specific.'

'Let's inventory your bedroom then.'

'Yeah,' she replied, still shivering a little, 'let's.' She looked in on the kids one last time. They were sound asleep. Bless their hearts. She didn't think she would sleep easily for a long time. Jasper was nestled between the children, a protective paw resting on Asia's small back.

She and Rico went into her bedroom. She noticed the gap in her entertainment unit immediately. 'He took all my music videos.'

'Who'd you have?'

'Janet Jackson, Sting, Mötley Crüe, Blondie, Michael Jackson.'

Rico raised an eyebrow.

'Asia wanted that one.'

'We'll come out tomorrow and try to lift some finger-prints. If this is the same crew who hit the other homes, we won't find any.'

Munch took off Ralph's bathrobe. Rico stopped talking.

'Come here,' she said.

★ ★ ★

Twenty minutes later, Munch asked Rico if he wanted some water. The blankets were kicked to the bottom of the bed. Her head rested on his chest.

'I thought you girls liked foreplay,' he said, wrapping his arms around her.

'Didn't anyone ever tell you not to make generalizations?' Munch said a silent prayer of thanks to the god of big mouths. She had almost said, *Didn't your mother . . . ?*

He ran his foot up her leg. 'God, you feel good. Your skin is so soft.'

She formed herself to his side. He kissed

the top of her head. 'What do you think the expression *the buck stops here* means?' she asked.

'I don't have a clue.'

Her fingers ran along his scalp lightly scratching, rubbing. She got to his ears. The cartilage was supple, the skin warm. She would never have thought in a million years that someone's ear could feel so good on her hand. She didn't want anything to come between them again, ever.

She studied his face, memorizing the planes of his cheeks, the curl of his eyelashes. 'When you found out Kathy wasn't pregnant, how'd you feel?'

His eyes popped open. Studying the ceiling, he said, 'It would have been worse if she miscarried. If there had really been a baby.'

'Yeah, but were you disappointed?'

He sighed. 'Can we go back to the buck thing?'

'It's not a trick question. I promise. I just wondered how you felt about it all.'

'A little disappointed, a little relieved. Pissed off.'

'Were you hoping for a boy or a girl?'

'It wasn't all that long that we thought she was pregnant.'

'Boy or girl?'

He sighed again. Surrendering. 'A son would have been nice.'

'I thought so.' She wasn't satisfied to be right. But people couldn't let fear of the truth stop them from asking the important questions.

He lifted his head so that his face tilted toward hers. 'Really, all you hope is that the kid is healthy.'

Maybe he thought he was redeeming himself. She felt herself shrink back into the loneliness of her own thoughts. As the poet Ogden Nash so aptly put it, 'that cell of padded bone.' As thirty loomed, she was just coming to terms with what her infertility meant to her emotionally. It wasn't fair to expect Rico to know how it felt to be barren.

She had lied to him.

All questions between lovers were tricks.

She touched his forehead and he relaxed back on to the pillow.

'What do you think the motive was in Steve Koon's murder?' she said.

'Does the term *afterglow* mean anything to you?'

'No, seriously. Why would someone kill him?'

Rico folded his arms behind his head. 'The kid was trying to go straight. Maybe his coconspirators wanted to keep him quiet.

From blowing it for them.'

'Probably that Mouseman asshole.'

'Good possibility.'

'How about in the car?'

'What car?'

She stroked his belly, tracing the swath of hair that began at his navel and headed south. 'The treasure trail,' she and her friends had called it, when sex and dicks had been subjects they discussed frequently and openly. In many ways, those were simpler times, when the most important thing was the act itself and damn the consequences.

'The car you found him in,' she said.

'It was burnt, remember? There were some videos and cassettes melted beyond recognition. Papers we couldn't identify.'

'Had he packed a bag?'

'Just a minute,' Rico said. 'I want to check something.' He pushed her gently on her side so that her back was to him. She didn't resist. She felt his tongue trace her spine and moaned as an orgasmic aftershock shook her. He brought his mouth to her ear. 'Shh.'

'I'm trying,' she said into the pillow.

He bent her leg back and sucked on her toes. His fingers probed her. She lifted herself to meet him, feeling his breath on her neck. After that, she left the known universe. Time passed, maybe a few lifetimes, then they both had to surrender to the limits of heart and muscle. The sheets were soaked with their sweat.

'Wow,' he said.

'I hear you,' she said. She wondered if it was possible to find a way to make this work.

20

Rico awoke first and dressed quietly. Munch watched him from her cocoon of blankets. She couldn't believe it was light out already. Her mouth was dry and she felt as if she had a hangover. The place between her legs was pleasantly sore.

'Hey,' she said, 'good morning.'

He stopped tying his shoes and twisted around to kiss her. 'Want me to make some coffee?'

'All I have is instant.'

'I know. I'll put the water on.'

She stretched. 'God, I feel like shit.'

'I knew I had an effect on you.'

She laughed. 'No, not that. That was great. I'm just drained from everything else.'

He sat on the edge of the bed and brushed the hair from her face. 'Why don't you play hooky today?'

She considered for a moment, then dismissed the notion. She had played hooky for the first twenty-one years of her life. She had a lot of catching up to do. 'Can't. But it's Friday so the weekend's almost here.'

'Do you have any limo runs this weekend?'

She visualized her blank limo calendar. 'No, nothing scheduled, but hope springs eternal.'

He stood. 'You're going to have to call the phone company and get your line fixed.'

'Yeah, I can do that from work.' She turned at the sound of Jasper's approach, heralded by the music of his new tags jingling against each other. A moment later, the spaniel leaped on to the bed. He came up beside her and rolled on his back. She scratched his chest while he worked his face over the pillows, reintegrating his scent.

Rico leaned across her to pet the dog. Jasper allowed the overture, and before long the dog was making prolonged grunts of pleasure.

'Looks like you're in,' Munch said.

'I'll call you when Lisa is released,' Rico said. 'Should be mid-afternoon. I'm going to go see her while she's still in custody. I want to show her the sketch of the delivery driver for Mobile Pet Supply, see if she recognizes him.'

Munch had a mental picture of Lisa's blank face, behind which lay a very bad attitude. 'It would probably go better if I showed her,' Munch said.

'All right, I'll bring you a copy.'

She threw back the covers. 'I guess I'd

better get up.' She stood naked. He looked at her and smiled.

'Cold?'

She crossed the room to her closet and retrieved a bathrobe. 'I'll get the kids up.' She wanted to ask: *Do you love me? Will you stay this time? Will we get married and be happy and live euphorically ever after?* But what she said was 'Lots of cream and sugar.'

'Hot, white, and sweet,' he said. 'Got it.'

'First things first,' she said to herself. One day at a time.

Asia had a leg out of the covers and was snoring. Jill's pajamas were bunched into a ball on the floor. Munch lifted the blanket. Sometime in the night, Jill had put her clothes back on. Even her shoes.

Munch sat on the bed and shook the kids gently. 'Wakey, wakey.'

'Isn't it Saturday yet?' Asia asked.

'Almost, honey. Time to get up.'

Asia sat up groggily and rubbed her eyes. There was a clattering of pans in the kitchen.

'Who's here?' Asia asked.

'Rico.'

'No wonder you're smiling,' Asia said.

Munch looked at her daughter. The expression on Asia's face was completely guileless. Asia was just observing the obvious, something that escaped Munch from time to time. She tweaked her daughter's nose. 'Make sure your cousin gets up.'

'I'm up,' Jill said. 'My mom comes home today. Maybe Charlotte, too. I dreamed about her last night.'

'What did you dream?' Munch asked, curious. This was the first time this week Jill had expressed an interest in her sister.

'I dreamed she was in the ocean, in the waves. We were yelling for her to come in, but she wouldn't listen.'

Munch nodded. She had a lot of ocean dreams herself. She was usually on the shore or climbing rocks at the water's edge. The waves were always monstrous tsunamis, but breaking straight up and down. So as long as she didn't go in the water, they didn't harm her.

And even though she loved everything about the ocean in real life, in her dreams the waves scared her. She had looked up the symbolism once. The dream book reported that water signified emotion, and a turbulent sea meant danger. Made sense. That she was always on the dry land while the biggest waves hit was even analyzed. This scenario meant that the dreamer had narrowly avoided great danger.

Sometimes the shoreline was the width of a tightrope.

'You're lucky,' she said to Jill. 'I never had a sister.'

'Me, either,' Asia said. She looked at her mother. 'Maybe someday? Please?'

'I'll see what I can do,' Munch said.

'That's all I can ask,' Asia said.

Munch laughed and ruffled her hair. 'Get ready for school.'

Coffee was drunk, breakfast was eaten, and good-byes were said. Munch put an old bedspread and a plastic bowl for water in the car.

'What's this for?' Asia asked.

'Jasper's coming to work with me today,' Munch said. 'You think Lou will mind?'

'I don't think Lou tells you no about anything,' Asia said.

'He must love you,' Jill said, and the two girls exploded into gales of laughter.

'What's not to love?' Munch said, deflecting the observation. 'We love each other like friends.'

'Uh-huh,' Asia said. 'Yeah, right. Friends.'

The girls put their hands over their mouths, but their smirks were plain in their eyes.

'C'mon,' Munch said, 'let's not dawdle.'

Munch left Asia at the gas station to catch her bus. Lou promised to make sure she got on board safely. Then Munch drove Jill to school in a customer's Volvo that had an intermittent clunk in the front end that she was trying to pin down. She kept the radio turned off.

Jill sat upright beside her on the passenger seat, seat belt on, and hands folded primly in her lap.

'I remember once years ago,' Munch said. 'Before Asia was born. I was over at your mom's house. I was sitting on the couch and you and your sister came running by me. She had her fist in the air, her thumb just showing between her first and middle finger. Her head was thrown back and she was laughing so hard I thought she'd fall.'

'What was I doing?' Jill asked.

'You were mad as hell. You were chasing her and screaming, 'Give me back my nose, you son of a bitch.''

Jill grinned. 'What a potty mouth I had.'

'What I also remember is that Charlotte and you always had each other.'

'She's different now. Sometimes we hate each other.'

'I hope you guys find a way to work things out. You're blood. Don't ever forget that.'

'I'm not the one always making trouble.'

Munch wondered how much of the sisters' acrimony was due to limited resources. Maybe in Jill's childlike logic, with her sister gone, there would be more stuff for her. Maybe that reasoning never surfaced to her consciousness but festered in some dark, insecure region of her psyche. Maybe Munch didn't know what the hell she was talking about. Then again, what was life but guesswork?

One thing was certain. The three Slokum females formed an odd triad. They were like the points of a triangle. Bitter Lisa, who managed total denial of her failure as a mother and role model. Intelligent but overaware Charlotte, who was *too* cognizant of life's unfairness. And then there was Jill. Carefully cheerful, capable of dismissing that which interfered with her optimism. Munch was sure that Lisa, Charlotte, and Jill would each tell her different versions of any given event and that the truth would always lie somewhere in between.

She looked over at Jill, who was humming now. It took a lot of work to be consistently happy. The kid deserved credit. 'How many times have you been to Disneyland?'

'This year? Five times.'

'Really? You must like it a lot.'

'Better than Knott's Berry Farm, but Universal Studios is pretty good, too. They have an E.T. ride where you get to fly through the air and E.T. says your name at the end.'

'Who do you go with?'

'Friends.'

'Do these friends have names?'

'Sure.'

Munch waited a few seconds, then realized that Jill was perfectly content to say no more. 'Would you tell me a few of them?'

'You wouldn't know them.'

'Humor me.'

Jill spread her fingers. 'Brenda and her mom. My friend Randy and his dad. I went to Knott's Berry Farm with school. I'll never forget that day. I have this one friend Sarah who likes this guy named John, so she asked me to ask his other friend Christopher if John likes Sarah, but I like Christopher, so I felt kinda shy about it all, you know?'

'Boy, do I.' Munch checked the rearview mirror. 'What happened?'

'Well, then Sarah asked Christopher if he liked me and he said yes, even though I'm taller than him.' Jill took a breath. 'It was magical.'

'Sounds like he needs to grow,' Munch said, enjoying her own double entendre. 'Who do you go to Disneyland with?'

Jill pushed her hair behind her ears, perhaps preening for Christopher. 'Well, Micky took us all to Disneyland two times last summer and we went again last month.'

'And who is Micky?'

'Oh, just this guy. He does lots of stuff for us.'

'Is he your mom's boyfriend or something?'

'No. My mom only likes gay guys now. She goes dancing with them for exercise. She says they're much more fun than regular guys.'

As if Lisa had ever known a regular guy. The term *fag hag* came to Munch's mind. Basically, she couldn't give a shit what consenting adults did behind closed doors. She had a few friends, even women friends, who happened to be gay. Okay, maybe not real close friends, but people she knew to say hi to and to care how they were. But she knew she wouldn't be comfortable with the whole gay subculture social scene. She'd probably laugh at all the wrong times and get everyone pissed off at her.

She was still working on not mentioning a person's sexual orientation or race if she was telling a story. As in, Joe went to the store. He's gay. Or my friend Debra called the other day. She's black.

They stopped at a red light. Munch looked at her niece. 'How often does your mom go dancing with her, uh, friends?'

'Probably not as much as she should. Charlotte is always after her to eat healthier and go to the gym. My mom tells her to mind her own business.'

'What do you think about all that?'

'Well, I have to agree with Charlotte. Mom would probably be happier if she was healthier.' Jill shrugged her thin shoulders. 'But it's her body.'

'It doesn't hurt to nudge her in the right direction, especially with the diabetes and all.' The light changed and they turned left. They were within shouting distance of Palm Elementary.

Jill fidgeted and kept her face averted, unwilling to comment any further on what diseases her mother might be afflicted with.

'Micky,' Munch said out loud. 'When we went to the storage unit, your mom asked for Micky. Same guy?'

'Yeah, that's where we met him, I think. He's the owner. He gives us a good rate.' Jill affected an air of sophistication.

'In exchange for what?'

Jill sighed with exasperation, as if her patience was really being tested now. Maybe she was annoyed at having her bluff called. 'He's just a nice guy, okay?'

'Did I say he wasn't?'

Jill studied her hands. Munch felt a distinct chill.

'Mickey Mouse,' Munch said. 'Mouseman.'

Jill didn't look up, but she flinched ever so slightly.

Munch pressed, even though she knew it was probably useless. Some kind of psychology was called for here. Jill had to be convinced that she wasn't betraying a loved one, turning her over to the storm troopers who threatened her world. Munch gave it one final try. 'Just tell me if you ever heard anyone call him that. Maybe Charlotte or your mom said something once that you happened to overhear.'

With exactly wrong timing, they had arrived at the school. Jill rolled down her window and yelled hello to one of her friends. Munch drove past the driveway.

'Hey,' Jill said. 'I'm going to be late. I get in trouble if I'm late.' There was real panic on her face and her color was high.

Munch pulled the car over to the curb. She made her expression sympathetic, but firm. 'This is important. It might have to do with where Charlotte is.'

'I don't know anything,' Jill said. 'Can I please just go to school now? I don't know anything.'

'You said that already.' Munch didn't believe her either time but she wouldn't keep her in the car. She let Jill out and watched her until she was safely through the gates. As Munch headed back to work, she replayed what she knew and what she didn't. It was like trying to piece together a movie being played on the wrong speed or with the frames out of order. Discordant, sometimes blurred, but with flashes of recognizable images. A sequence formed that began to make sense. Micky or Mouseman had broken into Lisa's storage locker looking for whatever. The whatever fell into two categories. Something he wanted or something he feared others having.

If it was something he wanted, then it was probably some valuable loot that had passed through his hands. Maybe the thief had been ripped off by his young crew. Steve and/or Dave and/or Charlotte. Three kids, two of them dead, one missing. Maybe his little disciples had something on him. What could that be? Proof in some form that could get him arrested?

She thought about the Koons' home and all those home movies on videotape. And the intruder at her own home had made off with her music videos. What was it with videos?

'Shit,' she said out loud. 'Of course.' She checked the rearview mirror and then signaled. It took three car lengths and some pissed-off motorists before Munch could manage a U-turn. Something in the right front clunked, and the steering wheel lurched ten degrees to the left.

She pulled into the parking lot of Palm Elementary, left the car without stopping to lock it, and ran to the office.

A woman was on the phone, explaining something to somebody about immunizations. Munch drummed her fingers on the counter and looked at the clock. A bell rang throughout the school and a voice came over the loudspeaker. The assembly was asked to stand for the Pledge of Allegiance. The woman on the phone held five outstretched fingers in Munch's direction.

The seconds stretched on endlessly as the voice over the loudspeaker system led the children: ' . . . and to the republic for which it stands . . . '

Munch gathered her thoughts and composure.

'Are you here to help?' the woman asked.

'I just dropped my niece off and I need to get something from her.'

'What room is she in?'

'I don't know.'

'Who's her teacher?'

'I don't remember.' Munch knew how suspect she sounded. 'Her name is Jill Slokum. She's in fifth grade. If I could just pop in her classroom for a second . . . '

The woman looked at Munch over her bifocals and then reached for a large student roster. Munch bit back her impatience as the woman dragged her finger over the list of names.

'Surely, it's in alphabetical order,' Munch said. '*Slokum* with an *S*. *S* as in *sh* — , uh, *shipwreck*.'

The woman looked at Munch again, clearly not amused. 'The students are listed according to classroom. If you knew her teacher, this would go quicker.'

Munch nodded and forced a smile on her face. The phone rang again and the woman answered it. Munch felt like screaming. It was like dealing with the Department of Motor Vehicles.

'She'll have to bring a note from her doctor,' the woman said into the phone. 'We're here from eight-thirty to four . . . Yes, I'll have the nurse call you.'

Munch covered her face with her hands. *Just give me the room number*, she thought, *you idiotic fu —*

'Your niece is in Mrs Zimmer's class. Room 310. Do you know where that is?'

'No.'

'Third bungalow, turn left. You'll see the number.'

'Thank you.'

'You'll need to sign in.' The woman leisurely rose to her feet.

Exactly like the DMV.

Munch found the visitor sheet on her own. She clicked her pen open and wrote in her name, phone number, time in, and room she was visiting. Before the clerk could say another word, Munch was out the door and running toward the classroom bungalow. She found room 310 and pulled the door open. Thirty faces turned her way. None was Jill's.

A tall woman who had to be Mrs Zimmer looked at Munch expectantly.

'Sorry to disturb you,' Munch said, scanning the children. 'I'm looking for Jill Slokum.'

'She seems to be absent today,' Mrs Zimmer said. 'Or she's tardy.'

'I just dropped her off.' The edges of the world turned razor sharp, all Munch's senses ratcheted up a notch. 'She should be here.'

Mrs Zimmer addressed her class. 'Did anyone see Jill this morning?'

Rachel, the kid whom Munch had given a ride in her limo, raised her hand.

'Rachel,' Mrs Zimmer said.

'I saw her by the gate. She was with her sister.'

21

Munch ran back to the parking lot, looking for any sign of the girls. If they had left in a car, there was no telling what direction they'd gone. She got in the Volvo and began circling the block, hoping to glimpse them. The clunking and shifting in the right front suspension was consistent now. Great. Why couldn't the problem go back to phantom mode?

And why hadn't she walked Jill to her room? Had Charlotte been by herself or acting under duress? Munch had had some experience with the Stockholm syndrome, the phenomenon whereby captives become brainwashed and end up assisting their captors. Could this have happened with Charlotte?

Why hadn't Munch played hooky today as Rico had suggested? She felt those metaphorical waves lapping at her feet. The kids were in the water. What could she do but go after them?

Munch returned to the school. She hadn't signed out so she went straight to the classroom.

Mrs Zimmer looked up again. 'Did you find her?'

Munch shook her head. 'Can I ask Rachel a few questions?'

Mrs Zimmer summoned Rachel and told the rest of her students to work on their math.

Munch knelt before Rachel, bringing them eye level with each other. 'Did you see Jill go with her sister?'

Rachel nodded, no doubt wondering if she was in trouble. 'Yes. They went out to the parking lot.'

'Were they happy or sad?'

Rachel looked down and to her right. 'Kind of both.'

'What were they doing?'

'They hugged each other. I guess they were happy. They both smiled. Charlotte smiled, but then she was crying, too. I think it was happy crying.'

'Was there anyone else with them? A grown-up maybe?'

Rachel scrunched her nose in concentration, then looked at the two adults wide-eyed. 'No, and you know what?'

'What?' Munch asked.

'Charlotte had car keys and she got in the driver's side. She's not old enough to drive, is she?'

'Not legally, but that doesn't always mean a whole lot.' Munch patted Rachel's cheek.

'Thanks, honey. You've been a big help. You didn't happen to notice what kind of car it was, did you?'

Rachel nodded importantly. 'A green one, but not as big as yours.'

Lisa's Dodge Dart had been green. Munch thanked the kid again. As soon as she was out of the classroom, she started running. She burst into the office. 'I need the phone, now.'

The woman who had been sluggish before stood at once. 'Has someone been hurt?'

Munch lifted the receiver without answering and dialed Rico's direct line.

'Chacón.'

She explained where she was and what had happened.

'Do you know the Dodge's plate number?'

'No. It's a sixty-eight, I think.'

'I'll see if it's registered in her name.'

'Are you going to talk to her?' Munch asked. Lisa was going to freak. Or not.

'Yeah, I'll call the jail right now.'

'I think you should go see her in person. See how surprised she is.'

'You think she's involved in this, too?'

'I wouldn't put anything past that bitch. Listen to this.' Munch ran down the connection between 'Micky,' the owner of the storage business, whom Lisa had known, and the nickname Mouseman.

The woman behind the desk raised her eyebrows. Munch didn't owe her an explanation. Maybe an apology for the language, although in truth she was being restrained.

'What are you going to do now?' Rico asked.

'I'm in a customer's car. I have to take it back to work. If you hear anything, call me there.'

She hung up and turned to the woman. 'Thanks. I'm sorry for the uproar.'

'Will you let us know when you find Jill?' The woman seemed genuinely concerned.

'Sure.' Munch hoped that the next report wouldn't come from the evening news. She feared an ending to all of this that would make the headlines.

Outside, in the parking lot, Munch lifted the Volvo's hood. The source of the clunking noise was soon evident. Shavings of bright silver metal caught her eye. The three nuts that fastened the strut assembly to the body had worked loose. The tie-rod ends of the rack-and-pinion steering system attached to the spindle assembly at the bottom of the strut. So all the symptoms were accounted for. Her drastic U-turn must have worsened the condition. Fortunately, the nuts were seventeen millimeter, same as the lug nuts. She went in the trunk, retrieved the lug wrench, and snugged the hardware back on to the strut housing studs. The car would need a wheel alignment, but now it was safe to drive.

Pulling into the station, she was surprised to see she'd only been gone forty minutes. Lou was only a little perturbed with her.

'You've got this guy's been waiting for you,' he said, jerking his thumb toward a brown Datsun 280Z. Munch glanced at the license plate. The first three letters were *VFW*. *Veterans of Foreign Wars*, she thought to herself.

'Where is he?'

'He said something about getting coffee.'

Munch explained about what had happened at the school and what she had found was wrong with the Volvo.

'At least something good happened,' he said.

'Yeah, I feel very blessed.'

'Here comes that guy with the Datsun.' They both turned.

The owner of the Datsun was Chet Lombardi, Charlotte's guidance counselor. He smiled when he saw her.

'I was in the neighborhood,' he said.

'I've got some flyers for you, although you might not need to put them up.'

'Have you heard from Charlotte?'

'She just took her sister out of school. I don't know what she's up to but at least she's still in one piece.'

'Did you speak to her?'

'I just missed her. Have any of her friends at school been in touch with her?'

'Not that they're saying. She needs to stop this nonsense and come home.'

'*Nonsense* is a little strong,' Munch said.

He looked at her sharply. Munch supposed that in his business he was finely tuned to sarcasm. She felt a twinge of remorse. It wasn't him she was mad at.

'Will she go to your house?' he asked.

'I don't know. I hope she does so I can help her sort out her problems. I'd like to get her some professional help. She might need to be on medication.'

'Do you think she's delusional?'

'Possibly. There's a lot of that going around.' Munch thought that in Charlotte's case, she probably felt that her life was crappy and was not going to get better anytime soon. Any therapist or counselor would have difficulty saying that wasn't so. But there was hope. That's what Charlotte needed to know. That's what Munch would tell her if she got the chance.

Lombardi was studying her. He was probably thinking that she was the one who needed medication. At times she wished she wasn't an addict and that she *could* take drugs. The problem with that was she knew if she used any form of mind-altering substance, she would be using said substance all the time. Therein, ladies and gentlemen and children of all ages, lay the rub.

But this situation wasn't about her. 'Did Charlotte ever mention a guy named Micky?' she asked the counselor, chastising herself for her self-absorption.

'A boyfriend?' he asked.

'I hope not. This guy is older. He owns a business and he takes the kids to Disneyland. From what I've gathered, I think he's also this guy known on the street as Mouseman, runs a burglary ring of kids.'

'A modern-day Fagin,' Lombardi said.

'Something like that. Let's not romanticize it. This guy screws up these kids' lives under the guise of being a friend.' Munch noticed Lombardi's coffee was getting cold. 'Don't you have to get to work?'

'I have sliding hours. Is there anything I can do to help you? Can you think of anywhere the girls might have gone?'

'No. I'm in much the same dark as you.'

★   ★   ★

Thirty minutes after Lombardi had left, Colin Webster pulled up to the gas pumps. Munch recognized the bright red car. She made eye contact and he gestured for her to come over.

'Check your oil, sir?' she asked.

A gleam of excitement was in his eye. 'I have news.'

'Someone offer you the merchandise?' She spoke out of the side of her mouth, sensing he would enjoy the air of intrigue.

He nodded. 'I made them describe the cameo in detail. I'm sure it's the same one. I told him I would need to inspect the goods.'

'What arrangements did you make?'

'I asked him to meet me at a restaurant in Westwood this evening.'

Munch smiled. 'How would you like to arrive in a limousine?'

He gave her his address and they agreed on a seven o'clock pickup.

Rico arrived at noon with a composite sketch of the delivery driver for the now nonexistent Mobile Pet Supply. As composite sketches went, it wasn't bad. It easily narrowed the search to fewer than six thousand young white males in Los Angeles County.

'Any word on the girls?' she asked.

'No, you wouldn't believe how many

sixty-eight Dodge Darts are on the road. We've pulled at least fifty traffic stops this morning already, and not one of them a hit. She's either long gone or the car is stashed in a garage somewhere.'

Munch was disappointed, but not as worried as she had been all week. From what she'd seen of her nieces, they had good survival skills. She looked at the sketch again.

'This could be the kid who died in Hollywood. Dave Limitz.'

Rico chewed on his lower lip. 'The Hollywood PD has located his family. I'll check with them and get a photograph. Maybe one of the burglary victims can pick him out of a six-pack.' By *six-pack* Munch knew Rico was referring to a group of six photographs of similar-looking young men. It was the police's two-dimensional version of a lineup.

'Wouldn't really do to stand a corpse up alongside five other guys, would it?' she asked.

'No,' he said. 'That's what we would call a dead give-away.'

When her hysteria finally died down, she decided she loved him. That she had never stopped loving him and couldn't picture herself with anyone else. What she said was 'You're a sick man.'

'That's my charm,' he said. 'We went back to the storage company with a warrant and searched the other units.'

'Find anything?'

'It was strangely vacant. Your buddy with the bare feet was gone and several of the larger lockers were cleaned out.' He lowered his voice. 'I found some food wrappers, empty water bottles, and a couple of strands of hair. They might have been Charlotte's. We're testing them now.'

Munch absorbed the information. 'How about the owner, Micky. Did you get a line on him?'

'The business is registered to a corporation. It's going to take a little time to unwind the paperwork and come up with a name.'

'The name of the corporation wasn't Sullivan Development, was it?' Weren't Irishmen referred to as micks? Could Meg's husband be Mouseman? Were the burglaries a source of merchandise for the antique store in Westwood?

'No,' Rico said. 'But corporations can be formed by anyone with a little bit of money and paperwork.'

She told him about the stolen jewelry and her planned sting with the cameo.

He thought a moment, then said, 'When the seller produces the goods, and your buyer is sure it's the stolen property, roll a stop sign. I'll have a black-and-white pull you over. You just get out of the car like you don't know what's going on and we'll take it from there.'

'Sounds simple enough.'

'Simple is best,' he said. 'But even simple can go very wrong.'

'What about Lisa?'

'That's the other thing. She's no longer in custody.'

'Since when?'

'They kicked her out early this morning. The last thing she told the public defender was that she was going to sue us.'

'Sue who? The police?'

'You and me.'

Munch scowled. 'For what?'

'Emotional duress.'

'I'll give her duress,' Munch said. 'I've got her duress hanging.' She aped an impression of a tough guy. A tough guy who would use the word *duress*. She didn't know whether to be really pissed or to laugh. 'The nerve of this woman.' She pronounced *nerve* á la Curly of the Three Stooges. 'What did the public defender say?'

'Nothing, they hear that kind of shit all the time. I wish I'd known she was going to court this morning. I would have delayed her paperwork.'

'What you should've misplaced was her insulin.'

Rico looked mildly shocked. 'You don't really mean that.'

'I guess not.' Munch didn't see herself capable of premeditated murder, but that didn't stop her from wishing certain people would do the honorable thing and die. Her morning reading of the obituaries was part morbid curiosity and part competitive interest. The Italian checklist.

'Has Kathy called again?' he asked.

Speaking of certain people. 'No, why?'

'She called my house last night and left a message. She wants to see me.'

'Have you considered changing your number?' Munch's tone was light, her thoughts were anything but.

'She'd just call me at work. I'm going to call her tonight and ask her to move on. I'm going to tell her I already have.'

Munch felt this conversation was long overdue. If he had told Kathy the truth back in February, they might all have been spared a lot of grief. But then again, in February, Kathy thought she was having his baby and nothing would have changed. Rico had chosen the baby, or the promise of a baby, over what Munch and he had.

'I thought you'd be happy,' Rico said.

Stupid man, she thought. 'Let's just find those girls. When they're safe, we'll talk about what's going to make us happy.'

'You're right. When you're right, you're right.'

22

Somehow Munch got through the rest of her day. She was numb with self-recrimination. Jill had been entrusted to her care, and now she was out there somewhere in the big, bad world. Charlotte had taken her sister, and if Munch's assumptions were correct, Jill's disappearance meant that a valuable key to this whole puzzle was gone. Now with Lisa on the loose, anything was possible. That she hadn't contacted Munch was telling. There was a good chance the three Slokums were together again. What a mess.

The shop phone rang at three-thirty. Munch had a weird sensation as she approached the instrument. There were three incoming lines and the phone rang constantly for all different reasons. Customers, suppliers, salesmen, personal calls to the various workers, and the occasional wrong number. She gave out the number for line two to her friends, partly because it was the easiest to remember, and partly because it wasn't the primary number on the work orders and business cards. That would be line one, the number most often used by customers. Line three was dedicated to the modem on the smog machine, but could be utilized when the other lines were tied up.

The time between when the ringer sounded, line two lit up, and when she held the receiver to her ear stretched long enough for her to know with certainty that the information she was about to receive was critical.

'You were right.' It was Rico.

'Which time?' she asked.

'Dave Limitz has been positively ID'd as the driver for the pet food supply business.'

'Was he from the Venice area?'

'As a matter of fact, yes. Why do you ask?'

'Did he go to Venice High?'

'That's the other thing,' Rico said. 'The same school as Steven Koon and Charlotte.'

'His last name started with L.' The inside of Munch's head was screaming, *Oh-God-oh-God-oh-God-shit*. 'That means Chet Lombardi was his guidance counselor, same as Charlotte and Steve. He was here at the station earlier.'

'The counselor? He came to your work?'

'Yeah, he said he had a sliding schedule. He seemed just as anxious as I am to locate the missing kids. Now, I have to wonder, how pure are his motives? He asked me twice if I'd spoken to Charlotte. Maybe he's afraid of what she'll tell me.'

'Okay, you might have something. I'll check it out.'

'Check it out? Go pick him up. He might be the one. He might be this Mouseman guy. If so, he's killed two kids already. Two more won't be so hard.'

'Whoa,' Rico said. 'Don't worry, we'll find him and put a team on him. If he's the guy, he won't get a chance to hurt anyone else. I have to follow procedure here.'

'What if you can't find him? He's on the road. He's driving a brown Datsun 280Z, seventy-eight, I think. The plate is *V-F-W* something. I can't remember the numbers.'

'How do you even remember the letters?'

'I always look at plates, it's how we keep track of the work we've done. I make a game out of the letters or sound them out. That was an easy one. Veterans of Foreign Wars.'

'All right, we'll check out the counselor.'

'Lombardi. Chet Lombardi.'

'I'm on it.'

'Roger that,' she answered, but Rico had already hung up. Asia's school bus arrived at four-fifteen. Munch felt her chest loosen. The bus only stopped here to deliver Asia. At least she hadn't lost all the children in her care.

'Is Jill here?' Asia asked.

'No, I don't know where she is.' Munch

explained the circumstances. How Jill had been seen leaving with her sister and that neither had been heard from since.

'Is she going to be all right?' Asia asked.

'I hope so. I'm worried about them. Jill shouldn't have left school.'

'I'm sure you did your best.'

Munch pulled her daughter to her. Asia was such a nurturer.

'Do you have any homework?' Munch asked, trying to return some sense of normalcy to their world.

'I have some math, and we're supposed to write three paragraphs about the missions, and one page on what we think we'll be doing in twenty years.'

'I'd like to see that one.'

'You want me to do it now?'

'Get started on it anyway and keep Jasper company. We'll go home in about twenty minutes.'

Munch followed Asia into Lou's office. The wood on the bottom of Lou's door was deeply grooved by Jasper's claws. Munch was touched at this evidence of his devotion. She hoped Lou wouldn't be too pissed. Asia used to draw on his walls when she was a toddler.

She watched her daughter unload her backpack. Her delicacy was a recent development. First came her pencil box, then her diary. Two books followed: a math primer and an illustrated text about the missions. The last item took Munch's breath away. It was the video box with the Beta tape.

'Isn't this Jill's?' Munch asked.

'She said I could borrow it.'

'Have you watched it?'

'Not yet. Who do we know with a Betamax VCR?'

'Well, there's Garret.'

'Oh,' Asia said. As if Munch, in mentioning her old boyfriend, might as well have told Asia she knew of a cassette player on the moon.

'Pack up your stuff again, honey. We're going to leave now.'

Munch made quick arrangements with the night crew, going over the work orders and explaining which vehicles needed to be parked inside the bays overnight, which customers were expected to be picking up their cars, and whose check was all right to take.

She told the other guys she'd see them on Monday, then loaded Asia and Jasper into her car. They all drove to what could have been their house.

She wondered if Garret was still living with that woman he was teaching to work on cars. The one he'd met at the aquarium store before Munch and he broke up. Jenny, her name was Jenny, and she was a bit of a snot or had been on the last occasion Munch had seen her. Maybe she thought Munch would try to steal back Garret.

'What's so funny?' Asia asked.

'Just thinking about something,' Munch said. 'Nothing worth going into.'

Garret Dimond lived in West Los Angeles, which was a small area for such a big name. It was nestled among the towns of Rancho Park, Westwood, and Palms and bordered by two major freeways. As much time as she spent in, and as many recent connections she had to the neighboring communities, she had managed to avoid that particular grid of streets as if they were lined with plague bacteria. She didn't know what scared her so much. How bad could it be to chance upon an ex? Well, two exes if she counted Derek, who, if he hadn't moved, lived six blocks away from Garret. Nothing about Derek had ever frightened her.

Maybe she felt guilty for dumping Garret. He had loved her, but she couldn't return the feeling. A part of her always felt guilty about that. Maybe she was apprehensive about how she would handle seeing his organized, straight lifestyle, knowing that if she had stayed with him, she could one day be one of those upper-middle-class ladies in a station wagon with credit cards. If nothing else, Garret was steady and reliable. There were moments when she wondered if she had given up on the relationship too soon.

Maybe that's why she avoided seeing him. Her reaction was similar to the philosophy she applied when playing the slot machines in Vegas. Once she gave up on a machine, she moved to an opposite corner of the casino. Nothing felt worse than seeing the next gambler hit the jackpot and knowing all it would have taken her was six more quarters and two more pulls.

Twenty minutes later, she pulled into the driveway of Garret Dimond's house behind a Saab Sonnet. An older 99-series model was on the street. Obviously, he still lived here.

These old Saabs were rare beasts, and mechanics who knew how to work on them were even rarer. Garret could pick and choose his clients. Lou had a good-old-boy distrust of foreign cars and those who chose to work on them. She loved the big American cars, too, but the German and Japanese imports were obviously the wave of the future. She doubted if Saabs would ever catch on.

Garret's front yard wasn't landscaped, not with any color anyway. A large pine tree shaded hard-packed dirt, which looked as if it had been raked. The redbrick flower box under the front window was filled with more dry dirt and topped with brown pine needles. With Asia and Jasper in tow, she rang the doorbell.

Garret answered after several long minutes, just as Munch was thinking she should have called ahead. His expression wavered between bewilderment and pleasure. He leaned toward her and kissed her cheek. Very civilized, and to give him credit, the gesture was sincere.

'Hi,' she said. 'Can we come in?'

He opened the door wide.

'Who's this?' he asked, bending down to pet Jasper.

Asia made the introductions before Munch had a chance.

'Sorry to barge in on you like this,' Munch said. 'I have this Beta tape I need to watch and I was wondering if you still had that — '

'Cool!' Asia interrupted. Her outburst had been elicited by a hundred-gallon saltwater tank complete with its own coral reef and layers of fish of exceptional color and variety.

He smiled. 'You like?'

Munch looked at the tank and then took in the rest of the room. His walls were painted a nice shade of apricot. Baskets of varying weaves, tapestries, and a collection of African masks decorated the walls at eye level and up. Small shelves held interesting vases and artifacts.

'Nice,' Munch said. 'Why didn't you decorate like this when I knew you?'

'I don't want to tell you. It would just piss you off.'

She took him at his word. She was there for a favor. This was not the time to introduce subjects that would require angry responses.

Munch held up the tape. 'Can we do this now?'

'Sure, help yourself. It's set up in the office.' His office was a converted back bedroom where his Saab clients could sit on a couch and read a magazine while they waited for their car.

Asia stayed with Garret to admire his tropical fish.

'Don't touch the glass,' Munch heard Garret say.

She remembered how he wasn't really good around kids. He hadn't seen Asia in months, and he was worried about her fingerprints leaving smudges instead of enjoying her company. Munch had made the right choice with him. He wasn't a bad guy, but he wasn't the right guy either. Munch and Jasper walked down the hall to the back rooms. She made a point of not turning her head and looking in his bedroom. Nothing that went on there was any of her business.

She loaded the videotape and pushed PLAY.

The bumpy frames of a home movie materialized. Three kids walked up to a house. She paused the picture. She knew the two boys. Steve Koon and Dave Limitz. It took her a second to recognize Painter Dave. He was wearing jeans, sneakers, and a polo shirt. His hair was short and neatly groomed. This tape must have been made at least a few months ago.

She resumed the action. Steve was holding a baseball. The boys put on gloves and tossed it between themselves. The ball rolled into the bushes. Steve Koon went after it while Dave walked around the side of the house. A moment later the front door opened and a young girl stood in the doorway inviting them in.

Munch paused the tape again. The girl was Charlotte, her hair tied back in a braid, but not dyed any outlandish colors. She was also wearing gloves.

Munch pushed the button that allowed the film to continue. Nothing happened for a while, just the image of the house. She advanced the tape at a faster speed until there was new movement.

The garage door opened and a car emerged with the three kids inside. Charlotte was at the wheel. Munch adjusted the player to resume at real time.

She turned up the volume in time to hear a dog's high-pitched bark. Jasper stood and stared at the television screen. A voice offscreen said, 'Queenie, hush.'

Munch knew that voice. It was the voice of the man who had called Lisa's house the day after Charlotte's disappearance. She'd heard the voice since this whole mess had started, too, but she had been too distracted by other things to put it all together. She'd made a terrible mistake. Possibly a fatal mistake. She'd overlooked the obvious, what was now very obvious. She ejected the tape without rewinding it and ran back to the living room.

'I need another favor,' she said. She hated to ask, hated to incur the debt, but she knew her limitations and this was no time for ego. Garret was still big and strong, and that might come in handy. 'First, can I use your phone?'

'Local call?' Then he caught himself. 'Whatever, help yourself.'

Munch called Rico. The phone rang ten times. With each ring, her impatience grew. Finally, an answering machine picked up. She waited the interminable seconds for the outgoing message to conclude, then told him where she was going and to meet her there. She also told him it was urgent.

She hung up and turned to Garret. 'Would you take a ride with me? I don't know what we'll find. It might even be dangerous. I'd appreciate the backup.'

'You'll explain on the way?'

'Yes, but we need to hurry.' Mouseman had crossed the line and was eliminating everything that tied him to his crimes. Painter Dave had been killed because he had become a liability. Everyone tied to Mouseman had now become a liability.

23

The Jag was in the Koons' driveway. The Range Rover was not. Munch knocked on the door. No answer. She walked around to a side window and peered inside. What she saw made her run back to the front door and try the knob. The door was locked.

'What's up?' Garret asked.

'There's a body on the floor in there. I can see her feet.'

Munch popped open her trunk and retrieved her tire iron. Garret was already at the door, kicking at the jamb. It gave a bit, but held fast.

'Here,' Munch said, pushing him to one side, 'let me.' She forced the tapered steel tip of the tire iron into the space between the frame and the door. Garret grabbed the curved end and pried. The door gave with a crack of splintering wood. Munch pointed at Asia. 'Stay in the car. Lock yourself in.'

Asia didn't have to be asked twice. Munch rushed to the body on the floor. Empty bottles of booze and pills littered the carpet around her head. Cheryl was barely breathing. A photograph of her dead son lay under her cheek.

Garret lifted the phone and called 911. Munch heard him explain that they had found a woman unconscious. 'She appears to have overdosed on drugs and alcohol,' he said. He covered the mouthpiece and said to Munch, 'They want me to stay on the line until the ambulance gets here.'

'Tell them to send the police, too,' Munch said. 'This was no accident.' It wasn't a suicide attempt either, she thought. The props were too obvious. This scene had been staged and she knew by whom. 'Garret, keep an eye on the car. Please.'

Munch quickly searched the rest of the house.

'Should you be doing this?' Garret asked nervously. 'Did you find something?'

'It's what I'm not finding that's more telling.' All the home movies were gone.

The ambulance and the police arrived within minutes of each other. Cheryl was loaded on a gurney and whisked off in a riot of sirens and flashing lights.

At the patrol officers' insistence, Munch and Garret waited outside. Asia was still in the car, but she'd rolled down the window.

'Would you call dispatch,' Munch asked the nearest cop, 'and find out if Detective Chacón is on his way?'

Garret raised an eyebrow.

'That's her boyfriend,' Asia volunteered. 'His name is Rico. He's a cop.' She sounded pretty smug about it.

Munch stroked Asia's cheek and smiled. Jasper was shaking so she made reassuring noises and stroked his head. She finally looked at Garret, realizing that she had been avoiding just that.

'Thanks for coming here with us,' she said.

Garret shook his head. 'I guess you don't need me anymore. I'd leave now, but we came in your car.'

She wished she could zap him home magically. 'It was nice seeing you again, whatever the circumstances.' She stroked Jasper again. 'How's Jenny, by the way?'

'Probably wondering where I am.' It had started to get dark. Dinnertime for most of the normal world.

'I'm glad that's worked out for you,' she said. 'You deserve it.'

Rico arrived and made his way over to them with long, confident strides. He went to Munch first. 'Are you all right?'

'Yeah, sure, don't worry about me.'

Rico turned his gaze to Garret. 'Hi, and you are?' One thing about cops, they were trained to be direct.

'This is Garret Dimond,' Munch said quickly before Asia had a chance to comment. 'Garret, this is Rico Chacón.' There, that wasn't so bad.

The two men shook hands.

Rico stared at her. His eyes looked almost black. She felt a small thrill at his apparent jealousy. She knew she shouldn't.

'He had a Betamax VCR,' she said. 'I had this tape that Jill had and I thought it might have important information — Shit. What time is it?'

Rico looked at his watch. 'Almost six.'

'We've got to come up with a different plan,' Munch said. 'I can't show up in the limo now.'

'Why not?'

'I'd be recognized. Michael Koon knows I have a limo. I was driving it the day I came here to talk to Cheryl.'

'Call the buyer and tell him the plan is off.'

Munch nodded. 'Garret needs a ride home.'

Rico turned to Garret. 'Where do you live?'

'On Moore, near Rose,' Garret said.

Rico held out his hand. Munch, understanding what he wanted, retrieved the tape from her car and handed it to him. He crooked a finger to Garret. 'You can ride with me.' He turned back to Munch. 'Will you go home now?'

'I think that's best.'

'I'll come over later,' Rico said. Then he bent down and kissed her. He wasn't given to public displays, or at least he had never been before. She could get used to this.

She watched the two men leave in Rico's car.

'I wonder what they're talking about,' Asia said.

'Maybe Rico will tell us later.'

'I wouldn't hold my breath if I were you.'

Munch looked at her daughter and wondered for not the first time which incarnation she was on.

Munch went back to her house and called Mr Webster. 'There's been a change of plans.'

'How did you know?'

'What are you talking about?'

'The seller contacted me. He's coming here, to my house. He said his schedule had changed and we needed to make our meeting later.'

'No, you can't do that. This guy is dangerous.'

'Oh, dear,' Webster said, 'he has no reason to harm me.'

'He might try to rob you. The guy is serious trouble. He's killed two boys and maybe a woman. He's got nothing to lose and he's running on desperate.'

'I'll call him back. Oh, no, I don't have his

number. I'll leave a note on the door and put out the lights.'

'When do you expect him?'

'He said to look for him around seven-thirty, but he might be as late as eight. That's why he thought I'd be more comfortable in my own home.'

'What's your address?' Munch wrote down the street and number. 'Okay, lock your doors and call the cops.' She gave him the direct line to Dispatch and told him whom to ask for and what to say.

'I'll call you right back,' he said.

Munch hung up. Two minutes later, the phone rang again. She was surprised he'd been able to get through so quickly.

'Hello?'

'Auntie Munch?'

'Where are you?' Munch felt her knees weaken and realized she had feared she would never hear Jill's voice again, a fear she had refused to acknowledge until this second. 'Where are you? Are you all right? Is Charlotte with you?'

'It's my mom. She's really sick. We took her to the hospital.'

'What's wrong with your mom? How did you hook up with her?'

'She went to her friend's house, Charlotte figured she would. The guy sells her medicine, but it must not have been the right kind. She had one of her attacks. I really don't know what's happening and I'm kinda scared.'

'Where's Charlotte?'

'She's talking to the doctors or somebody, trying to find out what's going on.'

'Which hospital?'

'Daniel Freeman.'

'In Inglewood?'

'Yes. But we're going to leave as soon as Charlotte talks to the doctors.'

'Stay there, I'll come get you.'

'Charlotte said to ask you if we can pretend the ten years is up.'

'Sure,' Munch said, understanding immediately. Ten years had been too long to begin with. 'Jill?'

'Yeah?' Her voice sounded very small. Munch wished she could wrap her arms around her. She had to get to her first.

'Don't worry, honey. This is all fixable. Just stay safe.' What she meant was 'stay alive' but she figured Jill was savvy enough to figure that out.

* * *

She parked on the street in front of the Slokums' former home in Inglewood. The

Dodge was wedged against a wall in someone's carport, mostly hidden by a large Dumpster.

She stood and looked around, making herself visible. A jet flew overhead and Asia covered her ears with her hands.

Charlotte emerged from the bushes. She had actually put on a few pounds. The goth makeup was gone and her skin had a healthy glow. Jill followed, looking subdued.

They spent a long minute in a wordless hug, then Munch put Jill in the backseat and Charlotte next to her. Jasper curled in Asia's lap, resting his head on the girl's knee.

Munch considered the picture they presented. A car full of kids. A cocker spaniel. A mom. She wished it were all as idyllic as that. Would other drivers glance their way and think, *How nice?*

Munch was seized with an urge to stop for ice cream, to prolong the fantasy, or more accurately, to delay reality.

'I watched the tape,' Munch said.

Charlotte nodded. Tears filled her eyes.

'Tell me what I was looking at.' Munch was pretty sure she knew already. She needed to know if Charlotte was ready to come clean and begin putting this all behind her.

'What you saw,' Charlotte said, 'was a burglary in progress. Mouseman taped us all.'

Her voice broke and the next words she said were uttered through her tears. 'He kept the tapes and said they would help us learn.'

'Any job worth doing is worth doing right,' Munch said.

To her credit, Charlotte laughed. It was an important skill to be able to laugh and cry at the same time.

'So how did you get the tape?' Munch asked.

'We stole it,' Charlotte said.

'We?'

'Me and Steve. I wanted to take it to the police and explain everything, but my mom had another idea.'

'Your mom knew about this?'

'I wanted her to go with me to the cops, then Steve was murdered. She said we couldn't bring Steve back, and that the cops would bust me, too. She said we could make Mouseman leave us alone.'

'By blackmailing him?' Munch was sure that Lisa had convinced herself that she was doing the right thing. She had for sure felt justified, and knowing Lisa, she had probably felt even a little noble, as if she were striking a blow for the greater good.

Charlotte buried her face in her hands. 'Dumb idea. I know. But she said Jill and I would be taken away from her if the cops found out that I had been breaking into homes and stealing. I only did it a few times, and I am, like, a minor. I wanted her to ask you for help, that's why we called you.'

Munch remained quiet, waiting for Charlotte to fill in the rest.

'Mouseman was supposed to bring the money to our house Monday night, but instead he broke in on Sunday night when we were all asleep, grabbed me, and tied me up. He locked me in one of the storage units in the same building as ours. He said he'd keep me there until Mom gave up the tape. I could hear you guys when you came that day, but I was tied up and gagged and I couldn't make enough noise for you to hear me.'

'Oh, God,' Munch said, and shot Charlotte a sympathetic look in the rearview mirror. 'To think we were so close. I'm so sorry.'

'I knew you were looking. I knew my mom was looking, too. That made me feel better. I left a hank of my hair in our storage locker when Mouseman searched it. When he changed the lock, I was afraid no one would find my clue.'

'How did you get away?'

'My friend Painter Dave. Mouseman had him bring me food and water. He said he met you and you offered him a reward. He thought he could use the money to get away.'

'He helped you escape?' Munch asked.

Charlotte nodded again. 'I gave him the dog tag as proof. He said he was going to call you.'

'He did, but something happened to him.'

'I know,' Charlotte said. 'He's dead. I saw it in the paper. He's dead because of me.'

'No, not because of you. You don't have that much power. He's dead because he was in the wrong world at the wrong time. You have to make your life count now. You have to rise above all this.' Munch considered Lisa's dilemma. Once Charlotte had been snatched, Lisa knew that if she handed over the tape, she would lose all leverage and quite possibly seal her daughter's fate. Blackmailers preferred to avoid the police, too.

'I want to live,' Charlotte said, sounding somewhat surprised to be making this proclamation. 'I want to make something of my life. For a long time, I didn't care if I lived or died. I was leaning toward death. But when someone wanted to take my life away from me, I realized I wanted to live after all. I'm going to make the most out of this second chance.'

Throughout the conversation, Jill and Asia had remained quiet. Munch knew they were listening. Asia was even holding her breath so as not to miss a syllable. Munch reached across the seat and stroked her hair.

She caught Charlotte's eye in the mirror again. 'You won't have to do it alone. I know about your compulsions. The need for order, your obsessions with your temperature. The good news is that it's an illness, and there's a treatment if you're willing.'

'I think I'm cured,' Charlotte said. 'I haven't taken my temperature since Sunday. I haven't felt I needed to. I haven't had to straighten things or pull my hair, any of it.'

'I'm glad, but you don't get better overnight. I used to be able to put down dope when my life reached critical mass. I know you can thrive under extreme pressure. It's the mundane times that people like us can't handle. And then there's your mom.' Munch looked at both of her nieces. What a load these kids had been given.

'I know my mom needs help, too,' Charlotte said. 'I'll make her go to counseling and start a diet and exercise program. She needs to stop drinking, too.'

After all this, Munch thought, *the kid still cares about that bitch.* 'Was that her vodka we found in your room?'

'I took it to stop my mom from drinking it.'

'It takes more than that,' Munch said.

'I know, but we're not going to pretend we're okay anymore. I know you'll make sure of that.'

Munch smiled. The kid was all right.

'What happens now?' Charlotte asked.

'We're going to the police.' Munch didn't add, *What you should have done in the first place*. There would be time enough later to discuss all of that.

★   ★   ★

They parked in the visitors' lot in front of the police station. Munch left Asia, Jill, and Jasper under the watchful eye of the desk sergeant and took Charlotte upstairs to be debriefed. Rico produced the Beta tape and said, 'Let's all watch this together, okay?'

'You've got a Betamax here?' Munch asked.

Rico said, 'All you had to do was ask.'

'I'm working on it,' she said.

They played the tape for Rico, stopping when they got to the part where the man called out, 'Queenie, hush.'

'Hear that radio-announcer voice on the tape? That's Cheryl Koon's husband, Michael. Michael, Micky, Mouseman. I recognized the voice. It's not one you easily forget. See? It all fits.' Munch thought about her first meeting with Cheryl Koon. Cheryl hadn't known what her husband saw in her. Munch knew now that he hadn't wanted Cheryl. He wanted her son, Steve, the boy with the fast hands, and all his disenfranchised little friends.

Charlotte repeated her story for Rico, minimizing her mother's involvement in this telling, Munch noticed.

'What these tapes also did is keep us tied to him,' Charlotte said. 'Steve just wanted out. We thought if we had the goods on his stepdad, he'd let us go. Most of the kids didn't want out. He treated them well.'

'The trips to Disneyland,' Munch said, looking over at Rico, who was sitting quietly letting Charlotte do the explaining. There was no judgment on his face, no anger, only a patient quiet.

'And shoes and sports equipment for the boys,' Charlotte added. 'Clothes or whatever for the girls.'

'Music?' Munch asked, keeping her voice even, her face calm, trying to follow Rico's example.

'Music, paying the gas bill, keeping our phone hooked up. He even saved us from getting evicted once.'

'Did he touch you?' Munch asked quietly, fearing the answer.

'No, it was never about that. You're talking about sex, right?'

Munch could only nod.

'It was' — Charlotte searched for the word — 'the parenting. All the kids had to keep up with their school-work, do their chores at home. He even lectured us on brushing our teeth regularly, and he was really down on drugs and smoking cigarettes.'

'So what went wrong?' Munch asked.

'We started growing up. Mouseman wanted the younger kids.'

'Like Jill,' Munch said.

'Yeah,' Charlotte said. 'She thought I was trying to run her life, but I wanted to protect her. Someone was going to get caught one of those times. Mouseman got caught once because a silent alarm called the police. He had to go to jail. He said none of us would make it in jail. He only wanted to keep us safe, he said.' Charlotte snorted. Her eyes looked a thousand years old, but when she cried, she looked fifteen.

'Can I take her home?' Munch asked.

Rico shook his head sadly. 'We're going to have to hold her. She'll be all right.'

Charlotte seemed accepting of this, too. Munch hugged her before she was led away to be processed. Rico accompanied Munch to the reception area and helped her explain to Jill and Asia what was going on. She'd also made arrangements to drop the kids at the St Johns'.

'Why aren't we going home?' Asia asked. She was tired and cranky. Munch realized that she hadn't fed them dinner.

She knelt so that she was at eye level with her daughter. 'I have one more thing to do. It might be kinda late before I'm finished.' She didn't want to tell Asia that home wasn't the safest place anymore. Not until this was over.

'Does it have to be you?' Asia asked, an uncharacteristic whine in her voice.

'I need to see this through. I know what this guy looks like. I'm going to help Rico catch him.' And then it would be safe for all of them to go home. She thought again about that voice on the tape, representing the adult, the parent. Not to mention that he was the guy with all the goodies. Everything but a conscience.

'I'll make it up to you,' Munch told her daughter. 'I promise.'

'Yeah, right.' Asia sighed one of her too wise sighs. 'Let's just go.'

24

Munch and Rico drove to Colin Webster's house. It was in Marina Del Rey, on one of the small bays carved out of the coastline to create more boat slips. The avant-garde sculptures in the front yard, twisting, soaring figures cast in bronze and Plexiglas, reflected the art collector's eclectic tastes.

The moon was full and was reflected in soft ripples on the black water. The scene would have been romantic if they hadn't been there to catch a killer.

Colin Webster's house was dark save for his house number flickering in purple neon. Munch pictured the man inside, sitting in the dark, scared and thrilled at the same moment. Sounded a bit like her love life.

The Range Rover was parked in a curve of the cul-de-sac, no doubt poised for a quick getaway.

'Not this time, buster,' Munch murmured to herself.

The police had met for a brief huddle several blocks away. There were eight uniformed officers in four black-and-whites. Rico made nine. Munch had been included in their powwow. The inclusion flattered her. They decided to take down Michael Koon once he was back in his car and pulling away from the curb.

'We'll do a jam,' a sergeant in uniform said.

The other officers nodded, an excited ripple running through them. Munch felt like a little kid around these guys. Not one of the guys was under six feet. They were all physically fit and confident. She was in the presence of gladiators, gladiators with guns who were operating under the color of the law. Michael Koon didn't stand a chance.

She felt a strong and unexpected wave of pride to be one of the good guys.

'When he gets in his car,' Rico said, 'we'll surround him. One car will pull in front of him, another behind, and a third will pull up alongside the driver's door pinning it closed. The rest of us will take position on the sidewalk, under cover of the remaining cars, weapons drawn, and order him to exit. He won't have an option.' Rico reached down and put his hand on her shoulder. 'We'll go on your word. You just point him out.'

Now Munch was waiting to do just that. Suddenly, a movement inside the Rover caught her eye. Koon was knocking at Colin Webster's door; somebody else was inside his car.

'Wait,' she said.

The police had tuned their Handie-Talkies to the same frequency. Rico's finger depressed the transmit button.

She pointed to the Rover and then to her eye.

They watched, straining to make out a movement behind the Rover's tinted glass. Had she just caught a reflection from somewhere else? A night bird? Or were her overtuned and hypervigilant senses playing games with her mind?

Koon had given up on getting a response from the darkened house and was beginning to walk toward his car. Rico looked at Munch. She shook her head. She wasn't sure.

Then . . . There it was again. A small head raised up on the passenger side of the Rover. Koon raised his hands to the small figure and shrugged as if to communicate, *Nobody home*.

Munch let herself out of Rico's car before he could stop her.

'Michael,' she said. 'Michael Koon.'

He looked her way. She took a step toward him, forcing him to face her.

'I've got something you want.'

'What are you talking about?' he said, wary now, looking back at the Rover. His keys were in his hands. She didn't know what he might have tucked in his waistband.

'I found my niece. I've got the tape, but it's going to cost you.' So far, she hadn't lied.

'What do you want?' he asked. He took a few steps closer to her. Munch forced herself not to look at the Rover or back at Rico's car. She heard the click of the radio, five engines idling quietly, and hoped Michael Koon hadn't picked up the noises that didn't belong in this otherwise quiet scene.

'Did you bring the money?' she asked. She moved closer to the Rover. A click of the door opening made them both turn. The dome light flicked on and illuminated a young boy's features, a kid maybe twelve. 'I'm not doing anything in front of a kid,' Munch said. 'We deal now or I'm out of here.'

Koon licked his lips and then smoothly told the kid in his car, 'Stay put, Sam, I'll just be a minute.'

Munch pointed toward the shadow of one of the larger sculptures. 'Over there.'

Koon took five steps and then the neighborhood blazed alive. Five sets of high beams put the moon to shame.

A helicopter swooped overhead, its loud-speaker splitting the night. 'Down, now!' the voice commanded. 'Down on the ground.'

Munch dropped and rolled, seeking cover under one of the sculptures. 'Freeze!' the voice said. The command was soon echoed by nine cops with drawn weapons. The beating of the helicopter blades overhead made the air concuss in her ears and kicked dust in her eyes.

She couldn't blink. The cops screamed at Koon. Their voices had a touch of hysteria that filled her with more fear than the guns they held. Perhaps that was the desired effect.

Finally, Michael Koon got the message and sank to his knees. He laced his fingers behind his head, holding his elbows akimbo. One of the uniformed cops came up behind him and pushed Koon's shoulder until the man went prone. Another cop kicked Koon's feet apart.

Munch wondered if this final humiliation was all part of the master plan.

She watched Michael Koon's face. He looked dazed as they cuffed him, but not surprised. Rico grabbed his arm and helped him to his feet. They walked over to Rico's unmarked, where Rico searched Koon's pockets, emptying the lot on the hood of his car.

The black velvet pouch was in Koon's jacket pocket. Rico dumped the contents in his hand and Munch identified the stolen jewelry. Most of it. The cameo was there, and the locket. Only two of Meg Sullivan's rings remained. The one with the blue stone was not one of them.

Munch felt a twinge of disappointment.

Michael Koon was led away and placed in the back of one of the patrol cars. The boy in the Rover was taken off in a separate car.

Colin Webster's door opened and the large man called out, 'Did you get him?'

'Yes, sir,' Rico said. 'We did.'

'Show him the stuff,' Munch whispered. 'It'll make him feel good.'

Rico and Munch joined Colin Webster in his doorway. Webster had turned his lights on.

'Sir,' Rico said. 'I'm told you're an expert in antique jewelry.'

Webster beamed with pleasure. 'I dabble.' He opened his door wider. 'Please, won't you come in?'

They gathered around a table made of some rich dark wood. Rico showed their host the cameo. Webster pulled a jeweler's loupe from his pocket and examined the piece carefully.

'Oh, my. Very nice.' He turned the brooch over and studied some scratches on the back.

'What do you see?' Munch asked.

Webster spoke without taking his attention off the jewelry. 'Please inform the owners that I'd like to make them an offer.'

'Is it valuable?' Munch asked.

'Not for the workmanship or materials.'

'A piece of history?' Munch asked.

Webster let her peer through the magnifying lens of the loupe. She saw that the scratches on the back were letters. She didn't understand the foreign words, but could make out a distinct few capitalized letters in stylized script.

'This cameo,' Webster said, almost beside himself with excitement, 'was a gift between lovers. If I'm not mistaken, to Josephine from Napoleon.'

'I guess I earned my reward,' Munch said.

★ ★ ★

They returned to the police station. Munch stayed while Rico wrote his report. He called the hospital and learned that Cheryl Koon was going to recover. Munch had no idea how the woman would put the rest of her life back together. Her son was dead, her husband had betrayed her in the worst possible way. Fortunately, that wasn't Munch's problem. She had plenty of other issues to which to devote her attention.

Rico was fairly certain that if Charlotte continued to cooperate with the police and the district attorney, she would come through her ordeal with nothing on her permanent record.

As for Munch and Rico, they ended up not

picking up the kids from the St Johns' that night, which was just as well.

★ ★ ★

On Saturday, Munch contacted the Sullivans. The couple were generous with their reward. The price negotiated for selling the cameo to Colin Webster more than offset the reward money they paid Munch. Mr Sullivan, Munch learned, was exactly what he appeared to be. A nice man with money. She'd like to find someone like that for Asia one day.

★ ★ ★

On Sunday, after dropping Jill off for a supervised visit at her mother's, Munch, Rico, and Asia returned to the petting zoo.

They took two cars: Munch's GTO and a radio-equipped police car. Rico had also suited up for business.

They wandered among the animals, trying not to look as if they were hunting.

When they got to the pen where the hooved animals were kept, Asia froze and pointed at a man in designer jeans and a Members Only jacket. 'That's him.'

Munch looked where Asia had pointed. She expected the guy to be older. Maybe she had painted him in her mind to resemble her father. This guy looked about thirty. He was clean-cut and well groomed, of normal appearance to the casual observer. He was bent over a girl who looked about Asia's age, his nose almost in her hair. The little girl was pointing at the llamas.

'Shoot him,' Munch said.

'Let me handle this,' Rico said.

Munch was happy to let him. Asia had ahold of her fingers. Munch wasn't about to pry her loose or let her get anywhere near the guy.

She watched Rico approach the man. The guy straightened immediately, his gestures exaggerated as if he was lying.

Rico said something to the little girl. She shook her head and pointed off toward the bathrooms.

Rico said, 'Go get your mother. I want to speak to her.' The little girl ran off toward the bathroom and Rico turned his attention back to the guy with the hair on the backs of his fingers.

Rico flipped his coat back, showing his badge.

The little girl returned with her mother.

'Do you know this man?' Rico asked her.

'No, should I?' the woman asked, looking more confused than concerned.

'We've had a complaint about someone matching his description being overly solicitous to children.' He looked at the woman's daughter. 'Especially to little girls who he finds by themselves.'

The woman looked horrified. The guy tried to spin away, but Rico anticipated the move. When the guy feinted to the other side, he exhausted Rico's patience. The blow came quickly. A punch delivered with cool precision to the solar plexus. The guy doubled over and crumpled to the ground.

He had been resisting arrest. Munch would swear to it. She was pretty sure the other mother would back her story.

Rico cuffed the guy where he lay, then dragged him to his feet and marched him back to the police sedan. Munch and a wide-eyed Asia followed. Munch figured that seeing justice carried out was one of the better field trips Asia'd ever been on.

The guy's name turned out to be as innocuous as his appearance: Fred Moore.

Rico called it in for wants and warrants. When that came up empty, he contacted a relatively new database of sex offenders. There he scored. Fred Moore, age twenty-nine, white male, was on probation for lewd conduct. According to the terms of his probation, he was prohibited from loitering in venues created to attract children.

'That's it for you,' Rico said, his face grim.

Freddy looked as if he were going to cry. It was always the same with these monsters. The only sympathy they ever felt was for themselves.

'You don't understand,' Moore said. 'I love children.'

'No,' Munch said, 'you use them. It's not the same at all.'

Rico requested a cage car to come pick up Freddy-boy. Munch was glad that Rico wasn't going to leave the petting zoo immediately. She had something to discuss with him.

They had to wait only five minutes for the transport vehicle. Sometimes, the cops were just where they needed to be when you needed them. In fact, that seemed to be the case a lot lately.

Asia relaxed, letting go of Munch's hand and wandering toward the animals that were available to pet. Munch told her they could stay for ten more minutes and then they needed to get home. Jasper didn't like to be alone.

When Asia was out of earshot, Munch turned to Rico.

'I'm going to have to take care of my nieces for a while,' she said. 'I talked with Lisa and she's checking into a rehab. I told her the kids could stay with me.'

'Of course,' he said. 'You're family. It's only right. I'll help any way I can.'

'What about all your buddies? Your cop friends. What would they think of you spending time with me?'

'It's nobody's business but ours. Besides, there's nothing wrong with you. Nothing.'

That wasn't strictly true, she thought.

They walked along, keeping parallel to Asia as she tried to portion her handfuls of feed equally among the animals clamoring around her. They heard the sounds of children at play. Rico took Munch's hand. She concentrated on the place where their flesh met.

'You know,' she said, 'I've never really had my infertility checked out. There was just the one doctor who told me eight years ago that I had probably damaged my fallopian tubes. I mean, I know he was right. I haven't ever taken birth control and I've never gotten pregnant, but that's not to say that I couldn't have surgery or maybe take some kind of medication.'

'Why don't you look into it?' he said.

'I have. I went to see this specialist at UCLA. They want to do a laparoscopy. They make a small incision at my belly button and then go in with this tube-shaped instrument that lets them look at my internal organs. They inject dye from the other end and see if it makes it through.'

'Do you have to be knocked out?'

'Yeah, but it's outpatient. I wouldn't spend the night. Check in at nine and out by the same afternoon. The important thing is, then we'd know.'

'It's always better to know,' he said. They had slowed their pace, perhaps unconsciously, but certainly noticeably. 'You want me to go with you?'

'You wouldn't have to.' She made her voice bright, almost cheerful. 'I could get Ruby to drive me home, or Caroline.'

'I wouldn't mind. You'd probably need some help once you got home. I could make you soup. Tortilla or *albóndigas*.'

'Anything but *menudo*.'

'Your choice.'

Munch smiled at him, wondering why happiness felt so much like heartbreak. 'Well, here's the thing. I was thinking, what if they go in there and see that it's hopeless?'

'You don't know that.'

'Let me finish.' At some point they had stopped holding hands and she now folded her arms across her chest. She took a deep breath before she spoke again. She wanted to get it all out at once, without pausing. 'If they

351

find out the damage is too much, the scarring too severe, we'll stop seeing each other now.' Munch felt she was being brave, practical. It wasn't easy. The right thing often wasn't. That's why they called it fortitude.

'Or how about this?' he said, taking her face in his hands and meeting her eyes. 'Why don't you skip the procedure altogether and we stay together? Why even put yourself through the trauma? I love you. Don't you get that? I want to marry you.'

Munch couldn't speak. She didn't have a snappy comeback or a sly observation. The most honest thing she could say was nothing. The tears filling her eyes felt cool and cleansing as she nodded her head yes.

Acknowledgments

A special thanks to Paul Bishop and Gary Bale for the cop stuff; Anna Miller for her willingness to share her jewelry expertise; Nanette Heiser for her insights into psychosis from a medical professional's point of view; the good people at NAMI; Debbie Mitsch for her terrific PR services. I also want to acknowledge my wonderful editors, starting with my critique groups; my agent Sandy Dijkstra; and the gifted, hardworking Scribner folk: Susanne Kirk, Sarah Knight, Angella Baker, and Steven Boldt.

And a special nod to those who make the journey worthwhile. I am rich in the love of my husband, Ron, our furry babies, my family, and friends. Not the least of whom is my newest, bestest: Stephen J. Cannell.

We do hope that you have enjoyed reading this large print book.

Did you know that all of our titles are available for purchase?

We publish a wide range of high quality large print books including:
Romances, Mysteries, Classics
General Fiction
Non Fiction and Westerns

Special interest titles available in large print are:
The Little Oxford Dictionary
Music Book
Song Book
Hymn Book
Service Book

Also available from us courtesy of Oxford University Press:
Young Readers' Dictionary
(large print edition)
Young Readers' Thesaurus
(large print edition)

For further information or a free brochure, please contact us at:
Ulverscroft Large Print Books Ltd.,
The Green, Bradgate Road, Anstey,
Leicester, LE7 7FU, England.
Tel: (00 44) **0116 236 4325**
Fax: (00 44) **0116 234 0205**

Other titles published by
The House of Ulverscroft:

WAKE UP LITTLE SUSIE

Ed Gorman

In September 1957 the Edsel made its long-awaited debut in Black River Falls, Iowa. The local Ford dealership was hosting a baton-twirling celebration to welcome the car of the future . . . But the future can't be taken for granted — a fact made all too clear by the discovery of Susan Squires' body in the boot of one of the brand-new cars . . . Now private eye Sam McCain must find out who killed the wife of the town's most prominent lawyer before the guilty party hits the road.

KILLER SWELL

Jeff Shelby

Life for Noah Braddock, living in sun-drenched San Diego, is good. Just shy of thirty, his job as a P.I. gives him plenty of time to surf. He makes enough money to keep his beachfront apartment, and a six-pack of beer in the fridge . . .Suddenly his life gets a lot more complicated when Marilyn Crier, the mother of his former high school girlfriend Kate, calls him out of the blue and tells him that Kate is missing — and she wants Noah to find her.

WHISPER MURDER

Marjorie Stiling

Lorraine Barclay is busy creating the perfect home for herself and her fiancé Jeffrey in the sleepy village of Drayford. Her dream of domestic bliss is shattered by the arrival of Jeffrey's fourteen-year-old daughter Kim — loud, abusive, thieving and promiscuous — the teenager from Hell. Kim's disruptive presence poisons the idyll Lorraine has tried to create. Soon, almost everyone is ready to strangle her — and then she disappears. Jeffrey and Lorraine are now subject to the suspicious scrutiny of their neighbours, and the villagers are forced to rake up the past in order to unearth clues which might solve Kim's disappearance.

DEAD AIM

Iris Johansen

Photojournalist Alex Graham's assignment at a dam collapse in Arapahoe Junction, Colorado, forces her across a dangerous line. Alex witnesses a conspiracy that will shock a nation. For the collapse of the Arapahoe Dam was not an accident. The official story is a cover-up for a truth so frightening that anyone who threatens to reveal it must be silenced. Forever. Alex's ally, an ex-commando, has a price on his head and an assassin at his heels. When a reporter does more than report and becomes involved in the story, she ends up marked for death by enemies who've got her centred . . . dead aim.

RULES OF ENGAGEMENT

Bruce Alexander

Sir John and Jeremy are confronted with a series of bizarre deaths on the streets of London, and when Lord Lammermoor plunges to his death from Westminster Bridge, suicide is deemed to be the cause of death. But Lammermoor's fatal leap coincides with the arrival of Dr. Goldsworthy, a student of Dr. Anton Mesmer and his research in animal magnetism. Sir John discovers that Goldsworthy's patron in London is Lady Lammermoor. Meanwhile, Jeremy's sleuthing uncovers a web of intrigue within the Lammermoor family and reveals more suspects who stand to gain from Lammermoor's death.

TEMPORARY SANITY

Rose Connors

When Buck Hammond's seven-year-old son is abducted and murdered by Hector Monteros, Buck takes justice into his own hands. Unfortunately, the TV cameras were rolling as he aimed his hunting rifle at Monteros's head. Attorney Marty Nickerson has a tough role acting as Buck's defense attorney. How can the jury acquit him when the shooting is on the screen for all to see? On the very eve of the trial, a battered and bleeding woman staggers into the office of Marty and her partner, Harry Madigan. The woman is in deep trouble — her attacker's body has just been found, viciously stabbed, and he's an officer of the court. Now Marty has two seemingly impossible battles to win . . .